LATE ARCADE

ALSO BY NATHANIEL MACKEY

Fiction

Bedouin Hornbook
Djbot Baghostus's Run
Atet A.D.
Bass Cathedral
From a Broken Bottle Traces of Perfume Still Emanate: Volumes 1–3

Poetry Books and Chapbooks

Four for Trane
Septet for the End of Time
Outlantish
Song of the Andoumboulou: 18–20
Four for Glenn
Anuncio's Last Love Song
Outer Pradesh
Moment's Omen
Lay Ghost
School of Oud
Eroding Witness
School of Udhra
Whatsaid Serif
Splay Anthem
Nod House
Blue Fasa

Criticism

Discrepant Engagement: Dissonance, Cross-Culturality, and Experimental Writing
Paracritical Hinge: Essays, Talks, Notes, Interviews

Anthologies

Moment's Notice: Jazz in Poetry and Prose, with Art Lange

Recordings

Strick: Song of the Andoumboulou 16–25

Late Arcade

Nathaniel Mackey

A New Directions Paperbook Original

Late Arcade is volume five of *From a Broken Bottle Traces of Perfume Still Emanate*, an ongoing work. Volumes one, two, three and four are *Bedouin Hornbook, Djbot Baghostus's Run, Atet A.D.,* and *Bass Cathedral.*

Sections of this book have appeared in *Amerarcana: A Bird & Beckett Review, Blues for Smoke, Conjunctions, Current Musicology, Fence, Floor: Poetics of Everyday Critique, Golden Handcuffs Review, Hambone,* and *Women & Performance: A Journal of Feminist Theory.*

The author would like to thank the John Simon Guggenheim Memorial Foundation, whose award of a Fellowship for the year 2010–2011 contributed to the completion of this book.

Manufactured in the United States of America
New Directions Books are printed on acid-free paper
First published as a New Directions Paperbook (NDP1368) in 2017

Library of Congress Cataloging-in-Publication Data
Names: Mackey, Nathaniel, 1947– author.
Title: Late arcade / Nathaniel Mackey.
Description: New York, NY : New Directions Publishing, [2017]
Identifiers: LCCN 2016037893 | ISBN 9780811226608 (alk. paper)
Classification: LCC PS3563.A3166 L38 2017 | DDC 813/.54—dc23
LC record available at https://lccn.loc.gov/2016037893

10 9 8 7 6 5 4 3 2 1

New Directions Books are published for James Laughlin
by New Directions Publishing Corporation
80 Eighth Avenue, New York 10011

for my cousin
Kenneth Ray Kahn

Late Arcade

Dear Angel of Dust,

Djamilaa brought a new composition to rehearsal today. It's called "Sekhet Aaru Struff," a title that immediately, as you can imagine, got my attention, alluding, as it does, to my own "Sekhet Aaru Strut." Putting "struff" in "strut's" place, it alludes as well to the piece from which it borrows the term (if it can be called a term), Johnny Dyani's "The Robin Irland Struff" on the *African Bass* album he did with Clifford Jarvis a few years back. I'm inclined to say it pointedly alludes to both, albeit its "point" would appear to be a diffusion of point, an advancement of blur (with overtones of slur) tending to dislocate point. What, that is, was Dyani getting at with "Robin Irland" if not an ambiguation of "Robben Island," a pointedly malaprop version bordering on slur? And doesn't "struff" go on in the same vein, subjecting "stuff," "strut," "straw," "fluff," "bluff" and any number of other phonically related words to an ambiguating fusion and diffusion, upping the ante on the already indefinite "stuff"? Djamilaa perhaps had this in mind. Perhaps she meant the replacement of "strut" by "struff" as an ambiguating move, a deflationary tack perhaps.

However much the replacement of "strut" diffuses and deflates a certain self-congratulation at the titular level, however much "struff" does indeed mess with "strut," does indeed mush it up, taking the wind out of the sails its apparent pleasure with itself could be said to be, I say "perhaps" because the music itself does anything but diminish or deride. "Struff" notwithstanding, it conveys no loss or ratcheting down of dimension, no lack of majesty. It's better, perhaps, to simply say a certain modesty obtains, a shying away from the presumption self-nomination can't but entail. "Struff" wants to lighten up, walk lightly, outflank if not entirely break free from such presumption.

"Sekhet Aaru Struff's" light tread compounds a sense of light as trepidatious gait with a competing sense of light as bouyancy, a saltatory élan nowhere more notable than in the bounding figure Aunt Nancy sustains on bass. Atop and to a degree at odds with the bass's throb-inflected walk, I pursue a more tentative approach on trumpet, the trepidatious advance adumbrated by "struff's" unraveling of "strut's" edges, a frayed, fraught excursion bereft of any but ad hoc assurances. Drennette steps away from the traps in favor of bongos and conga for this piece, peppering and otherwise abetting Aunt Nancy's bounding figure while helping propel and punctuating the piece on other fronts as well. Djamilaa herself plays synthesizer, though "presides on" would be a more accurate way to put it, so fully does she avail herself and the piece of a sense of ultimacy, majesty and moment, an incumbent cosmicity or an abiding ethereality the synthesizer is famously able to impart.

The most unusual aspect of the piece's instrumentation is that Lambert and Penguin don't play their horns, assigned instead to something Djamilaa variously terms extended voice (nodding to Meredith Monk), prepared voice (nodding to John Cage) and amended voice or (further accenting her own intervention, underscoring her nodding to no one if not herself) amended mouth. Each is given a text to read, excerpts from a chapter of the *Chapters of Coming Forth by Day*. Lambert's is taken from Chapter XV, "A Hymn of Praise to Ra when He Riseth in the Eastern Part of Heaven," which mentions Sekhet Aaru toward the end: "Let him mingle among the Heart-souls who live in Ta-tchesert. Let him travel about in the Sekhet Aaru, conformably to thy decree with joy of heart—him the Osiris Ani, whose word is truth." Penguin's is taken from Chapter CX, "The Chapters of Sekhet Hetepet," which concerns arrival in Sekhet Aaru and living in the city of Sekhet Hetepet, e.g., "Let me go forward. Let me plough. I am at peace with the god of the town. I know the water, the towns, the nomes, and the lakes which are in Sekhet Hetepet. I live therein. I am strong therein." Lambert recites first, then Penguin.

By extended voice, prepared voice, amended voice or amended mouth Djamilaa means that Lambert and Penguin each clamp three clothespins to their lips for the piece, two of them clamped to and hanging down from the sides of the upper lip, one of them clamped to and hanging down from the middle of the lower lip. The aim is to alter their elocution, to pidginize, as Djamilaa puts it, the papyrus of Ani. She instructed them not to let it stop simply at that but to assist the aleatory work done by the clothespins (or, as she sometimes terms it, the amendments) by furthering it, consciously recasting the text, at the point of enunciation, as universal patois, idiosyncratically conceived. "Think of Pharoah's 'Japan,'" she exhorted. "Think of the long line of scat behind it. You could do worse than think of Slim Gaillard or of Clark Terry's 'Mumbles,' to say nothing of all the vatic chatter outside the music."

Lambert and Penguin wondered if Djamilaa was serious at first (Aunt Nancy, Drennette and I wondered as well), especially when Penguin noticed the sentence "Behold my mouth is equipped" in the text he was to read, at which point he started laughing and, sure it was all a joke, said to Djamilaa, "Okay, you got us. Touché." Djamilaa, though, looked at him as if she had no idea what he meant. Quickly enough, we all saw that indeed she had no idea what he meant. She was nothing if not serious, though she did allow, responding a bit later to a question Lambert raised regarding "amendment as endowment versus amendment as obstruction," that the tactic might be viewed as a bit quirky. "But who says quirky can't be serious?" she rhetorically asked.

Lambert and Penguin, then, approached their parts (in many ways the linchpin of the piece) with all due seriousness, holding any impulse to ham it up, go tongue in cheek or in some other way play for comic effect at bay. Each adopted a damped inflection, whisperlike but a whisper less in volume than tone, conspiratorial—open, even so, to exhortative, declamatory moments now and again. The clothespins did their job of detour, inhibiting certain habits of pronunciation while enabling alternatives, conducing to a pestered, repercussive manner of speech that did indeed, thanks to the synthesizer's choric hints and empyrean laminates, seem the issue of a pidginizing "celestriality" (to use Alan Silva's term), universal patois. I need to stress that this wasn't arrived at quickly, that there were a number of false starts and a good deal of trial and error before Lambert and Penguin found the right vocalic balance and blend, the requisite pace and restraint to make it work.

As I've noted, Djamilaa extracted a lush but buried oratorio from the synthesizer, interred, if one could so say it, in the firmament, a streaming advance and a sheeting sweep thru the heavens. Solemnity and moment, neither untouched by requiem, were hers to maintain, universal bounty both mourned and extolled. Swell had to do with it, as did surge, emanation, pulse—pressed amenities it was all one could do not to be borne away by, however much (yet all the more) one felt allied.

As for my part, it especially fell to me, as I've already said, not to be borne away, to offer an astringent bounding bass and universal bounty could be qualified by. Counterpoise and parry were typically my lines' relation to Lambert's and Penguin's readings, moments of convergence not altogether absent. Moot sublimity, all such rally was earned assurance's emptying out, a hollowing out. Incertitude vied with assurance, earned assurance hallowing hitch, hesitation, sputter's recondite remit. Lambert and I or Penguin and I, as were the trumpet and I, were each the other's hollow extension.

We played the piece a good number of times, even after we finally got it down (especially after we finally got it down). I'm enclosing a tape of the best version.

As ever,

N.

Dear Angel of Dust,

We played a gig at the Comeback Inn over in Venice night before last, a place on Washington about a third of the way between Lincoln and the canals that's been around for about ten years. I heard Joe Farrell there five years ago. We were pretty surprised to get the call, our stuff being more outside than what they normally book. Evidently it had a lot to do with last year's Kool Jazz Festival, a lineup called "New Directions in Sound and Rhythm" that most folks in town still haven't gotten over—some in a negative way, some positive, as appears to be the case with the owner of the Comeback Inn. It was an unlikely lineup for a Kool Jazz Festival, especially one here in L.A., a bit like an invasion from Chicago, the AACM side of Chicago: Muhal Richard Abrams, Anthony Braxton, the Art Ensemble of Chicago, Air, Lester Bowie's From the Root to the Source, Leroy Jenkins's Sting, Roscoe Mitchell's Sound and Space. Also on the bill were James "Blood" Ulmer, the World Saxophone Quartet, John Carter, Laurie Anderson and the Nikolai Dance Theatre. Though we had mixed feelings about this kind of music being presented under as commercial an imprimatur as Kool (Aunt Nancy at one point claimed to wonder if the balloons would begin emerging as smoke rings), it was all rather beautifully anomalous, inspiringly so, nowhere near business-as-usual. One funny thing we've heard is that the night Laurie Anderson, Leroy Jenkins's band, the Art Ensemble and the Nikolai dance troupe performed at the Santa Monica Civic more than a few people showed up expecting to hear Sting the rock singer. Anyway, the owner of the Comeback Inn specifically mentioned the Kool Festival. "It really opened my ears,"

Lambert told us he told him when he called, going on to joke, "It might've even grown me a new pair." He went on to say he'd been meaning to get in touch for a while and asked if we'd play there some night. Lambert said yes and they decided on a date.

It's a small restaurant with not much in the way of a stage, just a spot in one of the corners where they clear away a few tables. It was no great shakes, but a number of friends showed up and it all went well, with a few moments here and there that more than simply went well. Penguin took an alto solo on "The Slave's Day Off," for example, that had Aunt Nancy, draped over the bass like a rag doll, sustaining a rafters-rattling walk that belied her rag-doll diffidence, a walk whose lowest note repeatedly served as Penguin's moment of truth. Repeatedly, Aunt Nancy's walk's furthering pulse notwithstanding, Penguin, with a broken gait and ghost timbre recalling John Tchicai, took stock of the wherefore of going on, assaying, it seemed, every reason not to. A rummaging hover, low to the ground it seemed, the horn's low-register audit, Hamlet-like, left no dissuasive stone unturned. Repeatedly, Penguin pulled free of such hover by way of an angular but oddly damped move into the middle and upper registers, refusing to posit such ascent as triumphant ("flat" refusal, lateral dispatch), a resolution of the quandaries by which he was beset. Repeatedly, he offered no resolution, as though resolution could only be false, the more false the more triumphalist, the more false the more defeatist as well. It was some of Penguin's headiest, most heartfelt playing ever, a mesmerizing insistence upon and abidance in a third way that wasn't just a middle way, a hypnotic hum, hover and run of a solo that didn't so much finish as fade, beg off ending, beg off going on, Penguin pulling away from the mike playing less and less loudly. As I've said, there were other moments as well.

Arguably, however, the gig's aftermath upstaged the gig itself, its most eventful moment occurring afterward, as though a time lag of some sort were in effect. Drennette, that is, tells us that two balloons followed her home (as she puts it) after the gig. She says that yesterday as she was unpacking her drumset, setting up to practice, they emerged as she lifted the lid to the parade snare's container. Before she took the drum out of the container, before she even reached in to take hold of it, a balloon floated up out of the container, emerging from under the slightly lifted lid as though the opening effected by the lifting were the container's mouth. The balloon, floating just above the opening, contained these words: *Too funky. Too forward. So rude the way of the world, too crude. The nerve of him to come on that way, slick-chivalric.* "Be my queen," he said. "Let my face be your throne. I'll lick your pussy, I'll sniff at your ass-crack." *So crude a way to put it, so rude the way of the world.* It hung there a while and then vanished, at which point a second balloon floated up out of the container and hung just above the opening. Inside the second balloon were these words: *"You oughta not be so funky with it," I should've said, semisung, Aretha-like, mock-operatic, and would've said, semisung, Aretha-like, mock-operatic, had I only thought of it in time. Instead, I stood speechless, taken aback.* It hung there a while, just above the parade snare's container's opening, and then vanished.

Drennette says the balloons (the first one in particular) remind her of the X-rated balloons that emerged from the dancers' fists during our record-release gig at The Studio back in February, the emergence our recourse to a 4/4 shuffle meter brought about. She can't help surmising, she says, that the two balloons might be tied to a somewhat similar moment during our second set at the Comeback Inn, a passage during "Tosaut L'Ouverture" in which Aunt Nancy touched ever so lightly upon a 4/4 shuffle, not so much committing unequivocally as alluding to it. In response, Drennette resorted to an obliquely stated backbeat, bordering on tongue-in-cheek, a manner of statement that had it both ways, both advancing the backbeat and beating it back, holding it at bay. It was a passing moment, not at all drawn out, but Drennette says it was that moment, she's convinced, that passage, that gave rise to the balloons in the parade snare's container. That they hid and followed her home, she says, rather than emerging right there during the gig (no balloons appeared at any point during the gig) adds a new wrinkle to this whole balloon phenomenon that we need to think seriously about.

Drennette went on to say, as we talked about this during rehearsal, that she noticed a certain concord (as she put it) between the leverage she and Aunt Nancy had applied to the backbeat and the 4/4 shuffle and the casting of the first balloon's X-rated material in quotes, to say nothing of the explicit distancing from and disapproval of that material the balloon expressed. She wondered if, consistent with this, the balloons' delayed emergence doesn't bespeak reserve, a sense of restraint, modesty even, albeit the business of hiding away and following her home does have, she can't help feeling, a sinister side. Or does the delay, she went on to speculate further, have to do with the speechlessness or the inability to immediately respond, the being less than quick on the uptake, to which the second balloon confesses? What also strikes her, she went on to say in an outrush of questions and thoughts that made it clear how deeply the balloons had gotten to her, is that the balloons appear to have a sense of history, so unmistakably, in this instance, harking back to an earlier emergence.

A good amount of discussion ensued, none of us quite sure what to make of this new development but each of us, notwithstanding, venturing a comment or two, a question or two, a surmise or two. Lambert, for example, led off by all but asking Drennette, whose manner was ponderous, weighty, bordering on distraught, to lighten up, noting that it wasn't the balloons' sense of history he was struck by but their sense of humor, especially the second balloon's reference to Aretha's "nasty gym shoe" ad lib on the *Hey Now Hey (The Other Side of the Sky)* album. Aunt Nancy, on the other hand, agreed with Drennette regarding the rapport between levered backbeat and 4/4 shuffle and the balloons' recourse to quotation, adding that the use of the conditional tense appeared to her to have to do with this as well. Thus, things were off and going.

Much got said during the discussion but we all continue to give this new development thought. And though much got said, not everything that might've been said got said. Djamilaa mentioned to me later that she didn't bring it up, for obvious reasons, but there seemed to her to be a strongly personal element to the balloons' manner of emergence and their content both, that it seemed they wanted to say something about Drennette or even that Drennette wanted to say something about herself: putatively hard-ass Drennette, putatively repercussive Drennette, Drennette Virgin. "'Slick-chivalric,'" she said, "rhymewise and otherwise, has Rick written all over it."

More anon.

Yours,
N.

Dear Angel of Dust,

More balloons last night. It was during the John Coltrane Birthday Concert we took part in at the Century City Playhouse. The folks at Rhino Records organized it and a good number of bands played. The usual suspects from around town were there: Badi Taqsim's trio, the Boneyard Brass Octet, SunStick and the Chosen Few, Horace Tapscott's quintet. Bobby Bradford and John Carter came in from Pasadena, Roberto Miranda came in from the Valley. It was a marvelous event. Weatherwise, what had been a beautiful day turned into a beautiful evening, somewhat on the warm side, a touch of Indian summer, but unusually clear, sparkling, a bit of burnish left over from the day. Most of the musicians hung around outside when not playing. One could still hear the music and it was nice to see and talk with folks one hadn't seen in a while. We milled around in front, some of us strolling a block or two up or down Pico. Badi Taqsim and I stood gazing thru the fence at the Rancho Park Golf Course at one point, talking about recent bookings at Hollywood's Catalina Bar & Grill. Anyway, we played a couple of pieces, "Sun Ship" and "Sekhet Aaru Struff." It was our first public performance of "Sekhet Aaru Struff" and it was during this piece that the balloons emerged. It was actually, to be more precise, during a section toward the end of the piece that was a bit of a detour, a turn toward rumba initiated by Drennette.

We'd been talking about rumba earlier in the day, listening to and talking about an album by Totico y Sus Rumberos that came out a couple of years ago, so the turn Drennette initiated didn't entirely come as a surprise. Their rendition of "What's Your Name?," the old doo-wop hit by Don and Juan, had especially caught our attention, getting us going on the mesh between doo-wop's mellifluous come-on and rumba's courtship mimetics. Exactly how apt or effective a mesh it is was what we discussed, opinions ranging from endorsement, even outright rave, a claim that the merger isn't only beautiful but long overdue and that the piece is the best on the album by far (Penguin), to reservations regarding the advisedness of literalizing what's otherwise more subtle, productively so, otherwise more dynamically understated (Drennette).

It wasn't entirely a surprise, then, as I've said, when Penguin came to the end of his recitation and Drennette began to beat out a guaguancó rhythm on the conga, not only beating out the guaguancó but singing a lalaleo or diana, the introductory song-syllables "ana na na ana, ana na na ana," which in fact made the detour less jarring, contributing to and thereby continuing Lambert and Penguin's theme or thread of universal patois. Soon after finishing the lalaleo, however, she sped things up, switching from guaguancó to giribilla, a more strictly musical, nonmimetic form that has been called the bebop of rumba variations.

Aunt Nancy was the first to respond to Drennette's detour, letting the bounding figure go and imitating, in the bass's upper register, a segundo's giribilla pattern. Djamilaa's synthesizer turned its interred oratorio into a chorus answering Drennette's lalaleo, a bank of antiphonal echoes Djamilaa granted galactic reverb, intergalactic reach. I temporized for a few measures before letting my sputters give way to a golden run worthy of Chocolate Armenteros, but it was Lambert who most decisively responded to Drennette's detour. Removing the clothespins from his lips and putting them in his coat pocket (the clothespins, by the way, had drawn laughter from several people in the audience when the piece began but they'd gotten used to them and quieted down), he picked up his tenor, put it to his mouth and motioned for me to pull back.

Lambert began by going back to the sputter my golden run had come out of, blowing a barrage of expectorant bleats and pops not unlike an attack of hiccups. Beginning there, he indeed never left, thriving on what sounded like obstruction even as he ran the gamut from belly laughs at the horn's low end to a wistful quizzicality in the

upper register that at times took him to the spoons. More than Toti-
co's "What's Your Name?" he appeared to have Frank Lowe's "Broad-
way Rhumba" in mind, rummaging around the horn as though it
were a hot potato or a goose's neck or as though it were a clothespin
pinching his tongue. He sustained a blustery tone, bursting, it seemed,
with things to say, albeit more things than could be said it seemed.
It was during this solo that the balloons emerged, the first of them
lifting heavily up out of the bell of the horn bearing these words:
*An Egyptian rumba she said it would be, abstract, angular, undulant, pulse
beaten out on a salted cod box, an Egyptian giribilla she said it would be. No
BaKongo cloth kicked in a circle, no guaguancó, no lifted skirt edge, no not
being caught by the vacunao. A giribilla, no euphemistic vaccine, she said it
would be, an Egyptian rumba, ardent, austere.*

Following the first balloon's emergence Lambert took a more con-
fidential tack, sputtering as before but as if under his breath, resorting
to the sotto voce forage he pursues to such resounding effect. It was
a more gauzy sound but one with which he parsed not a whit less,
having no less recourse to angles, inversions and reversals, breaking
rumba apart, it seemed at points, and by turns putting *ba* before *rum*
and putting *rum* before *ba*, an Egypto-Caribbean conjugation having
to do with soul (spirits' bearing on soul, soul's bearing on spirits). It
was at one such point that the second balloon came out of the horn
bearing these words: *"Isis to his Osiris, I dreamt he stayed inside me all
night, forever, stiff, unyielding," she said. "Damsel in distress, dread virgin, I
lay scared stiff. Isisn't to my own Isis, stiff but not unyielding, I lay afraid, flat
as a board beneath his weight."* The balloon disappeared when Lambert,
put upon by a strain of quizzicality stronger than any that had come
before, paused ever so slightly. When he resumed playing the third
balloon floated up from the bell of the horn bearing these words: *"I
lay afraid but unafraid, feigning frailty," she said, "stiffness answering stiff-
ness, yielding even so, faux fragility stiffening him throughout all eternity.
Stiff intruder I welcomed in and regaled with my own stiffness, he likes it
when I start off stiff and begin to loosen."*

After the third balloon's emergence Lambert stepped back from
the mike, let the balloon vanish and put his tenor back in its stand,
the audience applauding loudly. Drennette ever so subtly blushed, as
though the balloons had peeped her heart of hearts, but she held her

head higher than before, her back straighter than before. She let go of the giribilla pattern, Aunt Nancy returned to the bounding figure, I came back in on trumpet and we took the piece out, the audience applauding loudly still.

As ever,
N.

Dear Angel of Dust,

Hotel Didjeridoo would have none of it. Hotel Didjeridoo, the once towering, long since fallen cathouse of wide repute I dreamt ages ago, reluctant object of the Resurrection Project's announced intentions, would have none of it. Strain as I might, it refused resurrection. The news the Hotel had fallen flew like bullets overhead, insisting I lay low, insisting I stay down. The news the Hotel had fallen continued to be news. My low reconnoiter had barely begun, the bullets cried out. No way was it to be risen up from in a hurry, no way hurried out of, no way made an edifice of. All such architectural conceit had long since been made moot. Limit-case dispatch à la Braxton's contrabass clarinet, low reconnoiter knew nothing if not crawl space, crablike sashay (if it could be said to be sashay) tending toward and touching on collapse. It knew nothing if not limbo's antithetic arc.

Bullets indeed flew, announcing and reannouncing the Hotel had fallen, insisting and again insisting I stay down. "Lay low" it seemed I heard and indeed I did. Hotel Jíbaro the Hotel appeared to have become in its demise. "Aylelolaylelolay" chimed inside my head. A glossolalic launch long the custom in Puerto Rico, it was an odd scrap, a bit of caroling debris, a curious run or recourse to non-, post- or presense lyrics I was nothing if not taken aback to hear inside my head. "Aylelolaylelolay / lolaylelolelolela," it ran and repeated, a talismanic loop whose repeated "lay low" I could no way ignore. It threaded its way thru the fabric the bullet barrage apprised me of, the accompanying quatro's wincing ping as piercing as a Portuguese guitar, needlepoint address I drew back from but welcomed (bittersweet pinprick, bittersweet vaccine).

It was an odd bit of music to be visited by while under fire, but on a certain level, the social fabric one heard so much about shown to be what it was, Puerto Rican scat's admonitory "lay low" made perfect sense, an involuntary reflex insisting stay down if one were already down, duck if not. Admonitory duck, moreover, bordered on earth-diver duck, a foundational drop or a compensatory plunge rendering save-oneself and save-the-world one and the same, bite of dust and beakful of mud one and the same. One lay on one's belly, having hit the dirt, bullets whistling overhead, one's jíbaro serenade woven into the guns' ongoing report. It all made perfect sense.

Hotel Didjeridoo, I had to accept, would have no rebuilding, no rebirth. A thread running thru the proverbial social fabric, "lay low" said let the proverbial dogs lie, what was done was done. Even so, as I lay I stood ready to ring changes on syllabic largesse, "aylelolay's" un-raveling rope a noose I sang or sought to sing my way out of, the fait accompli Hotel Didjeridoo resigned itself to. Or was it syllabic duress, a rope I ran the risk of choking up on if not dangling from? I rolled over and lay on my back baying at the moon, "aylelolay" my coyote howl. Caught feeling, fraught sonance, "aylelolay" culled a rapport harking back to what some said were Muslim roots, a derivation (or so, at least, I had heard) from *ilaha illallah*, not unlike bullfighting's *olé* (I had also heard) harking back to *Allah*.

Hotel Moro it might well have been and was, "lay low's" metathetic remit a reminder of Lole Montoya's voice. Husky, full-throated, the hull of a boat I lay on my back looking up at, it bore tidings from Egypt, Mohamed Abdelwahad's "Anta Oumri" and "Wdaret el Ayan" segued into out of "Sangre Gitana y Mora," an incendiary sunship scorching the water I lay under.

Still, I stepped forward and blew—stood up, stepped forward, took horn to mouth and blew, "lay low" notwithstanding. A bugling flutter and flex it was, the feather I could be knocked over by rousing me even so, requiem and reveille rolled into one. Brass but ever so inward (so cracked a wrinkle of sound as to risk erasure), it raised a hand, it seemed, all the same, hailing the ship's hull in the water above. Incendiary boat all the more inveterate rebuff, Lole's voice I would chase forever, its brass equivalent not quite to be arrived at. I would chase and be forever outrun.

I resisted making much of "low lay," the obvious play on jazz's reputed bordello roots. Lole's voice was a bit of husk in my throat, tightening it, constricting my airflow, choked-up endowment could it be said to be an endowment, poignant, unappeasable, possessed. I blew to be its equal or, short of that, to etherealize it, bodily husk an abidance never to be gotten free from, blow though I did as though I could. Brass, that is, was a way of getting by or going on. It afforded what solace it could, its by no means moot condolences. I had recourse to a coyness recalling Miles, the face-behind-a-fan retreat or seeming retreat heard on "Circle," demure but not without design ("See how that sounds, Teo"). It turned away from the ship's hull overhead, a blush or the beginnings of a blush burgeoning inward, a breathy spread of guile and regret. It was anything but "aylelolay" but not unrelated, nothing if not its compunction or its qualm.

It occurred to me it might also be Hotel Mita, "aylelolay's" Puerto Rican provenance bearing again but in a slant manner. The ship's hull was a message on high, "el mensaje de alto" sung about by the Rondalla del Templo de Mita in San Juan, the song's mention of Noah no doubt the connection, its "Como los tiempos de Noë vino el espíritu / anunciando que viene destrucción" resonating with Hotel Didjeridoo's fall. I brought this to bear upon the horn, put it into the horn as though the horn were the proverbial pipe, my blush or my beginnings of a blush combusted, nothing if not the Rondalla's heartrending chorus. "Amigo, ven y oyes la vóz de Dios," I said with my breath as well as under my breath, a smoked insistence I parried against the boat's unreachability, smudge and buff's newly made amends.

Husky, haggard, Lole's voice I already knew I would chase forever. The Rondalla's call I now knew I would chase forever, equal parts cry and confection, sweet smoke circling skyward. The sea I saw myself laid low in held me up, the ship's hull caulked as if coaxed into the water, insisting I blow my horn. I felt a salty-sweet buttress or brace whose rough accompaniment said, not outright saying it, stand tall.

I stood underwater blowing my horn, an Aquarian undulance inflecting each note. I blew as though aided by synthetic strings, a synthesizer's air of impendence, a watery element all its own. Urge and emanation rolled into one, doused alterity of an astral sort informed each note, a star having fallen into the sea and set it boiling, each new insinuation bugling no end. That star was none other than the sun, warily ensconced in Lole's Atet boat, the ship whose hull her voice was. The morning boat's fall or its failure to lift (if either, against all odds, was what it was) stirred the bottom of the sea and sent waves everywhere, roiling with insinuation, the very blush or beginnings of a blush I blew like smoke out the bell of the horn.

The mixed-metaphorical premises on which I stood—smoking water, undersea buttress, "lay low" vantage—turned my legs to rubber, propping me up even so. Bubbles came out of the bell of the horn, smoke bubbles, bubbles that were in fact balloons. Each balloon bore a message as it rose toward Lole's boat but burst when it got there, raining down bits of script, the words that had been inside. Gone up in smoke, such bits as *I caught myself* came floating down, water more like air than water, such bits as *letting myself lean back before catching myself*. A note-bearing bottle as well as a comic-strip balloon, each bubble as it burst blessed my undersea launch with incongruous ash, burnt bits of script consecrating my intonation, the words or the would-be words I bruited on high. "All this in the wake of Lole's boat," I said to myself, "the merging of hull and husk I'll forever be outrun by." It was a vow, a benediction even, a mandate I afforded myself. "Lay low" auspices notwithstanding, running after would never stop.

My horn wanted nothing if not to announce liquidity's advance beyond rectilinear form, the stiff amenities undulance and curvature so luxuriously annulled. Such amenities bend and slur would have nothing to do with (or would, were they to, only by way of contrast), just as Hotel Didjeridoo, root brass or root embouchure, would have nothing anymore to do with architectural conceit's dream of rise and rebirth. Hotel Didjeridoo, I reminded oneself, would have none of it, nor would Lole's metathetic morning boat, mixed-metaphorical ash ran in whose wake, burn and rescinded script rolled into one.

The morning boat's fall or its failure to lift was in fact a refusal. Lole's voice would allow no likeness. Stout reluctance I thought to call it, willed unwillingness, husk none else than a containment, heartfelt holding back. The boat sat taunting me, teasing me, flat on the water it seemed—flat but holding all there was of arc or ascendency, hold and hull nothing if not the same.

Water wet the horn I blew underwater. Wooing the boat's hull overhead, I imagined myself aboard ship, stowed away in the hold but aboard it even so, none other than the smoldering sun. It was a doused Osirian sun I saw myself as, adamantly of a piece with the smoldering horn I blew, the wet trumpet's blare an upsurge of bubbles ascending the sky the sea whose floor I stood on had become. Still, the boat stood me up in more senses than one. Each bubble, before it burst, gave me something to reach for, a note-bearing boat inside a boat-bearing bottle, the rendezvous of seed with husk Lole's boat's hull promised, destiny's proverbial date. Each bubble, having burst, left me dateless.

Datelessness notwithstanding, burst bubbles notwithstanding, I rallied, a hip variation on first call coming out of the horn, a bugling whose call was to carry on. Stingy-brim strut woven into a mustering charge, it was nothing less than a gauntlet hitting the ground.

What it was was that one horn wasn't enough, one voice not enough. There was something crowded about Lole's voice, precisely what one meant by husky. It was as though, no matter how subdued a turn her voice took, some indefinable something or a multitude of such were jostling for space. It was all she could do to contain strains that would otherwise undo the tenuous-accord-cum-strenuous-contention husk held in check.

Even from below I could see the boat bulged with voices, some stowaway, some aboveboard. It bore more than one voice, however much Lole's voice might've been the voice that fueled and kept it afloat, much as the smoldering sun it bore might've been no more than a smoke-filled bubble, burning-boat-bearing bottle inside an incendiary ship. To see it so cried out for a larger conception, a new perspective, Donald Byrd's recording of that name coming quickly to mind, only to have its eight-voice choir rejected as too pat or predictable for what was called for here. Voice ("chorality" or "choricity") needed to be more diffuse or more dispersed, more constituent strain or pervasive surge as in the sort of emic or seemingly emic effusion, aqueous or atmospheric, a synthesizer might provide.

I stood ready to acknowledge this need and, indeed, almost before one knew it, I already had. The bulging boat swollen with voices would be ratified beforehand, if the performance now underway became part of the antithetic opera (theoretic opera some called it) of which for a while there'd been so much talk. A quote I had not only long savored but knew might one day prove useful popped into my head as I continued to blow bubble after smoke-filled bubble. Should the underwater, boat-wooing performance come to be included in the opera, the quote would serve as Aquatico-Solar Epigraph #1:

> Osiris represents the Nile and the Sun: Sun and Nile are, on the other hand, symbols of human life—each one is signification and symbol at the same time; the symbol is changed into signification, and this latter becomes symbol of that symbol, which itself then becomes signification. None of these phases of existence is a Type without being at the same time a Signification; each is both; the one is explained by the other. Thus there arises one pregnant conception, composed of many conceptions.

Isis to the epigraph's Osirian *mise en abîme*, I quickly resorted to circular breathing, a tack whose underscoring of reciprocity verged ever so lightly on rotundity as well (swollen belly and swollen boat rolled into one).

Stingy-brim strut had come a long way, a diffuse, omni-voice dilation or solution absorption knew no way to constrain. No more than a mere hint of oratorio, no more than a mere hint of chorale, it furthered an aqueous consort of carolings coincident with the medium itself— coincident but not by that to be contained or ingested, an attenuation beyond (while residing within) liquidity's confines. Liquid's exhalation of gas was what it was like if not outright amounted to, an exhalation that oddly wafted within even as it wafted while standing in wait beyond. Such wafture, multiple, immanent, extrapolative, was nothing if not the quantum stride (not only soulful in addition to quantum but quantum only insofar as it numbered soulfulness among its attributes) called for by stingy-brim strut and begun by it to be put into play.

Nonetheless, neither "aylelolay" nor "Mensaje de Alto" had been left behind, each a standing rope song's promise of ascent made a signpost of sorts I repeatedly made note of and, in so doing, made listeners make note of as well. A firemen's pole if not a laminated snake, it could hardly not also expostulate descent, bearing senses of emergency, alarm and even frantic dispatch, its croonfulness and reassurance at the strictly musical level notwithstanding.

It all went to insist again that Hotel Didjeridoo would in no way countenance easy elevation, that it would have no truck with facile rebirth or rebuilding. Hotel Didjeridoo would have none of it, as its three alternate names (Jíbaro, Moro, Mita) and its unstated but implied potential for even more names had meant to make clear, "lay low's" and/or Lole's blown smoke's amity with "lo alto" not to be taken as other than the qualm or qualification it assuredly was.

Ambient accompaniment, water maintained pedal-point armature, fluviality, surge and subsidence, light oratorical wax and recess. Stingy-brim strut's Osirian posture stood on friendly terms, it all but went without saying, with standing itself, obfuscating Osiris's coexistent rapport with recumbency, recline, supination. It was this blown smoke's ascendancy made clear.

So I bent my knees and squatted, continuing to play, not missing a note. I leaned back a bit, letting my ass rest on the seafloor, horn still in hand, continuing to play. I lay back farther, the back of my head coming to rest on the seafloor, my back flat against the seafloor, still not missing a note, continuing to play. I extended my legs until they too lay flat on the seafloor, horn still in hand, horn pointed upward.

Aside from the fact that I was breathing and not lying perfectly still, moving my arms and fingers to play the horn and keeping time with my right foot, I lay like a mummy, not only not missing a note but playing my heart out, serenading and seducing (would-be seducing) the boat overhead.

Sincerely,
Dredj

Dear Angel of Dust,

I'm writing about yesterday's letter. It was written, as you no doubt saw right away, during a cowrie shell attack. The attack seems to've been brought on by a chain of associations or a train of thought that began with me reminiscing about my early childhood in Florida. I was particularly nostalgic about conch fritters, which I vividly remember though I haven't eaten any since we left Miami when I was four. Was that enough to ignite the conch component of the cowrie shell attacks, the new, scalpel-edge wrinkle that seems to've motored recent attacks even more than the cowries themselves? Or was it my recollection of a family fishing trip when I was three, the incident everyone still laughs about, my uncle reeling in a fish, whipping the line back in a high arc, and me, standing farther up the bank in back of him, getting hit squarely on the head by the fish on the end of his line?

Whichever, if not something else and if not both, it got me going. Whether conch-implied incision or fish-upside-the-head wallop, something seemed intent on underscoring depth, subaqueousness, river if not sea. It seemed to merge with a watery, "oceanic" sense I'd felt while playing "Sekhet Aaru Struff" the day before (albeit not so much felt as felt surrounded by perhaps), a sense I couldn't quite shake of being underwater, cosmic or not if not earthly and cosmic both. Was yesterday's letter Dredj's attempt to convey that sense? Garbled attempt I'm inclined to say, so brimming with matters not particularly germane to "Sekhet Aaru Struff" the letter seems to me to be. Or are these departures from point the very "point," the diffusion of point I touched on in the letter that accompanied the tape? So maybe it's not so much a garbled as a "struffy" attempt?

In any case, call it Dredj Alley, for it was an alley Dredj ducked into before it became a body of water whose floor he was on, an alleyway just off the beachfront in Venice, I'd go so far as to say, up from which one looked out from a flat filling up with sharp Shostakovian light. From House of Dredj to Dredj Annex to Dredj Alley, the attacks appear to be on an anti-architectural course, a course of architectural undoing, Hotel Didjeridoo refusing resurrection, insisting solidity and solubility hold hands. "Sekhet Aaru Struff" or not, Dredj descried hand holding hand, hand on hand, held hands holding his writing hand.

A light attack, it lasted only a day.

As ever,
N.

Dear Angel of Dust,

I wouldn't say I'm taking a page out of the balloons' book, that I'm trying to beat them at their own game. Aunt Nancy suggested as much but I don't think that's it. No, this new thing I'm trying goes back to a story Yusef Lateef tells about the days when he was in Mingus's band, a story I was deeply struck by when I first heard it, a story I think about from time to time. Yusef says there was a composition on which he was to solo and that Mingus, rather than writing out chord symbols for him to improvise against, drew a picture of a coffin, that it was this that he was to base his improvisation on. A friend of mine once joked that Mingus simply meant that if Yusef messed up the solo he'd kill him, but I've long been intrigued by and attracted to the idea of getting musical information from a picture and it's this that led me to a certain experiment with my latest composition. Braxton's diagrammatic, pictogrammic titles and the solo concert of his I caught a couple of years ago, the scores for which looked like pen and ink drawings, nonfigurative but drawings even so, had a role as well.

The new composition is called "Fossil Flow." I wrote it thinking about oil spills, the increasing number of them and the damage they do. Just this year there've been two massive ones: in February, the Nowruz Field platform in Iran spilled 80 million gallons of oil into the Persian Gulf; in August, a Spanish tanker, the *Castillo de Bellver*, caught fire and spilled 78 million gallons off the coast of Cape Town, South Africa. I was thinking about the distant past (prehistoric apocalypse, collapse or catastrophe) achieving fluidity, the oxymoronic play between fossil and flow of such dimension as to put the present at risk. It's as though it were the dinosaurs and the mastodons' revenge, prehistory's grudge against what came after, a brief against preservation or containment, fossil solidity, an entropic brief against past and present keeping their places. It's as though, Dredj-like, I saw solidity's hand and solubility's hand, gripped though they were by one another, holding history's hand, leading the way as it broke. Or was it, oil and water notoriously not mixing, solidity's hand and insolubility's hand? I'm not sure it matters. Recalling the rationing and the long lines at gas stations a few years ago, I saw dependency's hand and depletion's hand take solidity's hand and (in)solubility's hand's places, presided over by an entropic sun.

Much of the piece is written out but I'm trying something new, something of a built-in improvisation approach, by leaving gaps at various points in everyone's parts, gaps of a certain number of measures (which varies) marked by the words "Wild Card." The latter refer to a drawing and text with which each musician is provided, an 8" x 12" posterboard "card" on which he or she is to base what he or she plays at that point. I'm enclosing one. As you can see, the "card" consists of a drawing, captioned "Molimo m'Atet's Figurehead Consoled on the Revival Bench," beneath which is a brief paragraph. I struggled over whether or not to include the latter, fearing it might be spelling things out too much, taking away from the suggestiveness of the drawing. I decided in favor of keeping it, realizing that it adds a suggestiveness of its own, that words, regardless of how much they point or specify, can't altogether escape indefiniteness or inference, that, indeed, specification has a way of being shadowed by implication. What, for example, is to be musically made of the fact that the figurehead's ribs show, simply enough, in the drawing but also show, in an augmented, not so simple way, in the words "visible, as were the planks of the ship's busted hull"?

I'm also enclosing a tape. Let me know what you think.

Yours,
N.

Molimo m'Atet's Figurehead Consoled on the Revival Bench

An oil tanker had run aground farther up the coast and broken apart. Brothers in black before they knew it, B'Loon and Djbouche washed ashore with the news of the spill. People gathered on the beach to help clean up and help rescue seabirds, oil and tar stuck to their feathers from alighting on the water or, standing or prancing on the shore, being caught by the tide. Bright sun and blue sky notwithstanding, the spill cast a pall over everything and everyone, not least of all Djband, who, likening themselves to a ship, the sun boat of Egyptian belief, felt as though they too had run aground. Epitomizing the "boat-bodied lightness, light-bodied bigness" one of them had once extolled, the female figure gracing the prow of the ship they took themselves to be (the goddess Maat, some said) stepped away, walked ashore and sat down on a bench facing the sea, head down, dejected, ribs visible, as were the planks of the ship's busted hull. Impromptu patron saint of shipwreck, ad hoc angel, Dredj immediately sat down beside her and put his arm around her, offering comfort, consolation, recondite sun, as if to look to and be lit by eclipse were the only amenity.

_____

Dear Angel of Dust,

Many thanks for your letter. I appreciate your comments on "Fossil Flow," your reaction to which, I have to admit, I was nervous about. Yes, you heard it right. "Stratified extinction," as you say, does pervade the piece, a tributary distinction between extinction and exhaustion woven in. I'm impressed by your picking up on the "Wild Card" sections of each band member's playing and what about the drawing and/or text informs how he or she plays. Drennette says you're right that the abstract bench Dredj and the figurehead sit on (and, by implication, the abstract revival available to them) particularly caught her eye and especially spoke to her, giving rise to the stroked, retreating figure she has recourse to with brushes that you note a couple of minutes into the piece (not unlike, she agrees, sand pulled away from the shore by a receding wave). You're also right that the "welter of double-reed hustle" Penguin and Lambert get into on oboe and English horn, respectively, the outbreak of metaphysical sweat with its needling or drilling insistence as if to answer a spiritual-materialist clot begging to be cut thru, is one of the places where two players' "Wild Card" sections coincide. And your surmise that Penguin's choppy, shenai-like drone has to do with a focus on the apparently oil-toed and oil-fingered extremities on the drawing's right side agrees with his account; a meditation, he calls it, upon those extremities' "tarpit premises." Likewise, Lambert's barking, dilated, alto-sounding complaints derived, Lambert says, from an impulse born of both pictorial and textual cues, an impulse to "occupy ribcage arena," as he puts it, those cues being exactly the depiction of and the reference to the figure-

27

head's ribs that you suggest animated his playing at that point.
Nothing much else to report. Just a quick thanks for your letter.

As ever,
N.

Dear Angel of Dust,

Penguin seems to have been heartened by the subtle blush the bal-
loons brought to Drennette's face at the Century City Playhouse. It
came up as he and I were talking today. "Lambert got it right," he
said. "Or should I say the balloons got it right? They blew the whistle
on Drennette's fake reticence, ripped away the blasé front she puts
up. With all that stuff about the balloons following her home, all but
about being stalked or maybe outright about being stalked, she got it
right as well, auguring a muse of pursuit and pursuit's engine or draw,
reluctance, a ruse of rebuff, a prude poetics." He paused a moment,
savoring the thought. "There was more to that blush than met the
eye," he resumed. "Her heart's blood flew to her head." It seemed it
flew to his as well, for he paused again, subtly blushing at the conceit
before going on. "The balloons not only blew the whistle," he then
went on. "They let the air, so to speak, out of an inflated self-regard.
They all but burst with Drennette's recondite desire to be found out,
contested, caught by lordly science alone." He subtly blushed again,
inwardly balked, twin to the balking inwardness that was more than
met the eye, the prude interiority he took to heart and took heart
from, the soul whose mating twin he'd be if he could.

"Just like Lambert likes to say about the griot," Penguin said when
he took up speaking again, gazing into the distance as if what he was
going to say came from afar, "the balloons, bless their hearts, have a
big mouth." He no longer subtly blushed but again he paused. "Dren-
nette's a little bit off," he said when he spoke again. I took him to mean
more than he said. I took him to mean the balloons call interiority out,

their mouths, insofar as they can be said to have them, open in awe at Drennette's abscondity, her becoming all the more an object of pursuit by not being all there. He sought leverage it struck me. He'd have made B'Loon's wan smile a satchel mouth. He'd have pried B'Loon's wan smile open, ransacked it, anything to get next to Drennette. Confirmation came at once. Penguin repeated, "Drennette's a little bit off," adding, "but the balloons would have none of her not-nearness. They would abide by nothing short of not-nearness beginning to see its end, not-nearness beginning to be sashay."

I could not have seen Penguin more clearly. I saw him in nothing if not namesake light, hallowed by eponymous aura: ripped, wingless bird, wind-afflicted, flightless, devout. "The balloons would know Drennette otherwise," he said, "knowing her by her being a little bit off no longer enough. They would have her no more than two bows' lengths away, no more than an atom's breadth away. The balloons would be her throne and her footstool." He was quietly raving, caught in a low-key agitation, a game of hide and seek (hers with him, the balloons' with the band), gnostic stranger, grounded bird.

Still, he would aver what was yet to be seen, given heart by the balloons' intimations. He now spoke explicitly of himself, changing the course it had seemed he was on, contrasting himself with the balloons. "I, however, would know her by her distant footfall, footsteps down a dark hallway, a rustle outside my door." I'd all along taken the balloons to be a stand-in for himself and I continued to see them that way though he now employed them as foil. He fell silent and I remained silent.

I had said nothing all the while Penguin spoke and it seemed he expected as much. It was a run of pure devotion, a poem, a paean, an oath.

Yours,
N.

Dear Angel of Dust,

Day before yesterday we drove up to Santa Cruz to play the Kuumbwa Jazz Center again. It was three years ago we first played there. It was good to venture north again and again we took 101 and then 1 where it branches off from 101 at San Luis Obispo. The coast was a feast of blue sky and blue water again, radiant sun and reflected sun's radiant sparkle on water. It was a feast we could hardly take our eyes off. Sunlight and sea lay hypnotically to our left all the while we put Morro Bay, San Simeon, Carmel and Monterey behind us.

We got going early in the morning, early enough to get to Santa Cruz by late afternoon. It was still dark, in fact, when we left L.A., so we pulled into Santa Cruz well in time for the sound check, the longer route we took notwithstanding. It turned out we got there with time to spare, which time we decided to burn by visiting the lighthouse. We walked around on the pathways and the sidewalk and the grassy field surrounding the lighthouse, watching the surfers, the bicycle riders, the skateboard riders, the Frisbee throwers. Waves crashed on the rocks. Wind wafted salt.

The smell of salt addressed us again as we stood outside Kuumbwa later that night between sets. The air smelled heavily of the sea, prompting Aunt Nancy to note "a coastal piquancy" she said demanded we play "Fossil Flow" during the second set. She couldn't help, she said, catching a recondite whiff—imaginary, she admitted, but all the more insinuative being so—an oblique hint of oil threaded thru the marine bouquet the night air wafted. "I can't get those rigs off my mind," she said, referring to the oil platforms off the Santa

Barbara coast we'd driven past in the morning, the site of a huge oil spill in 1969.

It was hard not to see the sense it made. The specter of the derricks had followed us up the coast, shadowing the sea and the sun's gleam and shimmer, dark prospect under an otherwise bright façade. "Fossil Flow" couldn't have been offered an apter setting, salt itself auguring future affliction, imaginary though the smell of oil might've been. The piece is one that wants to put pressure on flow, indemnify furtherance, bestow auspice and omen upon the undulacy it works. Ominous undulance had already, to an extent, come into play, a suppositious wave and waft Aunt Nancy picked up on mixing oil and salt. Bass player to the bone, she sensed a deep throb, eventual ache, dark unction, a waxing of promise and foreboding that was doubly on the tip of her tongue—oil she could almost taste, calamity she all but announced. It seemed all the more fitting that "Fossil Flow" begins with her playing a three-note ostinato.

There was no way not to see it made sense. We decided we'd end the second set with "Fossil Flow," a fitting end not only to the set and the gig but to the day, a fittingness Lambert would accent by switching from English horn to tenor for this rendition, more deeply resonating with dark unction. Flow, the more we thought about it, cut more than one way, not spoilage or spill alone but excursion. We had, after all, driven up the coast. We had, after all, enjoyed it. There was a principle of nonexemption we grew apprised of, automotivity a fluid aspect itself: we were part of the flow, in on the flow. (I remembered the Buick Dynaflow my uncle had been so proud of back in the fifties. I thought of Ray Charles mentioning a Dynaflow in "It Should Have Been Me.") Enjoyment lent undulacy a lilt unction wanted in on. This was the truth we both averred and would keep at bay.

We played "Tosaut L'Ouverture" next to last. When it ended we went right into "Fossil Flow," not waiting for the applause to subside, not announcing it. We came on with a slow lope led by Aunt Nancy's pensive, three-note ostinato on bass, a descending figure whose rotundity of tone edged over into omen, apprehension, foreboding, robust as it otherwise was notwithstanding. A table of sorts was being set—implicative, dark but brightened by the bit of shimmer Drennette's ride cymbal worked in, the calm, confident way she kept time.

Djamilaa took up with that bit of shimmer when she came in on piano five bars in, starting out with a subtly happy-hand garnish that had something of glimmer and gleam to it and a prance aspect as well.

The horns, when Lambert, Penguin and I came in, stating the head on tenor, oboe and cornet, respectively, had an unprompted sense of aside, sotto voce not so much as reaching out from it, doing so with annunciative blare. Call and cry factored in as well, as also did no small amount of tartness, a ribald arrest of all one thought one knew, knowing the pensive lope it was. It seemed we wanted to say something about moment and simultaneity, moment's dismay at simultaneity's largesse, its doling out, moment's dismay at sequentiality's parsimony; it even seemed we had already said that something. This was in large part, insofar as we already had or possibly had, the work of Djamilaa's tolling chords and her solemn, sometimes grumpy left hand. Chorded ploy contended with chorded plenitude, sequential disbursement pressed and vied with by both. How to both unbraid simultaneity's bounty and give it its due, unpack to the point or brink of undoing, was the question we were called to confront in our solos.

The first to solo, Lambert was all business. He restated the head, grudgingly it seemed, put upon by quizzical misgiving, pestered by qualms. Calling to mind, in that regard, the solo Joe Henderson takes on McCoy Tyner's "Contemplation" on *The Real McCoy*, he allowed himself a certain hesitancy, opening gaps in the head's articulation, not so much a stutter as being repeatedly given pause (albeit stutter, sputter even, was obliquely the case). Bellow and beguilement volleyed, haloed by complaint at every point. Caught in a related quandary, Drennette beat the parade snare as though beating back tears, choking up on the stick and holding it at midpoint, swiping—rare vulnerability, rare admission, rare forthrightness, a clipped, cutting pleat, cropped egress.

I stood to Lambert's left, looking over his shoulder. When he got to the "Wild Card" gap within the head's elaboration it seemed it was the oil-drop extremities in the drawing that caught his eye, the figures' oil-drop hands, toes, fingers and feet. Working changes on classic teardrop tenor, he built on Drennette's choked-up admission but also brushed it aside. A parodic, moanlike drop to the lower register picked a bone with lachrymosity and, by implication, unctuosity as well. He would have nothing to do with suspect suavity, he declared by way of a more forthright return to the horn's middle octave, no matter the oil on his and everyone else's hands. It was a beautiful boast, made all the more so by his maintenance of a sober, unflustered tone worthy of Dewey Redman, a soothing, unhurried—did one dare say suave?—uptake or attack.

(No, one dared not say suave. What might've seemed so or one might've said seemed so was in fact a heuristic roughness Lambert plied and parlayed into scoured sobriety, sensibility abraded, a bumped entitlement or sense of entitlement tending more than one way.)

Drennette saw that her choked-up address of the parade snare no longer held sway. She returned her hand to the base of the stick, took the rim of the ride cymbal between the forefinger and thumb of her left hand and began to slowly mark time, the stick's tip hitting the cymbal with a tolling insistence Djamilaa quickly joined in on, repeating a single note in unison with it. Together the two chimed, Djamilaa's "tallywise" limpidity (one-two, one-two, one-two…) auditing and all the more endorsing the ride cymbal's understated ring. They too now bore the figures' oil-drop extremities in mind. It seemed they especially wanted to say something about digits, counting, and what it was they said or wanted to say Lambert agreed with, moving to the high end of the horn while remaining sober, keeping calm, as if to give them his blessing, say their tolling rang true.

Lambert allowed his solo to end there, a light, breathy peal floating above cost, consequence, toll. It floated above but not free of toll, telling, in its unperturbed way, of debts paid and debts yet to be paid, soberly tolling but no less tolling than Drennette and Djamilaa's ritualistic audit. It lay there a beat and a half, a thin, breathy peal whose remaining aloft ritual audit implied but quickly drew back from, Aunt Nancy, whose repetitive pluck had become part of it, announcing a new direction by pulling out the bow and proceeding to play arco. She gave the bass a cello's Orphic swell, fraught songfulness and fret, a teetering on the edge of elation she let sweep thru the "Wild Card" gap she stepped into, treading gingerly as though her toes were dripping oil, her feet soaked in oil.

Aunt Nancy bowed with a wincing resonance, as though the bow were an exposed rib—as though, indeed, it were *her* exposed rib, as though she were the see-thru masthead whose ribs the "Wild Card" drawing apprised us of. She bowed as though coaxing the bow across the strings at points, a jittery luxuriance given uncommon reach, uncommon albeit reluctant reach. Drennette peppered Aunt Nancy's resonance and reach (plumb resonance and reach) with rapid-fire outbursts on the orchestra snare, sanctified, spasmodic, pentecostal hammerings à la Sunny Murray.

Djamilaa had all but fallen silent, serving up chords every now and then, a more slowly doled out tolling meant to recall what had gone before. This left Aunt Nancy all the more at the mercy of Drennette's infectious pepper, a fact or effect eventually made evident by the percussive tack she resorted to. She came to a point where she lifted the bow and tapped the strings with it, letting it bounce lightly on them, much as Ron Carter does on "Barb's Song to the Wizard" on Tony Williams's *Lifetime* album, a piece, a passage and a technique Aunt Nancy had excitedly turned us on to ages ago. Here she took it further, sustained and stayed with it to an extent barely broached by Carter's jagged innuendo. Rickety buildup grew possessed of growl and grumble, an aroused rattle and would-be rafter shake amassing senses of emergence or at least emergency, rummaging for voice, viability, ground.

The bow was a mallet, the strings a throaty dulcimer, Aunt Nancy's fingers, thumb and wrist exquisitely schooled. Though she made it seem the bow simply bounced, no aspect of touch or attack went without thought, throaty dulcimer by turns a croaking cimbalom, by turns a raspy santur.

It became clear, though, that the strings were neither dulcimer, cimbalom nor santur, that the masthead's exposed ribs were the focus of Aunt Nancy's solo, that the strings were indeed those ribs, vertically though they lay, the fact that the bow was itself a rib notwithstanding. Indeed, Aunt Nancy's rib-on-rib address accented intimacy and consolation, exactly the embrace the drawing shows the masthead held in, Dredj's embrace—rib-on-rib contact, rib-on-rib caress, rib-on-rib assumption of Dredj's counsel. Here, however, rib crossed rib and was let percuss upon rib, a fact that not only accorded with but in part conveyed the disconsolate tone of Aunt Nancy's solo, the worked arousal refusing to be put to rest it so starkly was.

Eventually Djamilaa fell completely silent and Drennette soon followed suit. Aunt Nancy's solo was now exactly that, Djamilaa and Drennette having bowed out as if to suggest the bass's taut strings had to do with tautology, the solo's disconsolate temper with self-induced or self-digested ordeal, self-conducted ordeal—a suggestion to which, given the way Aunt Nancy's bass revved its own ennui, the way she ransacked it for sound, there was more than a grain of truth.

Aunt Nancy played alone and was all alone, played along with being alone, left alone, "all alone in the world." She allowed a hint of self-pity in, part parodic host, part woebegone orphan, not unrelated to Lambert's recasting of teardrop tenor. More specifically recalling Carter, she put the emphasis even more on *rev*, letting the bow ride and bounce on the strings with new and old verve, new and old volatility, mimicking or mining automotivity's old and new dream. A Model T on a bumpy road the bow might've been, so loudly did brake and sputter vie with flow.

Aunt Nancy played for all the world to know she stood alone, for all the world to know we all, no matter rev's would-be amelioration, stood alone, as though flow itself stumbled, stuck. Sputter never spoke more eloquently but even so she would not be done with fluidity, full-bodied arco, letting the bow glide between bouts or outbursts of coughlike exhaust, Carteresque bow-bounce. Such answering fluidity was nothing if not outright elegy, forthright lament, Aunt Nancy allowing the bass its low-throated moan. She spoke from nowhere if not from the heart (ribcage apse, alcove, atrium), no way if not on two fronts, both fronts, deep throb and bow-bounce both.

Point made, she put the bow away and went back to playing pizzicato, plucking the strings with chill serenity, ritual aplomb. She stood with her back straight, addressing the strings with a churchical assurance, churchical rectitude, as patient a fingerwalk as there ever was. She closed her eyes, exuding meditative calm, each ascending run seeming to say, "Alas," each descending run whispering, "Amen." Abidance was the overall note she struck, if there could be said to be an overall note she struck.

Djamilaa had left the piano to pick up one of her guitars. As the audience applauded Aunt Nancy's solo she began to play, pointedly chiming in on strings. She started off in what initially struck one as a Spanish vein but as she went further along one recognized a Malian or

Guinean provenance, a *guitare sèche* excursion (it was an acoustic gui-
tar she picked up) whose ambulatory rhythm feasted on recurrence.
It sought to make its home in a reverberant ping a shade beyond the
upbeat, a treble chime not so much home as haunt but beckoning as
though haunt could make heaven home. Indeed, treble chime verged
on going out of bounds, off scale or off record, verged on heaven itself,
rang heaven's bell.

Aunt Nancy picked up on Djamilaa's Mande invitation and replied,
playing the bass like a big guitar (rhythm guitar to Djamilaa's lead,
bass to Djamilaa's treble), whereupon Djamilaa, gratified to hear her
call responded to, shot her an appreciative glance and began to sing.
Together they plied a Malinke roll built on repetition, the chords
fraught with a certain drama or an inference of drama (false drama
perhaps), an inkling, inference or sense Djamilaa took pains to fend
off, paradoxically furthering, in so doing, the very inkling, inference
or sense it was her one wish in life (or so it seemed) to hold at bay.
A buoyant bout with quicksand, were such possible, her voice took
solace in its ability to declaim while being taken out, courting hoarse-
ness to extol its testificatory prowess. Rescue was only what witness
one could manage, were there rescue at all, and witness, were there,
would suffice, it seemed she said or sang more than said or made
singing say. Witness or no witness, her singing summoned words like
aria, *recitative* and *recital* only to say that they fell short, failed when
what was really real was afoot, that exactly that, the really real, was
afoot. Strident, abrasive, bent on scouring the air itself if need be, her
voice built with a certain insistence toward something none of us,
her included, could name, imprecatory at points, complaint piled on
complaint, coax plied with complaint.

Drennette joined in with a repeating figure that marked the strong
beat on the high hat, setting it up with a tap on the bass drum, the bar-
est percussive presence one could want. The three of them effected
an ictic, riverine amble, Djamilaa's treble chime, as time went on,
arriving a lengthening shade late, a hitch or a gimp or an eddy in the
flow. It brought to mind, for me at least, the "Wild Card" drawing's
abstract bench. It sat one down and it gave one pause, giving one to
reflect on water's indifferent flow, time's indifferent flow. One sat on
a bench on a bank overlooking the Niger.

Lengthening shade suggested the drawing's black sun had caught

Djamilaa's eye, the river's consolation an intricate mix of solace and complaint. The river's destination was there by inference, the salt air that had nipped our noses complicating time's occult remit. Lambert, Penguin and I picked up on this and instinctively bowed our heads, letting Djamilaa, Drennette and Aunt Nancy's amble have its way with us as waves or rapids might. Shade-late arrival's beneficiary, Djamilaa's treble chime gathered extrapolative reach. Eking out a summons or a receipt that would be the chime's equivalent, her voice every now and again leapt, its timbral bound and embrace as raw-ribbed as Aunt Nancy's bow-bounce had been, a miraculous mix of stridency and grace.

Lambert, Penguin and I now lifted our heads. Carried in or carried out, we stood athwart all emollience, amenity's reset, lengthening shade's limp a new boon nonetheless. Listening to Djamilaa, Drennette and Aunt Nancy, one heard again and saw again, as though for the first and final time, that sound was the inner skin of things, the other side coming over, inside turning out. A fool's errand it might've been to see it so but one saw it so. It was ground we'd been over before, ground we'd go over again, ground that somehow never got old.

As Djamilaa's voice began to trail off, letting us know she'd had her say, the audience began to applaud and Lambert and Penguin glanced at me and nodded to say the floor, so to speak, was mine. I put the cornet to my lips and began with a run meant to recall Aunt Nancy's Model T on a bumpy road, eventually stating the head with a hesitancy aimed at recalling Lambert's grudging address as well. I stood with my back straight but churchical rectitude wasn't what I was after, at least not to begin with. Gaps and crackle made their way out of the horn, more "ahem" than "amen." Indeed, sputter might've been my middle name for all anyone knew, so hard-won was any articulacy (or seemed so at least).

I say "seemed so" because sputter was more than sputter. It was an archarticulacy, fraught with meaning, "meaning" meaning "wanting to say." It wanted to bear on exhaustion, eventual eclipse, fossil fluency's abject eloquence, black sun. It wanted to find fulsomeness in hemorrhage, bumpiness, unable not to know it fed on exhaust, extinction, fumes. Sputter was double-jointed. Wanting was to say.

I stood with my back straight, parsing, repeating, teasing out the slowgoing unfolding of black sun. My not aiming for churchicality notwithstanding, there must have been something of it to the way

I made my way. Lambert, that is, bowed his head and lightly put his left hand on my right shoulder, a deaconly hand (mock-deaconly perhaps), as if to say, "Take your time, son. Take your time."

I took my time. It took all the calm I could muster not to be caught up in fossil fluency's depth and dilation, not to be carried away. I offered myself every caution not to resort to barrage, the Gatling-gun spray of notes I'd have bugled had bump's double joint had its way. I picked my way as though I walked in a minefield. A novice at a typewriter hunting and pecking, I pecked at sound and the possibility of sound. Aunt Nancy, Djamilaa and Drennette picked up on my cautious tread and lent themselves to it, letting their riverine amble subside. We no longer sat or stood on the bank of the Niger. Time dissolved into an aroused momentariness peppered by random event or invention—bass interjection, drum interjection, guitar interjection—isolate, asymmetric, intermittent, each a law to itself it seemed. It wasn't that time stood still but that time twitched, a volley of quivers that went for how long no one could say, trumpet, guitar, bass and drums each other's ricochet, no less random even so.

After however long it was, Djamilaa put the guitar down and went back to piano. She played a series of chords at the low end of the keyboard, a slow tolling that was a call to order, ominous and wistful at the same time—one-two, one-two, one-two again, a two-beat rest between each pair of chords, a space Aunt Nancy noticed and filled with a two-note descending ostinato. Drennette heard the call and went from sticks to brushes, applying a tight, circular stroke to the parade snare, stirring the pot. The three of them laid down a midnight creep that brought "Mood" on Miles's *E.S.P.* to mind.

I took my mute out of my coat pocket and put it into the bell of the horn. I blew a needle of sound that rayed out as it went thru the air, a tremulous ribbon whose advancing edge was a vibrating blade. It wasn't that sputter had been seeking this, that obstructed speech ironically or fittingly found its voice in the mute. Sputter, I've been saying, spoke. Djamilaa's call to order, moreover, calling randomness to a halt, was itself random. There was no reason for it to flow out of what preceded it and equally no reason for sputter to be said to have evolved into mute fluency. What happened happened. It was as simple as that. Sputter had spoken no less than mute fluency now spoke.

No less had sputter called flow obsolete (fossil flow indeed) than the mute bestowed fluidity and focus (mute fluency). I not only blew, as the old saw has it, from my diaphragm but set my collarbones abuzz with a sense of yet more remote origins, a faintly remembered myth involving clavicular spillage I'd read about ages ago in some Dogon lore. I vaguely recollected a creational aspect to it, something to do with Amma's collarbone marrow spilling out. My sound thus had an occasional raspiness at its edges, escaping or expiring breath a constitutive leakage. My collarbones hummed and from time to time knocked, shook like radiator pipes in winter. Part leak, part letting off steam, it was a sound I let the valves tease out, expelled or expired breath conducing to a theme of extinct heat.

More immediate, though, was the impact of what had now caught my attention in the "Wild Card" drawing, the wishbone above the masthead's ribs. It was this that my collarbones vibrated in affinity with, humming like sympathetic strings on a sitar. No matter how whimsical or wistful, I couldn't help noticing, it was a wishbone as black as the sun, as though to acknowledge wish's role were a dark admission, which in fact it was. The fact that it was was a fact I couldn't get over, though I made my peace with it by way of a Dixonian recourse to flub effects, extenuating breath into what gave sound to my exasperation. Nothing could've been more slick than our midnight creep but Bl'under blew with me now and again. Mishaps would occur, I said or let Bl'under say, wish otherwise though we might.

Dinosaurs and birds popped into my head, the thought of them having wishbones in common. The wishbone struck me now as an emblem not necessarily of extinction, a harbinger of ostensible extinction evolved into flight. A furcula technically speaking (Latin for "little fork"), it was eponymously the fork in the road leading toward one or the other. Where there's a fork there's a chance I told myself, admittedly wishful but not, I hoped, overly so.

It was a quick train of thought, feather and scale. Almost before I knew it, the horn emitted a Bowie-esque ratchet of sound, a careening squib that had a Dixonian contour as well, shades of *November 1981*. Feather outran scale, run reigning supreme, skid's indigeneity to squib newly audible, flight's tangential drift. Drennette went back to sticks to keep flight in line, upping the tempo after an onslaught of rolls that announced a new-day disposition tending toward all-out sprint (scale train, feather train). Scale to Drennette's feather, I lagged ever so slightly, a syncopic microbeat behind the beat, an ever so exactingly maintained messianic stagger, the gap, looking forward, saving grace turned out to be.

Aunt Nancy jumped on the new tempo right away. The fingers of her right hand scurried back and forth across the strings, those of her left scurried up and down. It was an avian pulse if there ever was one. She bore down, biting her bottom lip as she played, as though the pulse, the proverbial bird in hand, would fly away were she not to or did indeed, from moment to moment, fly away, notwithstanding she did. The flying, flown altercation she laid under it all gave the music wheels if not wings, legs and feet if not wheels. Djamilaa prodded us with pianistic chirp.

Hearing the buildup and sensing we'd soon crescendo, Lambert and Penguin took up their horns, Lambert his tenor still, Penguin soprano now rather than oboe. They saw me my wishbone wager and raised me a ribcage crown, blurting out the head with cairologic urgency again and again, four times in all. We played more loudly with each iteration and peaked on number four, whereupon I took the horn from my mouth and stepped back from the mike as Lambert did likewise, Djamilaa, Aunt Nancy and Drennette pulled back on the tempo and took the volume down to a whisper and Penguin, as the audience applauded my solo, embarked on his.

It was clear why Penguin had switched from oboe to soprano. He made a point, it seemed, of putting the oboe's pinched, eked-out sound aside, its inturned embouchure aside, opting for a soprano sound as open as a duck's cry, open as all outdoors. It was an open-throated sound à la Steve Lacy, with no tightness or constriction to it, resounding of nothing if not laryngeal openness, nothing if not esophageal openness, nothing if not, in a word, flow. He seemed intent on saying something about acceptance, something about flow bearing on depletion, departure, fluidity's eventual arrest. It was a duck's cry but without its frayed perimeter, the firm inside part of a strand of spaghetti cooked al dente.

Djamilaa, Aunt Nancy and Drennette continued at whisper level as Penguin started off. It was an unrushed, riverine amble they found their way into, Djamilaa now reprising on piano the Malinke way of knowing she'd earlier offered on guitar. Penguin's accent on flow they backed up and embroidered with a subtle, sotto voce roll extolling furtherance, a felt, otherwise fugitive equation of brightness and time.

For all its accent on furtherance and flow, there was an elegiac strain woven into what Penguin played. The horn was somehow buoyed by sadness, a deep, thoroughgoing sorrow so abstruse it could only turn sanguine, moan though it otherwise did.

The river, in other words, was back and along with it the lachrymosity Lambert and Drennette had earlier touched on or choked up on. Silly as it seemed, one couldn't help thinking of Julie London singing "Cry Me A River," especially if one had, as I had, seen the movie *The Girl Can't Help It* as a kid in the fifties. That she sings it as a specter haunting Tom Ewell especially came back to me now, conducing or contributing to a theme of payback and retribution I'd have sworn I heard coming out of Penguin's horn.

Penguin repeatedly had recourse to an E-flat pedal in such a way as to suggest conscience and also to say (or at least to imply) that he too, as I had in writing the piece, wondered if prehistory's grudge against the present were at work. The horn cried a river of regret, disbursing mixed-emotional strains of remorse and recrimination, as though evolutionary succession exacted dues, which evidently it does. Not since body first met soul had confession so wed complaint. It was a cry surmising gnostic entrapment, thug gnosis, the most accusatory mea culpa one would ever hear. Retributive spill was our fault but no less retributive it seemed he said, fossil fluidity's ominous underside. That it was our fault was not our fault it seemed he said.

I took my cornet up again, put it to my mouth and offered punctuation, endorsing Penguin's theme of demiurgic sting with a braid of mordents around E-flat. It was no more than punctuation, no more than a quick, ratifying run, but I too admitted fault while claiming fault to be a setup, I too took sublime umbrage.

Penguin shot me a glance, an appreciative gleam in his eye, going on as though newly fired up, made all the more adamant by my corroborative run. Newly adamant or renewing its adamance, his tone blended *accepting* with *incensed*, a tendency toward trill making its way in or having made its way in, a descending trill bottoming out into drone recalling Jo Maka, the Guinean soprano saxophonist. There was no way this would've been accidental. The river was back, decidedly so, running with quaint strain, uncustomary hustle.

Hearing her Mande insinuation expanded on, Djamilaa took to singing again or, to be more exact, semisinging, humming a song from Upper Guinea, "Toubaka." A few words from the song's lyrics emerged from her humming now and again, but mostly what she did was hum, a one-woman chorus commenting on Penguin's solo. She sang or semisang from a position of elderly repose, wise, as the expression goes, beyond her years. All weight, all ministry, all measure endowed her voice, an endlessly calibrated "alas," an extended sigh. Penguin now shot her an appreciative glance. Her voice was drenched in time.

The river had come around again. Malinke ambit had come around again. Penguin blew beyond the horn, the river's quaint strain and uncustomary hustle prompting him to heave an arc of implied intonation not unlike a fisherman casting a line. This arc was Dredj's arm around the figurehead's shoulder, the feature of the "Wild Card" drawing that had most caught Penguin's eye, an extrapolative embrace whose coo and consolation he now beautifully brought to bear on the horn. His new recourse to diaphragmatic oomph aired a light-bodied bigness or a big-bodied lightness, his eye also caught by the figurehead's thoracic largesse.

It seemed all we could do to contain ourselves. We stood poised on a precipitous edge it seemed. With the merest abrupt move we'd erode or evaporate, the figurehead's thoracic transparency suddenly at large. All we could do, it occurred to Lambert, Aunt Nancy, Drennette and me at exactly the same time, was hum. All we could do was catch, as it were, Djamilaa's choral contagion and hum "Toubaka," which is what we did, the four of us easing into it, joining her, an antiphonal consort of sorts, a chorus beyond her chorus or, all of us having heard the version of "Toubaka" done by Les Ambassadeurs Internationaux, chorus to her Salif Keita.

It was an immediately soothing hum, a sonic lozenge at the roof of the mouth apportioning balm. Humming drew us back from the edge. We stood stout again, lodged resolutely where we stood, readymade remit, the fossils we'd eventually be. Hum's vibratory dispatch came into collaborative play with solidity's transit. It was nothing if not flow's disclosure once and for all, an aggrieved emollient.

Thus it was that aggrievement and approbation ran as one. So it was we sang, if it could be said we sang, or, if not, semisang with our teeth clenched. Peal and ping rang from the keys under Djamilaa's right hand as we hummed, as poignant as a Guinean guitar. Penguin worked and worried the arc Dredj's arm inspired, a breaking wave, he'd have had it, as it broke, less a wave than a trace, audible to an imagined ear alone. The river and what it went out to were back.

Penguin leaned back a bit, mentally and physically both. He let himself be caught by the cushion of sound our humming had become, so relaxed he became all breath, all respiration, resorting to circular breathing as the music peaked. Circularity said it all it seemed he said, "What goes around comes around," "Where there's a wheel there's a turn" and so forth, Malinke furtherance a dream of empathic escort come true. Breath was a ball rolling atop our Malinke hum, a wheel buoyed by and rolling on water, wind roughening water.

The ball or the wheel gathered momentum and the music sped up, Aunt Nancy's bass advancing a jump-up rumble as Drennette's high hat hissed, hum nearly brimming over, a collective croon. There was more and more swell to it, more and more lift as well. We rode a low-spoken undulance, borne or abetted by Penguin's extrapolative surmise.

Just as it had as I ended my solo, the music crescendoed as Penguin ended his. Djamilaa, Aunt Nancy and Drennette again took the volume down to whisper level as the audience applauded. All the while we continued humming—quietly so, at whisper level as well. Once the clapping subsided an insinuative quiet obtained, an almost ominous calm. Penguin now joined our humming, the six of us ever so low-key yet stalwart, savoring the impromptu vibration humming had brought, the low-key visitation humming had become.

It was a soothing song our humming amounted to. A lullaby it might've been except its unremittingness roused us. We hummed possessed of alarm and assurance, an agitant mix whose intensification varied inversely with the tempo at which we hummed. We gradually, that is, hummed more slowly, curiously building intensity while winding the piece down, agreeing, without having to say so, not to return to the head. We instinctively and collectively knew that this was the way it should end—not so much end as fade.

Aunt Nancy, Djamilaa and Drennette eventually let their instruments go silent and we all continued humming a cappella. Here and there a few people in the audience picked up the tune and joined in, humming along with us, but it would be a stretch to say we set the entire crowd humming. Still, an infectious vibration seemed to affect everyone. When our humming finally subsided the audience sat silent for a while as though entranced, as though unaware the piece had ended or taken by surprise that it had, lost in thought. We felt we knew what they felt. Applause was beside the point. Yet when they snapped out of whatever it was they were in they rose from their seats and gave us a standing ovation.

We too were affected by the reading we gave the piece. I'm not sure I can say exactly how but even now it stays with us. How long I've gone on about it is a measure of that no doubt but I'm not sure I can more precisely pin it down. I will, though, mention something we've been wondering about. We couldn't help noticing and now can't help reflecting on the fact that, fossil fluency's extremity notwithstanding, no balloons emerged during the performance. Could it be that the "Wild Card" drawing was preemptive? Could it be that the drawing, conceding to caption as it does, inoculated us? Could it be that "Molimo m'Atet's Figurehead Consoled on the Revival Bench" kept the balloons at bay by rendering them redundant? Elated over the performance though we were, we began to wonder not long afterward and we still wonder.

As ever,
N.

_____

Dear Angel of Dust,

No, it's not that the balloons have gotten into our heads. We're not Maxine Brown, we're not singing "All in My Mind." The problem is that it's not that. It's that the balloons are actually out there and evidently they have a mind of their own. They dwell, as I've said before, in a deepseated impulse toward caption, a deepseated captivity they seek to leaven with whimsicality—true to themselves, unable to help themselves, insouciant, insecure. They body forth inflated claims to translatability only to beg off or betray them, burst as balloons at times do. Sometimes they renege before the fact, backtrack in advance, decide not to show up. Sometimes they make themselves known by their absence, a conspicuous reticence one would need to be dead not to notice. But who knows? Maybe even then one would see or sense it, pick up on it somehow. We know they show up camera shy when they do show up. Could the difference between alive and dead be only that shyness?

I've been listening to "Autumn Leaves" on the _Miles Davis in Europe_ album, a record I cut my teeth on as a teenager. The vibratory blade Miles uses the mute to make sound into amounts to a balloonlike adjacency, an off-to-the-side reticence or recoil I can't help hearing as recondite presence and manifest absence's mix or mating dance. What but the implications of that sound could so be there but not there, what but the balloons' adjunct agenda, the occult itinerary none but they seem to know but that, possibly, not even they know? Miles's recourse to flutter early on in his solo might be heard as onomatopoeic by some, the "sound" of autumn leaves, falling leaves. I tend to agree but I take it further. We hear the sound, in hearing it so, of a concession to caption, the hovering fall oblique afflatus turns out to be. We hear that concession's glide into an offhand rumble, a sly glide that will agree to caption only to nudge it toward refractoriness, as if *caption* and *captious* were somehow kin. This, moreover, comes of a sound that could not be more introvert, more introspective. Shy sound. Sly.

I'd say don't get me started but you've gotten me started. Listen, then, if you will, to the hover-and-dip, hover-and-dash dexterity Miles brings to that flutter, a not quite flight-of-the-bumblebee élan and agitation, buzz the recondite balloons' masquerade. Falling leaves' equation with not-quite bee flight is nothing if not a fractious caption, a lateral feint bursting with drift and flotation, border on tissue paper and comb though it does, nothing if not wind-aided cascade. That he can go, soon after that, from Gatling-gun staccato to quasi-whimper is what I mean by feint, drift and flotation, a tremulous resolve to be to the side or get to the side of besetment.

Not as blatant as Dizzy's ballooning cheeks, Miles's autumnal bob and weave imparts a balloon salience nonetheless, a balloon detour from Dizzy's overtness and extroversion, a balloon extenuation or, to use Duke's term, extension. I can imagine listening to this track thirty or forty years from now and still finding it fresh, the advent of my own autumnal prospect lending it all the more relevance and resonance, a time-capsule bubble or balloon loaded with decades of what won't tell itself but does, caption after caption donned and auditioned only to be cast off.

Let me know what you think.

Yours,
N.

PS: I left out the good news. We've been invited to play at the Detroit Institute of Arts in January.

_____

Dear Angel of Dust,

Once again it will have come to nothing. Again we will have sat exchanging thoughts on what was to be. Again we will have heard music, albeit not music so much as music's trace, music's rumor, pianistic breakdown as an archetypal he and she gazed out drapeless windows. What stayed with us will have been a wincing, distraught right hand backed by a grumbling left on an abject keyboard, a right undone or done in as much as backed by a disconsolate left. We will have stood and stretched as gray, wintry, late afternoon light filled each window, a wounded look on what lay outside and on our faces as we looked out on it. An archetypal he and she alone but for the music, aloof to each other even but each the music's intended, we will have so seen ourselves but no sooner done so than drawn back. Something found in a wrinkle, something found in a fold, it will have been this that set our course and put us on it, collapse and come to nothing though it would.

So I thought, at least, earlier today at Djamilaa's. What will evanescent splendor have come to I wondered as she stood at a window and at one point leaned against the window frame, her left arm raised, her left hand touching the curtain rod. She stood that way only a moment but the way she stood highlighted her long beauty, lank beauty, her long arms and legs a miracle of limbs. For an instant something jumped out at me and at the same time jumped inside me, a mood or a mix of elation compounded with dread. I saw what so much rays out from and relies upon, however much it shook me with apprehension: lank intangible grace, nonchalant allure, love's modest body. It was the news of the moment but yesterday's news as well, something aspect and prepossession seemed intent on saying. What that something was, as Penguin would say, more than met the eye, but it did nonetheless meet the eye. My heart leapt and my stomach dropped.

"Leave it alone," Djamilaa said, demure as to what was at issue but sensing my mood.

"I wish I could," I said.

The right hand on the keyboard prompted me perhaps, apprehension of any kind its mandate, apprehension of any kind's fraught base. Thought's ricochet played a role as well. Momentary angst was its immediate heir, an ungainliness of thought in whose wincing retreat one felt elation well up and right away subside. Fear of being caught out, knowing no way not to be caught out, factored in as well.

"Things are that way sometimes," Djamilaa said, laconic, blasé, unperturbed.

"I know," I said. "Things are always that way."

It had to do with angles. The piano's legs buckled for an instant and rebounded, then they buckled and rebounded again. The right side of the keyboard crumpled. The hand that played it crumpled as well. Had they been glass they'd have shattered, besetting one's ears, by turns bodily and cerebral, with sharp, intersecting planes rolling Duchamp's descending nude and Picasso's weeper into one. But they were not glass, however much the keyboard's keening ping made it seem so.

Dressed in a light cotton shift whose hem touched her ankles, Djamilaa stood caught between bouts and volleys of agitation and arrest, her lank beauty all the more lank finding itself so caught but unavailable all the same, it struck me, not to be lastingly caught. A lack of lasting hold or lasting capture pertained to the music plaguing our heads, mine maybe more than hers but hers as well, a music it seemed we each heard with a distinct incorporeal ear or perhaps together with a shared incorporeal ear.

Djamilaa again offered generic solace, oblique as to what was at issue still, so compellingly we both felt it. "Not always," she said. "But their effect when they are is to make it seem that way."

"Yes, I guess so," I said.

The music itself seemed an oblique telepathic dispatch, however much it appeared woven into textile and skin tone, the music of Djamilaa's bare arms and bare neck emerging from her cotton shift. It obtained in her skin's lack of lasting hold and in the wrinkles and folds of her shift. Had she said, "Fret not thyself," I'd have said, "Amen," but we were beyond that now, the music insinuating itself, issueless issue, the nothing it let it be known it will have come to, the nothing that had never been. It wanted to keep convergence at bay.

It plied an odd, contrarian wish but it was moving and emotive all the same, anti-intimate while inviting intimacy, anti-contact while acknowledging touch. It plied an aloof tactility, love's lank tangency, verging on emotional breakdown but brusque, pullaway catch or caress.

It was an actual music we heard and let have its way with us, Paul Bley's "Touching" on the *Mr. Joy* album. No way could we say title told all.

As ever,
N.

Dear Angel of Dust,

Yes, that one has "Nothing Ever Was, Anyway" on it, as do several others. It does appear, as you say, we let "Nothing Ever Was, Anyway" infiltrate "Touching," title not telling all notwithstanding, title not telling all all the more. But there's an asceticism to Bley's playing that comes across no matter what the title. Djamilaa's been thinking about that, wondering about that, drawn to it a lot of late. It's not that less is more, she likes to say, nor that nothing is all, nor that nothing, as Ra says, *is*. All those ways of putting it only let sensation in thru the back door, she likes to say. No, it's not about that. It's not as recuperative as that, not as categorical. It's an angled attrition, banked extenuation, she likes to say.

It's as if, when she speaks this way, she'd come to me in a dream and vice versa, each of us the other's wished-for rescue, each the other's wariness as well. It's not unlike what sometimes happens when we play. One becomes the extenuation of oneself and the emanation of something else, someone else, ghost and guest arrivant rolled into one. What is it or who is it steps in at such moments? It could be anything, anyone, one senses, but the hollow one's evacuation puts in one's place appears to afford strangeness a friendly disguise. One's fellow band members pass thru that hollow, step into it, relieving the brunt of an attenuation one might otherwise be unable to bear. It's something like what Roy Haynes must have meant by saying that playing with Trane was "like a beautiful nightmare."

Come to as in a dream, yes, a dream dreamt on a rickety bed, springs creaking, home like as not an illusion of home. To speak was to bank one's breath within angular precincts, wall intersecting wall's proprioceptive recess one's being there had become. Stereotactic as well, one touched upon aspect, facet, crater, protuberance, grade finessing grade, tangency's wont.

As ever,
N.

Dear Angel of Dust,

I was trying to call back time. The time I was trying to summon I'd in fact found distressing at the time but I was trying to bring it back nonetheless. I put two records on the record player, Etta James's *At Last!* and Bobby "Blue" Bland's *Two Steps from the Blues*, records that had been staples during the time I sought to call back, certain Sunday afternoons when I was a kid and my mother would play them again and again. She would usually have played Mahalia Jackson and the Five Blind Boys of Alabama in the morning, music that I heard as pretty grim, going on about a life beyond life as it did. That by itself was enough to pervade the house with a heavy mood, a mood Bobby and Etta not only kept going but took deeper come afternoon. I understood—or felt, if not exactly understood—that theirs was an even more somber church.

It was always as if time had stopped. The music and the mood brought everything to a standstill, causing me the kind of unease I'd later read Melville write about suffering during calms at sea. The music or the need for the music seemed to come out of a suspended state of some kind—not only to come out of it but to usher us into it, if or as though we weren't already there. But we were already there and always there it said or made it seem. That we were, the sense that we were, hung heavily over everything.

The music and the mood took my mother to another time and place, it seemed, a time and place given over to reflection as it touched on regret. She'd sit nursing a drink, a sad, distant look on her face, beset by some deepseated sorrow. It was a sadness I couldn't keep from getting to me, a disappointment she appeared to feel not only with her own life but with life more generally, a disappointment that boded well for no one's prospects. She'd stack the two records, listening to the first side of one followed by the first side of the other, then turn them over to hear the two other sides and when they were finished turn them over again, start over again. She'd play them again and again—two, three, four, five or six times. It was hard to miss the mood or what it meant. It hung heavily over the house and over the afternoon—heavily over the world, it seemed. When I went outside to find my friends and play, it went with me.

It was the same when there were people over, when my mother sat not alone but with company, one or both of my aunts, a friend or a neighbor or a few. When they got to drinking and talking loud and laughing, with Etta and Bobby in the background, they couldn't fool me. I knew it was a ruse. I knew adult life was no fun, life was no fun. Neither my apprehension of the arrest underlying it all nor my distress was diminished by their festiveness. I knew Bobby and Etta were the truth.

Those afternoons, whether sullen or festive, filled me with desolation and dread. It's odd I'd want to retrieve them, but I did. Day before yesterday, Sunday, I played the two records. I hadn't listened to them in ages. Right away they brought those afternoons and all the feelings they were filled with back. I'd forgotten how many of Bobby's songs are about crying, forgotten the reliance on strings throughout Etta's album, forgotten the poetics of plea winding thru both. It was a world of adult longing the two albums conjured, a world of desperate affirmation where there was affirmation, one of dejection more often. I listened to them repeatedly just as my mother would, putting side one of *At Last!* on the turntable, followed by side one of *Two Steps*, then side two of *Two Steps*, followed by side two of *At Last!*, then starting again with side one of *At Last!*

I didn't set out to write a new composition when I did this, just to see if the music could return me to a certain mood and moment, just to relive, if I could and to whatever extent I could, my mother's blue Sunday afternoons. I did indeed call back time, did manage to recapture or be captured by those earlier afternoons, desolate and dejected as they were. It's almost as if I so succeeded in doing so, fell so deeply into that early apprehension and dread, that I had to write my way out of it, come up with a piece that, touched as it couldn't help but be by Etta, Bobby and my mother's blue Sunday distress, would take it to another place. In any case, I started the piece on Sunday, finished it yesterday, and we took it up today at rehearsal. I'm enclosing a tape. I call it, as you can see, "Some Sunday," meaning to draw on the utopic senses given to Sunday by Etta's "A Sunday Kind of Love."

The title echoes Duke's "Come Sunday" of course, but it was actually Monk's "Children's Song" I was thinking about, the rendition of "This Old Man," the traditional English nursery rhyme, that he plays on the *Monk* album. I wanted a folk song-sounding or a children's song-sounding phrase repeated on piano throughout, a simple, "childlike" melody built on an emphatic key variation. Djamilaa, as you'll hear, delivers on that in a big way, drawing out the phrase's evocation of childhood by seeming at times to take a learner's tack, a beginner's tack, mock-awkwardly "losing" the time only to regain it. Drennette's reliable conga throws that all the more into relief.

Please pay close attention to Lambert. He's the lead voice throughout on alto, Penguin on bari and me on trumpet offering choral support. Lambert's sound on alto tends toward tenor, without, of course, being tenor. I wanted that. "Bruised bell," I leaned over and whispered into his ear right before we hit. He got a gleam in his eye and he grinned. As you'll hear, he brings out the hollow the horn ultimately is, exacting a haunted, harried sound recalling John Tchicai somewhat. He plays hurt, I like to say. Hurt in his case, however, gathers an extrapolative whimsy, a wistful élan holding heaviness at bay, hailing some Sunday, soon come.

As ever,
N.

Dear Angel of Dust,

Just as I'd begun a letter to you Djamilaa showed up. The doorbell rang just as I'd finished the first paragraph. *Once again,* I'd written, *we will have stood in a drapeless room filling up with light. I will have held her close, held her tightly, my chest against her shoulder blades, my arms around her waist. We will have held hands looking into a mirror, her left in my right. Once again we will have imagined a life to come, a slice of time we looked in on, looked like we looked in on. Once again I will have held off breathing deeply, not daring to take in the smell of her hair and her neck. I will have had none of night's mare riding me, none of her my horse. The aromatic incubus will not have been let in.* The doorbell rang and I got up and went to the door and opened it. There she stood.

It was as though a balloon had turned itself inside out, a gloved hand ungloved itself unassisted, by itself, script gotten itself big and delivered itself both (vain presentiment, vacuous portent) right at my door. Djamilaa stood there, in one of her nothing-ever-was-anyway moods I could tell. She gave me a light kiss on the lips and came in.

"Would you rather love or write a love song?" she asked right off. "Play free jazz or be free?" There didn't seem to be much question or much choice. I laughed, hoping she would as well, but she only stared at me, the nothing-ever-was-anyway look now indisputable. She'd been listening to piano trios again I could tell.

"Have a seat," I said, not really needing to, not buying time so much as rejecting the questions. It wasn't even that so much. The questions, I knew, were rhetorical. Djamilaa had already been about to sit down on the couch and she sat down on the couch. She audibly exhaled, looked up at me in an almost moist-eyed way and laughed, a nothing-ever-was-anyway lilt of a laugh that nonetheless turned the sides of her mouth down. I sat down next to her. I touched her right hand with my left and took hold of it.

Looking away but with the sides of her mouth turned up again, she asked, "Would you rather celebrate the Beautiful One or be the Beautiful One?"

It appeared she'd read my thoughts and was alluding to a piano trio that wasn't, Cecil Taylor's bassless trio. I shrugged it off and said, deadpan, "Djamilaa, the Beautiful One Has Come," as she was indeed that, all of that, all the more that the more the nothing-ever-was-anyway look undercut surface allure, a demure, dissenting look that gave her close-to-the-bone beauty all the more depth.

Djamilaa turned back and looked at me but held off speaking, as close to a Mona Lisa look on her face as I've ever seen on anyone. For some reason, I thought of Andrew Hill's triplet-laden "Laverne," the mix of hurry and restraint he works into the head, the almost muzzled way the horns announce it on the quintet version on *Spiral*, Chris White's bass gallop on the trio version on *Invitation*, etc. For a moment I couldn't shake the way the horns, even as they play in unison, break the line between them, breaking bread it seems, a by turns beaked and bleary nudge, a drawn-out, busily punctuated nudge.

When Djamilaa spoke again I couldn't hear what she was saying. I was thinking about the almost perky uptake Ted Curson imbues the head with on certain edges, as though gesturing toward an audience that isn't listening as though they are. I was thinking that music is a way of going out of our way not to speak as we otherwise would. I could see Djamilaa's lips were moving but what she said I couldn't hear, whatever it was drowned out by the quintet version of "Laverne" in my mind's ear.

I was thinking about the first time I heard it, recalling it coming on the radio in the car. I was remembering it coming on as I turned off Beverly onto Spaulding. I remembered pulling to the curb and stopping to listen, so taken with it was I from the very first note. I was caught up wondering what the word or words would be for that opening triplet and for the way of stating it the horns have, caught up trying to figure that out, wondering whether "quip," which had just occurred to me, fit, wondering whether "sotto voce quip," which occurred almost immediately after that, fit better. Djamilaa's lips were moving but I couldn't for the life of me make out what she was saying, caught as I was between cerebral quip and corporeal audition. She might well have been casting a spell. "The carnal ear," she might well have been saying, "heareth nothing. The carnal tongue speaketh not."

Or was it that the horns' curt buzz and crackle took the words out of her mouth I wondered, her carnal teeth, gums, lips and tongue all the more inviting or alluring even so, their nothing-ever-was-anyway stolidity daring one to hungrily have at them hoping to prove otherwise. I found it was all I could do not to lean forward and press my mouth to hers, testing its philosophic pout, its meaty but reticent fullness, its nothing-ever-was-anyway remoteness and detachment, abandonment and containment rolled into one. Her mouth was nothing if not the muzzle my mouth cried out to be quieted by, clutched and covered by, music, muse, mute and removal all rolled into one. I wanted only a moan to come out of my mouth and her mouth were any sound to come out at all.

I was wondering whether "the meeting of quip and quizzicality" did the horns justice when Djamilaa's eyes locked on mine. I could see that she saw they were fixed on her mouth. Mine met hers and then they went back to her mouth, its fullness and potential generosity, philosophy notwithstanding. I was in Duke's prelude zone (kissical buildup, kissical prelude), not without reason to think she was there too.

Even so, the horns were still in my head, deep in my head, some gregarious animal's nuzzling snout it now seemed. When Djamilaa stopped speaking, finished with or simply breaking off what she'd been saying, I moved ever so slightly toward her, still not having heard a word she said. She moved her eyes off mine and to my mouth for a moment, returning them to my eyes while moving ever so slightly toward me. We leaned and moved our faces toward each other. I could feel the breath from her nose on my upper lip, our faces a couple of inches apart, her feeling mine as well.

We were in Duke's prelude zone, both of us now, kissical runup. Oddly, though, holding back was all and all was hesitancy, hover, an aromatic, haptic swell welling between us, pure draw, pure impending, willed and rested, ripening restraint. The word "prance" had come into my head as one that might possibly get at how the horns acquitted themselves, the equestrian way they had of bounding between triplets. It was exactly then that something else came in that I had no way of knowing from where or to whom it might be addressed, me or Djamilaa, if not both, or, for that matter, about what. "Hold that thought," it occurred to me to say, unexpectedly, out of the blue, looking straight into Djamilaa's eyes, her breath my breath, our noses now touching. "Hold that thought," I found myself saying, pulling back as I did. "Save it for the gig tonight."

Djamilaa pulled back as well, nonplussed, her Mona Lisa look back in place. "Yes, you're right," she said. "It would only have added up to nothing." Her eyes were on mine but it appeared she looked at something in back of me, some remote something I wouldn't have otherwise known was there. How was it her nothing-ever-was-anyway look or élan cast or captured something I wondered, the "Laverne" horns having at me still, their prancical nudge not affected by my pulling back. Nonetheless, we were no longer in Duke's prelude zone.

It turned out we did indeed hold whatever thing or thought that moment amounted to or that Djamilaa, at least, did, the remote something she saw in back of me the thing or thought it perhaps came down to for her. We did indeed take that something or that thing or thought, whatever it was, to the gig that night, last night, or at least Djamilaa did. We played the Blue Light Lounge in Long Beach again and during the piece that was the evening's highlight, "Book of Opening the Mouth," Djamilaa stole the show.

Djamilaa's show-stopping solo was all the more unexpectedly so, coming on the heels of a solo by Lambert that none of us envied her having to follow. If it could be said, that is, that anyone or anything had stolen or stopped the show up to that point it would be Lambert and the solo he took. It is, after all, his tune. He knows whereof it speaks and of whom it speaks and, pardon the pun, he ate it up. Following the statement of the head, on which he plays tenor, my solo on trumpet and Penguin's solo on soprano, he switched to sopranino (one-upping Penguin?) and built from a back-to-basics tack (if not a back-to-before-basics tack) to mount a thick disquisition on light, namesake light, the very light the venue we found ourselves in wants to credit itself with, blue light.

Lambert, that is, to begin, confined himself to a series of grunts in the horn's lower register, an expectorant tack that offered minimal musicality, bent, it seemed, on redefining musicality, if not discarding it altogether. He picked a bone with any sense of the pure and the proper, shoving these concepts aside and announcing himself done with them. He announced himself done with conceptuality itself even, down to his last nerve it seemed he said. The accent was on strain, exertion, the labor light exacted, effort, fraught sublimity, wrought remit.

It was as if someone had asked what sound itself was and he was intent on that inquiry, a starting-from-scratch tally and test meant to take inventory, an audit of all it might be at base. He grappled with the rub the thought of primacy subjected him to, taking to it as to a bath of ashes, dry but droll holdout against all odds. One wanted to be a duck sometimes he led us to infer, cracking us up as he did so, grunt gone over into quack before we knew it, Donald Duck ripe with complaint. Was it a way of warding off the balloons, we wondered, beating them to the punch to keep them at bay, no words coming out but the thought of comics or cartoons clearly there, the concept of cartoon broached only to be laughed at, conceptuality itself a joke, a cartoon?

The crowd at the Blue Light couldn't have been hipper. They saw Lambert's cartoon quack, cracking up, cackling, then raised him a hue and cry, a back-to-before-basics tack that had many of them up on their feet, pumping their fists, yelling, egging him on. Lambert heard them, their back-to-before-basics ratification both a boon and a caution. Could a critique of conceptuality be other than conceptually endorsed he wondered, a quandary he could only, could anything be done with it, find a way to let flow, not find a way out of, which is exactly what he set about doing, egged on indeed, a recourse to long tones and trills the way he now went. He was now looping the loop, threading the needle, even squaring the circle could such be done. He was now, in a word, *piping*, the mouthpiece and reed sheer birdsong, prodigal chirp tugging the floor out from under everything, majestic chirp announcing and annulling all advent.

The Blue Light, under Lambert's tutelage, became a live huddle, everyone wanting to know what sound was. We were all, band and crowd alike, bent on hearing blue light's call, the namesake sonance

Lambert let us know was out there, insistent what we heard wasn't what it was.

Lambert held the horn high, a bird on a branch, a bird on a wire, a bird bent on infinity worn out by infinity, a bird piping loudly as it flew. There was something weary to what he played, infinity's blue redoubt, a sense of having come to be daunted by endlessness, bask and abide by and celebrate it though he did. There was, that is, just the right touch of caution, a rind of complaint not inconsistent with the earlier accent on strain. This, one knew, was the meaning of his recourse to circular breathing, the long run of which he chose to take the solo to its crescendo with, conserving and exhausting breath both. The crowd met that crescendo with a bounding round of applause, some of them shouting out their approval ("Yeah, that's it!," "Tell it!" and the like), some putting their pinkies to the sides of their mouths and whistling, high-pitched, piercing whistles that were something like answering the sopranino in kind.

It was, as I've already said, a solo none of us envied Djamilaa having to follow, but she took the challenge in stride and took her time and went on, as I've also already said, to steal the show. It wasn't so much a solo she took as a walk over hallowed ground, the closer walk so long sung about in gospel torn a new ken. Right off the bat she made reference to the Paul Bley stuff she's been listening to a lot lately, the teasing, tangential way she had with it a remove or two or three away from straight quotation. A valedictory caress one couldn't help calling it, as if having distilled what there was to be gotten from it she bid it lovingly and lightly goodbye, all angle, all approach, all asymptote. By turns it was "Closer" one could've sworn one heard traces of, "Nothing Ever Was, Anyway" whose ghost one felt a nudge from, "Mr. Joy" whose prance and whose prod one took to have hold of her, "El Cordobes" one would've given an arm to have her come right out and play. Farther on it was "Touching" one was all but sure took the floor out from under one, "Seven" the run whose collapse made one wince put one in mind of, "Turning" whose faux dissolve accosted one's ear.

I can't emphasize enough that none of these tunes got anything near explicit statement. Indeed, soul to explicit statement's body, the tack Djamilaa took was one of ever so remote adumbration, the ghost of a chance body might be were it, she led one to ask, anything at all.

The remote probabilistic wraith all assertion came down to she ran thru a sieve of abstraction, all tune or even tone an extrapolation of aspect only the blind might see. Thus it was one saw in the sense of thought more than heard "Seven," "Mr. Joy" and so on, blindly saw in some jigsaw way that crossed over into hearing's near equivalent, listening-for, the closest one would come but still short of outright hearing, teasingly near and far both.

How close Djamilaa got to the Paul Bley tunes was also how far away she got from "Book of Opening the Mouth," so far, in fact, her solo seemed like another tune or like a tune inside Lambert's tune, a new tune or a detour of a tune I indeed couldn't help calling "Djamilaa, the Beautiful One Has Come." It also gave rise to something we've never had happen before. It was as she was wringing what sounded like the last possible drop from her say-it-without-saying-it allusion to and distillation of "Open, to Love" that it happened, the audience breaking out into loud, uncontrollable applause, yelling, stamping their feet and pounding on tables, some of them rising to their feet as they had during Lambert's solo, all of it so loud and raucous and all of it sustained so long it required Djamilaa, Aunt Nancy and Drennette to stop playing, the way we've heard it done on those Om Kalsoum albums where after one of her unbearably beautiful runs the Egyptian audience goes crazy and she and the orchestra have to pause for them to settle down again.

Whether it was a conscious homage to Djamilaa's North African roots or something the audience just couldn't help or both, it was, as I've said, something that's never occurred before. The three of them stopped playing and the ovation went on for a while after they did so, the audience, it seemed, pleased with the acknowledgment of their acknowledgment and the worked-up, wounded state they were in. It was as if they'd been begging for mercy and were pleased and relieved to have gotten it and could now quiet down, which they began to do. Once the ovation had completely died down and those who'd been standing were back in their seats Djamilaa, Aunt Nancy and Drennette started up again, their closer walk across hallowed ground picked up where they'd left off, Djamilaa's Paul Bley extract or extrapolation taken up long enough to be played against the next detour she took.

There was, that is, a strongly pronounced contrast when Djamilaa moved from Paul Bley to Bill Evans, to whom she's also been listening a lot lately. Radically changing her tack, she alluded to two of the tunes on the *Explorations* album, "Haunted Heart" and "Elsa," ever so nimbly quoting from one and then the other, a wisp of outright statement in each case that maintained her theme of ghostliness nonetheless, linking the two, an anonymous haunted heart lamenting some Elsa. Listening, one found oneself haunted by the ghost of "Elsa" and by that of the tune's eponym as well, mere wisp though it was notwithstanding, a wisp it was all one could do not to be lost in, so thrown one felt oneself to be. One couldn't help it. It was a wisp that would have none of being done with, a wincing, knee-weakening lilt it was an achievement not to fall over listening to. I for one, for the moment, renamed each and every person I'd ever loved Elsa, so put upon by the ghost of what, Djamilaa had set us up to feel, never was, anyway.

I also can't emphasize enough that Aunt Nancy and Drennette were models of co-conspiracy throughout, disbursing supplement and surmise alongside support. Aunt Nancy's bass waxed as the moment called for and ebbed as the moment called for, singing thru the gaps as Djamilaa's chiming touch hung in the air, an aroused "amen" or a bemused "alas" in which all possible sense, all apprehension, seemed tied up in a single note or a quick strum (throb and drop, it almost goes without saying, a never not available resort). For her part, Drennette would not let it be forgotten that the drumset commandeers light, cymbal shimmer and cymbal ping plied with water-wristed aplomb, so brightly the mind's ear's eye could only squint. She had a way of letting the side of the stick's tip roll with its metal address, a lingering ride or regard one heard as tambourine-like, tenor to tambourine's alto or soprano, baritone sometimes, bright even so.

The lamented Elsa was every loss, every lost hope, the charm gone from a charmed life. Elsa was the "was" that would've been had anything ever been, the "is" the "was" receded from as well. An elapsed albeit echoing recess, Djamilaa made clear, was also what Elsa was, a "was" we'd reminisce as though we'd been there, a "was" we'd spend forever not returning to.

The audience again got loud and went wild in the Egyptian style, interrupting in the Egyptian style, literally stopping the show again.

Again Djamilaa, Aunt Nancy and Drennette stopped playing and waited until the audience settled down to resume, picking up where they'd left off, Djamilaa reiterating her precept or prognosis regarding Elsa as elapsed, echoing recess. Elsa, she again made clear, now driving it across with all the more force, was a "was" we'd reminisce as though we'd been there, a "was" we'd spend forever not returning to.

It was a solemn prognosis Djamilaa laid out and she laid it out with a steady hand, tremulous truth no disabler, threadbare hope (if not lost hope) no hitch. Indeed, she let a certain stateliness accrue to solemnity or insisted it accrue, her last allusion and quotation, the one she began to end her solo with, coming from Federico Mompou's *Songs and Dances*, the opening strains of No. 9, a closer walk mingling near with far, the processional gait won by stoic resolve.

Djamilaa had sat slumped over the keyboard à la Evans while expounding on Elsa but with the Mompou she straightened her back and lifted her chin, sitting up with model posture as if to illustrate stoic resolve. Aunt Nancy straightened up as well. She no longer draped herself over the bass but stood erect, her head high and her eyes, when they weren't closed, on the horizon. Drennette did so too, her back ironing-board straight as she rode high on the drummer's stool.

Aunt Nancy went from wincing throb to mini-walk, swell to wincing stepdown, a Scott LaFaro reference that kept Elsa close by, but only until Djamilaa drove the Mompou home by humming it as she played, Drennette a muted waltz meanwhile on the high hat. A slow tolling, a slow noting of what one goes thru, prepared the way, toll a tally of cost and a chiming decree rolled into one. It seemed it said gait would be gate, an opening, as they eventually went from Mompou back to the head. Gait was indeed gate as they did so—which is to say, trite though it is to put it so, they *swung*, solemnity's unexpected boon or behest, closer walk nothing if not strut.

Indeed, they swung swing itself, swing so perpendicular to itself it sprang, spring the fey sense one had of it, a buoyant sway and a bit of swag, vintage Elmo Hope. The head, that is, was now a recombinant bounce Djamilaa worked and kept working, a host of collateral chatter among the fingers of her left hand. It all had a way of leaning back even as it sprang, not in posture so much as the actual sound, an acoustico-implicative stride at a slight angle, ambling yet relaxed, laid back. It had a way of bounding, even so, with namesake hope, all-out expectancy, Drennette's high clamor on the cymbals ladling release.

The Elmo Hope vibe was Djamilaa's nod to the audience's North African salute it occurred to me, oblique but necessarily so. I leaned over and said so to Penguin, who was standing next to me. He agreed and, grinning, added, "If she quotes from 'Stars Over Marrakesh' they'll go crazy again and I'll be out of here." He put his hand out when I laughed. I slapped it and turned my hand over and he slapped mine.

Djamilaa neither quoted from "Stars Over Marrakesh" nor needed to. She continued bearing down on the head, with not only collateral chatter but collateral clack, a nothing-ever-was-anyway bent and burr brushing everything aside. She, Aunt Nancy and Drennette did indeed speak of deserts crossed but that wasn't the point. Lambert, Penguin and I, given the nod by Djamilaa, came back in, ending the piece with three unison restatements of the head and a stop-on-a-dime return to silence.

The crowd again responded in the Egyptian manner, clapping, standing, stomping, whistling, shouting. It was a full five minutes before we were able to begin the next piece.

As ever,
N.

Dear Angel of Dust,

   We're in Detroit. Got here around noon after an early flight from
L.A. It's the first time in Detroit for all of us. After getting settled in
the hotel and resting up a while we went out to take a look—see, as
Rahsaan would say, what we could see. We walked around quite a
bit and took the bus for longer distances, anxious to see all we could.
It's hard to say, hard to sum up what it all adds up to, could it be said
to add up to anything. What it was was random vantages, random
veils, no such disclosure as we think a first-time exposure to a city
might yield. Detroit was there but not there. Or was it we were there
but not there, vantage indissociable from veil, red-eyed as we were? I
quickly found the expectation to see and say something about Detroit
an irritant, any summing up or desire to sum up an affront. Yes, the
monumental architecture seems to cry out for comment, the mas-
sive, no-nonsense rectilinearity of the General Motors Building bent
on eliciting reverence or ridicule. (Penguin went so far as to call it
"their new Parthenon.") The contrast between that blatant a claim on
eternity and the auto industry's recent troubles makes cultural critics
of us all, not to mention the charred, burnt-out neighborhoods, the
abandoned houses overtaken by vines and other growth, the naked
foundations, the empty lots. Yes, that all the more obvious contrast
would appear to put words in our mouths, easy words moreover, no
matter how stark what they report. Yes, them that's got, mostly white,
mostly keep getting while them that's not, mostly black, mostly don't.
This is axiomatic American cud we could chew for days and do chew,
chewing or not.

We strolled, at one point, up Woodward Avenue over to the Detroit Institute of Arts, where we'll be playing. It was beautiful, quite the promenade, with lovely buildings on both sides of the street, the Institute, perhaps, the loveliest of them. But likewise, once inside, yes, the huge Diego Rivera frescoes, the homage to industrial Detroit he painted in the early thirties, all but jumped out and took hold of one's tongue, tempting one to wax on about a discrepant relation to what one saw outside. The contrast between epic, heroic dimension and postindustrial diminution came easily to one's lips—too easily, all too easily, I thought. I found myself resisting the very observations I'd have made, something about them seeming too pat, too obvious perhaps. I had the sense there was an opaque Detroit, a recondite Detroit, a secret Detroit such observations don't even scratch the surface of. I bit my tongue.

It's not that any of that isn't true, not that easy sociologizing isn't true, probably more true the easier it is, not that that may not be the job society does. It's not that it's not true but that everyone already knows it and is maybe, at some level, okay with it. What, I was asking myself, does waxing on or waxing at all about it mean or do? Meanwhile, all the musicians that've come out of here and all the music that's come out of here are really staggering, really, as we like to say, saying something. If I named Howard McGhee, Tommy Flanagan, Betty Carter, Geri Allen, the Jones brothers (Elvin, Hank and Thad), Yusef Lateef, Julius Watkins, Ron Carter, Milt Jackson, Paul Chambers, Barry Harris, Louis Hayes, Alice Coltrane, Pepper Adams, Kenny Burrell, Donald Byrd, Lucky Thompson, Charles McPherson, Lonnie Hillyer, Sippie Wallace, Hugh Lawson, Frank Foster, Sonny Stitt and J. R. Monterose, I'd just be getting started, even without getting into gospel folk like Reverend C. L. Franklin, blues folk like John Lee Hooker, R&B folk like Aretha Franklin and George Clinton, rock and roll folk like Hank Ballard and Bill Haley, pop folk, Motown, etc. At the same time, I both care and don't care that they came from here. Music is always elsewhere.

After DIA, we took a bus down Woodward to go to Greektown. At one of the stops a man who I'd say was in his mid-sixties got on. He was wearing a rumpled brown suit that had seen better days, a white shirt that could've used washing and dress shoes that were run down at the heels. His hair was an unkempt, salt and pepper Afro, matted down on one side from having been slept on it looked like, his chin and jaws covered with salt and pepper stubble, in need of a shave. He headed for the back of the bus after getting on, muttering something under his breath and making a point of looking at each passenger he passed. His eyes were bloodshot and one could smell that he'd been drinking but he had a kind of elegance about him all the same, no matter his legs were a little shaky and he bumped against the edges of the seatbacks as he made his way down the aisle. He gave off the sense that, like his suit, he'd seen better days. After he and the other new passengers were seated and the bus began to roll again, one heard, coming from the back of the bus, his muttering slowly gain volume, reaching the point where one heard him say, a bit slurred but loud and quite intelligibly, "None of y'all don't know *nothin'* about this!" He repeated this again and again, pausing between repetitions as if to let it sink in throughout the bus or even, perhaps, to assess and be newly schooled by it himself. "None of y'all don't know *nothin'* about this!" he said again and again, his voice raspy, gruff, burning like whiskey.

The rest of us turned to look toward the back of the bus, one or two at first and then more and more of us, all of us eventually staring at him as he continued to announce, "None of y'all don't know *nothin'* about this!" (Every now and then he phrased it, "Don't none of y'all know *nothin'* about this!") He sat alone on the back seat of the bus, dead center, head up, back surprisingly straight given the wobbliness of his walk down the aisle, feet planted flatly and solidly on the floor, legs a little bit akimbo, hands on his knees. He stared back at us, panning the bus, intent on making eye contact with each and every one of us it seemed, something of a taunt, a challenge, a dare in the look he gave us. "None of y'all don't know *nothin'* about this!" he kept insisting, sometimes "Don't none of y'all know *nothin'* about this!"

It never became clear what he meant by "this," whether it referred to his condition in some micro or macro way (his tipsiness or his general disrepair, respectively), to a more general state of affairs, to life itself or to who knows what, but his vehemence, if nothing else, communicated, his adamance, if nothing else, had a kind of articulateness, the direness or the extremity from which he spoke was affecting and true. "The dead are dying of thirst," I thought, figuring him as a drunken Dogon elder chiding us for negligence or disrespect, for having fallen arrears on dues or debts owed the dead, owed history, a breach of ritual observance, ritual recall. It struck me that "this" was nothing if not the entire edifice, possession built on and put in place by dispossession, the disrepair of the socially dead. I thought this and I saw it all in a snap, a flash, but, no matter the truth of it, the historical and present-day relevance or resonance of it, I almost immediately lost patience with myself, guilty as I was of a deeper negligence, a deep non-observance of the hidden-in-plain-sight rite we were being offered, the initiation into not knowing the man in the rumpled suit invited us to. The simple fact was that he was right, we didn't know. We didn't know who he was, we didn't know what "this" was. All we knew was that there he was, announcing we didn't know, accusing us of thinking we knew but not knowing. "None of y'all don't know *nothin'* about this," he declared again and again.

Everyone in the bus looked at him for a while, a long while. The bus driver glanced up at his rearview mirror from time to time, checking out what was going on in back. It had started off with everyone being a little on edge, wondering what this would lead to, apprehensive as to what it would lead to, but after a while it seemed pretty clear that his mania, if mania was what it was, consisted solely of confronting us verbally and with his bloodshot gaze, that the always possible threat of violence didn't apply. He kept to his own space, clearly defined in the middle of the backseat of the bus, and his hands never left his knees—no flailing of arms, no gesticulation, not so much as waving a finger. What little violence there was, if it can even be called that, was confined to his face, a grimacing wince it got from time to time as he registered the effort it took to apprise us of our not knowing, a certain exasperation, bordering on exhaustion it seemed, with having to do so, with our not knowing and with our not knowing we didn't know. Once it was established that he was no danger, that he posed no threat, everyone in the bus relaxed. Everyone eventually turned away from staring at him and went back to what they'd been doing before. Drennette, Lambert, Penguin, Aunt Nancy, Djamilaa and I all looked at each other and rolled our eyes. There was a group of teenagers nearby who covered their mouths and giggled. The man in the brown suit, unfazed by no longer having everyone's attention, continued his tirade, his rant, his apprisal of our not knowing, "None of y'all don't know *nothin'* about this!" After a while it simply blended in, background noise, of a piece with the conversations going on in the bus, traffic noise from outside and whatever else came into earshot. At the fourth stop he stood up, went back to muttering, made his way shakily up the aisle and got off the bus.

I have to admit I found myself a little shaken, no matter nothing untoward had broken out. It wasn't even the possibility of violence so much as that I somehow felt singled out. He didn't look my way any more than anyone else's while he spoke and when he did make eye contact with me he didn't linger as if it were especially me his words were intended for. The fact that what he said, what he kept insisting, what he kept repeating, agreed so much with the way I'd been thinking, the random vantage being the random veil, is what shook me. It seemed he spoke from some unreachably occult place, a cautionary voice after my own heart, chastening and affirming me at the same time.

There are other things I could go into about our first day in phantom Detroit but I won't. We ended up leaving a diner last night, for example, when the waitress told Lambert he'd have to remove his skullcap, the kufi he was wearing. No way was that going to happen. We all just got up and left without exchanging a single word. We just glanced at each other and got up and left.

I'll try writing again while we're here. Our gig's tomorrow night.

As ever,
N.

Dear Angel of Dust,

We got back from Detroit yesterday. I'd have written again while we were there but it was all pretty whirlwind and we were going nonstop. The excitement our being there generated kind of took us by surprise. It all culminated in the gig at the Detroit Institute of Arts, the turnout for which impressed us—not just the number of people who showed up but the mix. It wasn't just the usual crowd of artists, intellectuals, college students, college dropouts and so on, but what Sly would call "everyday people," working folks who after pulling a nine-to-five came out to check us out. There was a range of age groups as well, teenaged to middle-aged, with some seniors here and there as well. We're not used to that, this sort of wide-ranging cultural appetite, especially amid so much that's down, depressed. Anyway, besides the gig at DIA, we did an interview and performed in the studio at WDET, the hip radio station that's not far from DIA, and we hung out a lot with some of the town's up and coming musicians, Griot Galaxy, A. Spencer Barefield and others, who took us around. There was lots to see but at the same time nothing to see, a deep sense of hollowed-out prepossession I couldn't get rid of. It wasn't just all the burnt-out or boarded-up houses and buildings or all the empty lots, the stretches that were destroyed in '67 (Destroyit some took to calling it) and simply left that way, but something else, something more to do with me perhaps. I did feel my forehead thicken from time to time. I barely staved off a cowrie shell attack.

It may have had as much to do with time as with space, not just being in Detroit but being half a month into 1984, the ominousness of the date taken from it by it getting here, as they say, without incident, failing to live up to its portent. Is it that or is it that it arrived, rich with incident and portent, seventeen years early if not more? This was the question that had me teetering toward a cowrie shell attack, the teasing sense of anticlimactic arrival on the one hand and before-the-fact arrival on the other. I couldn't help hearing Yusef Lateef's "1984," the title track from his 1965 album. It came on strong, piped into my head à la previous cowrie shell cuts, the abrupt, keening onslaught the track opens with showing no mercy. The whistling, the whining and the moaning quickly followed, ventilated by the dicelike tumblings on the piano, the ad hoc bass and drum acrobatics. It was all I could do to ward off a fullblown attack, having to do so more than once.

"1984" was a gremlin, an imp, it so kept coming at me. It seemed it insisted I appease it, a poltergeist, an offended ghost. It seemed the only way to do that would be to meet it head-on, so during the sound check I suggested we add a new piece to the program, one that "would honor one of Detroit's own," as I put it, "while getting some other business taken care of too." I told the band it was Yusef Lateef I was referring to and that the piece was "1984," something I wanted to work up our own version of, more a variation on it than a rendition, as much a departure from it. I told them about the sense of anticlimactic arrival I was beset by, the possibly before-the-fact arrival that also occurred to me, the repeated threat of a cowrie shell attack. I wanted to call our piece "1948" I announced, explaining that it was in that year that Orwell finished his novel and that he arrived at the title by having the last two digits trade places, a numeric anagram. I went on a bit about the arbitrariness of it, the concession to happenstance, the default on prophecy of something so often taken to be prophetic. I said something about the year not mattering, dates not mattering, something about the warning the book issued pertaining to no particular date, no particular time, but to all time, to every passing moment, something about hollowed-out prepossession holding all time, all futurity, hostage. I was on a run, a roll, prolix but both impelled and impeded by the sense that I hadn't yet said what I meant to say, that maybe there was no way to say it. I spurted, sputtered, cleared my throat, rambled on. It was Aunt Nancy who finally bailed me out, offering a phrase that both summed up and opened up what I'd been getting at, trying to get at. "We get it," she said demurely, ever so low key, as I stuttered reaching for a word. "We get it," she said, demure but decisive. "Moment's omen."

To make a long story short, one of our hosts at DIA got hold of a copy of *1984* and we listened to the track a few times, putting some ideas together as to how to both refer to it and take it somewhere else. We definitely wanted to retain its aleatory, strung-out, far-flung sense of space and its various recourses to vocalization, though we couldn't, we knew, use exactly the same instruments. Penguin came up with the idea of bringing Hendrix into the mix, reminding us of "1983 (A Merman I Should Turn to Be)" on the *Electric Ladyland* album, whose line "Oh say can you see it's really such a mess" he said he especially had in mind. "I like the way it messes with 'The Star-Spangled Banner,'" he said, "sort of the same way he did on the guitar." So we decided we'd each intone that line at some point in the piece, doing so hand-over-mouth, muffling it à la Yusef's whimpers and moans. And so on. Everybody came up with ideas. We ended up changing the title, scrambling it further and calling the piece "1489." "Right before Columbus," Lambert pointed out. "You land somewhere by mistake and tell the people living there it belongs to you. 1984 was around long before 1984. There've been a lot of 1984s." So we added "1489" to the set list and to our book.

The other news is that the balloons showed up again. It wasn't during "1489" but a piece we did later in the set, "The Slave's Day Off." It was during the solo Drennette took, a solo that began with the drumset seeming to collapse, come apart, the sort of thing Dannie Richmond would do with Mingus's band to mark a tempo change. Drennette came out of that collapse, that mock breakdown, with a figure that was all feet—clipped hisses, that is, on the high hat, hortative thumps on the bass drum. The first balloon emerged at once, slipping out between the two cymbals of the high hat as though they were lips. It bore these words: *I lay on my bed on my stomach, my head on my pillow, the sheet and the cover tossed aside. The sun rose, lifting the hem of my gown, warming the backs of my legs and my rump, bathing the bed in light.* The balloon, it seemed, harkened back to "The Slave's Day Off's" inception on Venice Beach—the rollerskaters, the cellophane jumpsuits, the publicized privates. When Drennette put sticks to snare the first balloon disappeared from the high hat and the second emerged from the center of the snare, bearing these words: *I felt him looking at* me, his eyes on my shoulder blades, the small of my back, my waist and my hips, tailstruck, I could tell, though I couldn't have cared less. He abruptly had at me, nose up my ass as though nothing else in the world mattered. He acted like his life was at stake.

Lambert, Djamilaa, Penguin and I looked at each other. The balloons appeared not only to be reaching back to the very roots of "The Slave's Day Off" but to be related to the X-rated balloons that followed Drennette home after the Comeback Inn gig a few months ago. The second balloon vanished as she went to the sock cymbal and came back to the snare with a series of rolls and paradiddles, whereupon another balloon rose from the center of the snare. It bore these words: *What was the point I lay there wondering, reticent, unresponsive, letting him have his way with my cheeks and the insides of my thighs, his lips and his tongue all over them, rummaging my ass-crack as well. No moans escaped my throat, no sound at all. Bored, blasé, I lay silent, unmoving, no grinding the bed, no lifting my ass to his face. My reluctance worked him into a fever, my reserve egged him on, as though he wanted what he wanted not to be wanted.* When Drennette turned her attention from the snare to the tom-tom the balloon disappeared and a new balloon rose from the tom-tom bearing these words: *He kept at it, head up my butt, ostrichlike. My ass and loins were his North, the Gourd he drank from and followed, my "back door" the place the sun would shine someday. Someday, evidently, had come, though I could not have cared less.* A few snickers could be heard among the audience.

Drennette kept at it on the tom-tom when the balloon disappeared, doling out a string of slow rolls. She played more softly as well, as if whispering, confiding, as though she herself was taken aback by what she went on to disclose. After three measures the fifth balloon emerged, rising from the tom-tom, bearing these words: *The world about to blow up, all he could do was bury his head in my behind, begging off. It wasn't his he said or it seemed he said, the world wasn't his. Muddy Waters was on in the background, "That Same Thing."* That same thong he might as well have said. More laughter rose from the audience, a little louder, more widely dispersed. Drennette worked the bass drum pedal as the balloon disappeared, a hurry-up insistence it fell to her left hand to learn from, which it did, quickening the tempo and passing the lesson along, both it and the right raising the volume over the next few measures, whereupon a new balloon emerged, this one from the bass drum: *Ripe with reticence, bottom-line romance, open-secret sex, the world was neither to be had nor held. He held me instead, my midriff and trunk some kind of surrogate, sweet respite no matter how moot it was to me.* No laughter greeted this balloon. The audience had grown somber, all ears, all eyes, absorbed. As the balloon disappeared a wistful sigh could be heard here and there.

Drennette took the volume back down, the hurry-up thumps on the bass drum a subdued patter she bought time with while putting the sticks down for brushes and then working the snare, all rub and stir. A new balloon, the seventh, rose from the snare, bearing these words: *What if it was otherwise his nudging nose and tongue demanded. What if governance were his it seemed he asked with each inhalation, each lick, each whiff, a new earth it was his to rule borne by the funk between my cheeks. What if my ass were a field his nose and tongue plowed, forty acres worth, what about that it seemed he wanted to know.* When the balloon disappeared Drennette left the snare for the ride and sock cymbals, applying the brushes with a malletlike or hammerlike address that crescendoed as the eighth and last balloon lifted off the sock cymbal bearing these words: *Planet Squat it seemed it all came down to, a dispatch, a dismissal, world without weal without end. World to be done with, done over, long wallow, world to so make it with me would remake.* The balloon disappeared and the solo ended. The audience erupted with thunderous applause and the rest of us came back in.

It was easy to see what the balloons had to do with "The Slave's Day Off," especially coming in a set that included "1489," but it was also clear, to Lambert, Aunt Nancy, Djamilaa and me, and to Penguin as well perhaps, that they had "Penguin" written all over them, the reference to another flightless bird, if nothing else, giving it away. As if that wasn't enough, Drennette, as we were leaving the stage, Penguin told Lambert and me later, looked back at him and said, "Nice gig, eh, Ostrich?" and quickly, smiling, corrected herself, "I mean, Penguin." Was it a come-on or a critique, he asked Lambert and me, maybe her way of getting back at him for the time he called her Djeannine.

It was indeed a nice gig, a nice visit, the audience receptive and especially excited that the balloons appeared, some of them thanking us after the concert for having, as they put it, brought them along.

Yours,

N.

Dear Angel of Dust,

We've been thinking about the expression a few people used af-
ter the concert in Detroit: "Thanks for bringing the balloons along."
Lightly spoken it may have been albeit sincere (they all smiled with a
gleam in their eyes as they said it), but it got us thinking about doing
exactly that, literally that. What if, we started wondering, we showed
up for a gig with a big bag of balloons, not comic-strip balloons but
literal balloons, rubber ones, the kind you blow up, and gave them
out to the audience before we hit, one or more to each member of
the audience, instructing them to use the balloons in whatever way
they could to accompany the music, contribute to the music? "It's an
idea that has a lot going for it," Aunt Nancy, who was the one who
suggested it, remarked, going on to elaborate that it would not only,
potentially at least, break down the distinction between audience and
band, listener and performer, observer and participant, not only add
further indeterminate elements to the music as we listened for and
responded to the audience's input, but also, perhaps, work as a "pro-
phylaxis" against the comic-strip balloons. The word was her choice,
"not unadvised," as she herself pointed out, "given certain connota-
tions and the balloons' recent X-rated content." She said this without
looking at Drennette, with no need to look at Drennette. We all knew
what she was getting at. Drennette herself laughed and quipped her
approval, "Prepared ensemble meets visual pun."

We're wondering what approach an audience would take. Blow the
balloons up and rub them? Blow them up and let the air out? Blow
them up and pop them with pins? Blow them up, put them on the

floor and stomp them? Leave them uninflated, stretch them tight and pluck or strum them? Leave them uninflated and snap them? Blow them up and thump them? All of these? All of these and more? We wonder but we also worry that were we to do this we'd be acknowledging the comic-strip balloons too explicitly, identifying with them, no matter how playfully, making them a trademark, inviting the audience to think of us in relation to the balloons first and foremost, making them a calling card of sorts. Is irony lever enough to fend off what could look like endorsement? And what if the comic-strip balloons themselves got the wrong idea?

We wonder if it's a risk worth taking. What do you think?

As ever,
N.

Dear Angel of Dust,

Thanks for writing back so quickly. I shared your letter with the rest of the band. We agree that a balloon is nothing if not captured breath. That it contains or seeks to contain something too inchoate to be contained we also agree. That the comic-strip balloon and the literal balloon, the rubber balloon, have that much in common we see as well. We agree that using containment (would-be containment) to open things up is a kind of coup. That putting the audience's will or wish to containment literally in their hands carries an element of poetic justice has also occurred to us. That it carries an element of poetic license as well has occurred to us too. The tradition of balloons as a sign of ceremony does recruit color, as you say, to the binding of breath, much as music does. We couldn't have said it better, except we'd maybe keep going and say balloons are in a sense already music, a ritual disbursement of caught or constricted breath meant to consecrate, even where it borders on asthma (if not especially where it borders on asthma), the blessing breath is. If asthma can be thought of as a wildfire, we'd say, balloons are a controlled burn. They marshall caught or constricted breath intimating breath's possible extinction, festive recruit's cautionary aspect or address. Balloons are also, we'd go on to say, chromatic festivity's dark tone, dark temper, so much depending on sacks of air. We'd want festive lightness given a gravity of sorts, each audience member holding a balloon as though it were his or her own lung.

We'll see what happens. We're more inclined to give it a try after getting your letter, more of a mind it's a risk worth taking. It's a moot question at the moment, however, as we don't have any gigs in the offing. As I've said, we'll see what happens.

As ever,
N.

Dear Angel of Dust,

I woke up remembering these words: *I plucked a plywood harp strung with fishing line, a crude instrument with rattly strings, a blunt instrument. No angel, I struck out at the world with it, disbursed its screw-loose harmonics (if they could be called harmonics) with a heavy hand, pure payback.* I awoke with them on my mind and tongue, mouthing them as I came out of sleep, under my breath as it were, muttering them close to my lips, tongue and teeth, a recitation by heart were there ever one. I remembered them from the dream I'd had, a legible, indelible burst within the dream, not unlike the balloons that on occasion visit our music. A balloon's balloon I'm tempted to call it, a cyst inside the balloon my dream was.

It was a dream in which I was back in school, junior high school. I had put off doing the project for my "Music Appreciation" class until the last minute, not getting going on it until the day before it was due. The project was to build a small musical instrument of some sort, either modeled on an existing instrument or invented. I'm not sure why I procrastinated, which was unusual for me, but my guess would be that my prior experiences with school assignments that involved building something, a science project on electromagnetism, a historical shadowbox, a terrarium and so on, did it. Such were among the times growing up without a father got to me most, as the best projects were always those done by kids whose fathers, with their well-appointed workshops and garages, all but did the projects for them. A girl in "Music Appreciation" the previous year had turned in a harpsichord that was much talked about and that went on to win a prize at the county fair.

So it must have been a kind of dread, a kind of trepidation, that kept me from getting to the project until the very last day, dread, trepidation and, the balloon within the balloon was telling me, anger, resentment. When I did get around to getting started on the project I rummaged around our garage, not with much idea of what I was looking for or of what I intended to make. I found an old sheet of plywood and I saw that we had a hacksaw, with which I proceeded to cut out a piece in the shape of a bass clef. It turned out we had some fishing line, a few spools of various grades, a can of silver spray paint and a packet of small nails. I spray-painted the piece of plywood I'd cut and once it was dry I cut several lengths of fishing line and used the small nails to secure them to the inner curve of the piece of wood, tapping the nails all but all the way in and tying the ends of the lengths of line around them. I'd made a harp.

It was a harp mainly to the eye if not in name only. I didn't pay much attention to how it sounded, just making sure the strings, the lengths of line, were pulled tight enough to make a sound when plucked. I made no effort to tune them. The thought never occurred to me. It was a perfunctory effort but, if I'm reading the balloon within the balloon right, subliminally more than that. I wanted it to visually signify harp but otherwise flaunt the meagerness of the resources available to me to make it, my absent father at the fore. Its rattly, measly, make-do sound was pathetic, an orphan sound I meant at some level to rub the teacher's nose in, the school's nose in, the world's nose in. The would-be elegance of the silver paint job only made it worse, more flagrant, an obvious compensatory move that highlighted how shoddy the harp was.

All this went on in the dream as it had when I was a kid in junior high. I turned the harp in the next day. It was one of the least impressive projects turned in, but when my teacher, Mrs. Keene, who was typically very stern and severe, took it up and examined it, as she did right there in front of the class for each and every project turned in, she plucked the strings and generously commented that several of them did indeed emit some of the notes of the scale. I was only more embarrassed and set emotionally awry by this though. She was also saying, without saying it, that most of the strings did not, which was true. No matter the harp had accomplished its subliminal mission, I was upset as she stood there plucking it.

It was at this point that the dream deviated from what had actually occurred that day when I was a kid. No, it's not that a balloon bearing the words I woke up reciting emerged from the harp as Mrs. Keene plucked. It was a little more subtle than that. What happened in the dream was that as Mrs. Keene continued to pluck I felt pressure against my forehead, exactly in the area where the cowrie shell attacks and the bottle cap attacks have occurred in the past. The pressure was intense and, reaching to touch the area, I felt it was made by extrusions of what had the feeling of type, as though the typebars or the typeball of a typewriter banged outward from inside my head, causing reverse-image letters to rise on my forehead. My fingertips were oddly fluent in the reverse reading the imprints on my skin required. It was as though I were a blind person reading braille and I did so preternaturally fast. I ran my fingertips across the text and there it was: *I plucked a plywood harp strung with fishing line, a crude instrument with rattly strings, a blunt instrument. No angel, I struck out at the world with it, disbursed its screw-loose harmonics (if they could be called harmonics) with a heavy hand, pure payback.*

When Mrs. Keene stopped plucking the strings the text went away and my forehead went back to being smooth, at which point I awoke with the words of the text on my mind and my tongue.

Sincerely,
Dredj

Dear Angel of Dust,

Thank you for writing back. I appreciate your response to Dredj's letter, which, as you guessed, was written during a cowrie shell attack, though maybe I should call it a reverse-image text attack. All the other hallmarks of a cowrie shell attack were there, but the protrusions on my forehead felt, as in the dream, like raised reverse-image letters rather than cowrie shells. You also noticed, I was happy to see, the conversation the letter seems to be having with the balloons that emerge from Aunt Nancy's "Dream Thief" solo on *Orphic Bend*, all that business about the cigar-box guitar. Yes, there seems to be some dialogue going on about absent fathers, makeshift amenity and string, as though the first were the third attached to the second, obligatory dues, anacrustic obbligato, something gone before saying but not without saying. You're also on point asking what dialectical residue accrues to fishing line's advance over straw, not to mention the other stuff you bring up.

The implied or potential chat between Dredj's fishing-line harp and Aunt Nancy's cigar-box guitar wasn't lost on the other members of the band. "It's as though the two played a duet," Penguin said at one point as we were discussing the dream at rehearsal. I'd brought up the cowrie shell attack, the reverse-image text attack, at the very beginning of rehearsal, still caught up in its resonances and its resistances even though it had been a light, shortlived attack as these things go. "Why would an embarrassing incident from junior high school come back with so much force?" I asked early on, a little bit rhetorically but not entirely so. I really did want the band's input into the process of decipherment and decoding, even recoding, I'd begun. We ended up talking for a long while, everyone pitching in, putting his or her two cents in, and it was Penguin who first brought up the relevance and apparent relatedness of the cigar-box guitar. "They might as well be cousins," he remarked of it and the fishing-line harp before noting their implied or potential duet or dialogue. Everyone immediately chimed in, saying the same had occurred to them, Aunt Nancy's not the least among the ratifying voices, "Yes, that's the first thing that struck me about it."

When I said recoding I meant exactly that. Drennette, after we'd been talking a long while, suggested we leave off talking by translating our talk, letting our talk extend into and take the form of a piece of music, "Dredj's Dream," which we would collectively compose, partly writing it out and partly, having done that, adding to what we'd written as we played. We all thought it was a good idea and Drennette went on to stipulate that we at no point allude to or in any way sound like either of the pieces the title brought to mind, "Monk's Dream" or "Sonny's Dream." She admitted, as she put it, that it would be especially hard to stay clear of Sonny Criss's piece, given its bottom-heavy propulsion's affinities with Mingus's *The Black Saint and the Sinner Lady*, thus providing an opportunity to say or to suggest something about an L.A. sound, but she insisted it was a temptation we would have to resist. I'm not all that sure we'd have found echoing or alluding to Monk or to Sonny so tempting or that we'd have otherwise gone that way, but we agreed to the proviso and got to work.

We decided that if we alluded to any other piece it would be our own "Dream Thief" and we did end up doing so. It was as if Dredj were the thief in question, the dream of the fishing-line harp siphoning aspects of the dream of the cigar-box guitar, just as we now channeled or alluded to certain melodic and harmonic elements in "Dream Thief" with an intermittent, subsidiary line running thru "Dredj's Dream" that bore roughly the same relationship to "Dream Thief" as Abdullah Ibrahim's "Sotho Blue" does to Oliver Nelson's "Stolen Moments," Abdullah upping the ante on "stolen" paralleled and upped further by the act of "theft" we made "Dredj's Dream" guilty of.

Yes, the line says or insinuates, we fish our premises, extend our precinct, our province, advance what sonorous catch we can. Still, we wondered if a more literal fishing line might not have a place in the piece, short lengths of it cut and tied around the strings of Aunt Nancy's bass à la Cageian "preparation." We agreed it did but the "line" Aunt Nancy ended up using was less literal than gestural, a symbolic substitute or simply a substitute, as there was no fishing line handy. We were rehearsing at Lambert's apartment and there was none there. Lambert, however, scrounged around and found some twistie bag ties in the kitchen. He offered them to Aunt Nancy and she tied some of them around her bass strings, a substitute for fishing line that could be seen or said to signify fishing line. Symbolic or not, the twistie bag ties, at the literal level, the aural and the tactile level, intrude and obtrude in a rattly, screw-loose way, in a manner not inconsistent with Dredj's fishing-line harp.

These are only a couple of the elements that went into it. After a spate of brainstorming, trial and error, disagreement, agreement, happenstance and what have you, we worked it out. It's funny that a few times, going thru it, one or another of us couldn't help referencing "Monk's Dream" or "Sonny's Dream" in the course of soloing, something, as I've already said, I'm not sure would've occurred had Drennette not brought it up. Prohibition carried the power of suggestion it seems. In any case, we ran thru it several times after pulling it together.

None of the takes were as good as we'll eventually make it. For one, we're wondering what it would sound like with actual fishing line and we intend to get some. I'll hold off sending you a tape, but "Dredj's Dream," collectively composed, definitely goes into our book.

Yours,
N.

——————————————

Dear Angel of Dust,

I dreamt I wandered in a maze, some sort of shopping mall it seemed, obliquely reminiscent of South Coast Plaza, the mall built on lima bean fields in Costa Mesa, the town right next to the town I grew up in. It was my birthday and I was there to meet someone, "a certain someone" as I put it, a special someone. I knew the sadness I'd see her struggling with would stir me, the struggle, to be more exact, more than the sadness, a struggle she and I would share. I knew her pouty, dry, slightly chapped lips would cry out to be wet by a kiss, the long, wet kiss my mouth was nothing if not made for. I knew it was that that my lips and tongue were there for, my teeth as well. I knew the bordering on bite our teeth would bring to the kiss was as much what we were there for as the press of lips and the meeting of tongues. I knew she was there somewhere in the maze, in the mall, though we'd forgotten to say exactly where in the maze or in the mall we'd meet when we arranged a few days earlier we'd meet.

As I walked about looking to see her, peeking into this or that store I could recall her liking, stopping at this or that bench we'd sat on before, this or that fountain we'd stood in front of, looking to find her but not finding her, her presence, a diffuse albeit palpable air, a presiding sense, suffused and pervaded everything, as though, there but not yet found, she was all the more there. At the same time, there was the sense of her as ultimate find, ultimate fit, the "one and only" of love lore, of course, but not only that. There was a sense of some long-sought attunement having been come to, a nestling sense of or-dainment, rest, no matter not having found each other yet. It wasn't some hackneyed business of her being with me though not actually so or not yet so, but it was. She was there as I looked, everywhere I looked, not in the way of thirst proving water's existence, not patly in the looking itself. She was there not so simply as that, though it can, in another way, be put simply: she was the dream.

Every so often during my waking life I'd glimpsed or gotten an inkling of agency and occasion run as one. In the dream it rayed out, sustained as never before. Her palpable air was nothing less than aura, a guiding sense that all was well, all would be alright, our not having decided exactly where we'd meet notwithstanding. She was there with me already and I was there with her already. An inner glow, an inner warmth, welled up in me at the thought. It was a thought I knew the dream dictated, the dream an expansive medium I knew now as at no time before. All this was true and of her it was true. She was as close as my breath, more near than my skin.

I came upon her in an odd room I couldn't recall ever having been in or ever having seen in the maze or the mall we were in. It was an open room, a pizza parlor or maybe a beer joint, with a wide entrance that wasn't a mere door but a whole wall pulled away. She sat around a table with a small group of people, engrossed in the conversation going on among them but my "certain someone" nonetheless, thru and thru. I knew this more viscerally than ever before and she knew it, though she didn't so much as look up from the conversation. She knew while not appearing to notice I was there, my "certain someone" to the bone, her not appearing to notice I was there notwithstanding.

She finally did look up and acknowledge me standing there at the entrance. She excused herself from the table and got up and walked over to me. She took my right hand into her left hand and she kissed me on the cheek, turning me away from the pizza parlor or whatever it was and beginning to walk out into the maze or the mall. She looked into my eyes and smiled. A jolt of sorrow shot thru me.

We had gotten our wires crossed it seemed. She was surprised to see me there she said and when I mentioned our arrangement to meet, my birthday and so on, she said we had left it hanging, with no follow-up, and she'd gone ahead and made other plans. I asked, "What now?" She explained that she couldn't simply up and leave her friends, the people at the table in the open room, and that she needed to get back to them. She hugged me and said happy birthday and turned around and walked away. I awoke with a sense of malaise that bordered on devastation, an extremely heavy sense of malaise, and with an even heavier sense that something was awry, that things didn't exactly add up or didn't exactly fit.

Later in the day, still bothered by the dream, I told Djamilaa about it, how much it had me disconcerted and how much it puzzled me. I went on and recounted it for her. After hearing it, she sucked her teeth and said, "Don't worry. It wasn't yours. You were dreaming someone else's dream. That was Penguin dreaming about Drennette." She would say no more.

I haven't had a chance to talk with Penguin but she said it so summarily, said it with such utter finality, confident to the point of dismissiveness, I can barely imagine she might be wrong.

What do you think?

Yours,
N.

Dear Angel of Dust,

I got a chance to talk with Penguin and I asked him about the dream. He says yes, he has dreamt it, more than once in fact, but he wouldn't go so far, he says, as to say it's about Drennette. The "certain someone" in the dream when he's dreamt it, he says, looks nothing like Drennette and doesn't, in the way she speaks, walks, carries herself and so on, resemble Drennette. "Anyway," he said emphatically, "I haven't dreamt that dream in a very long time. I dreamt it two or three times, the last about five or six months ago. Since then it seems to have gone away or been put away, like a tune a band retires from its book." I was struck by the analogy. He too, as soon as it left his lips, appeared to be struck by it, pausing as if hearing an echo of it, giving it further thought. "How strange," he went on to say, "that it popped up again, not to mention getting dreamt by someone else."

Why me? He couldn't help wondering nor could I. Is it my listening to his going on about Drennette, his bending my ear the way he so often has, my sitting still for it? Did that do it, did that open me up in some way? Did that in some way make me a surrogate or a host? "It's not about Drennette," he shot back when I asked out loud. "Of course not," I said, not wanting to make an issue of it, and went on to wonder, again out loud, what order of dream transfer it was we were dealing with, dream theft, dream contagion or what. Neither Penguin nor I could help recalling Dredj's dream, its roundabout exchange with "Dream Thief," ideas of dream transit, dream transport, crowding in on us. Was Dredj the connection, we wondered, the conduit, Penguin's dream's way into my sleep? Yes, that was it we agreed.

We no sooner agreed than Penguin looked at me and said, "Getting back to Drennette, whom it's not about, or getting back, I should say, to it not being about Drennette, I need to say about 'a certain someone' that she's the one we have that we don't have or the one we had that we don't have, the one we have by not having, that we have to have without having. You being new to this, I need to tell you she's the one whom to have would be not to have, to have let slip away in a presumption of having." He stopped as though winded by what he'd said, as though it were an hour-long speech he'd finished. I found myself set back, silent, not knowing what to say, and when he gathered himself again, got his wind back, he said, simply repeating himself, "I tell you this because you're new to it." He paused a beat before adding, "I haven't dreamt that dream in ages."

I wasn't sure anymore. I thought maybe I'd agreed too soon, settled on Dredj as the connection too quickly. Maybe, to begin with, "Why me?" isn't the question. What if Lambert dreamt the dream too, like the time the three of us dreamt the Djeannine dream? Maybe this was us dreaming a collective dream again, staggered instead of dreamt at the same time, and if Lambert hasn't dreamt the dream, could it be that he just hasn't dreamt it *yet*?

It may turn out to be inconclusive, I know, but I need to speak with Lambert and I'm going to speak with him next.

As ever,
N.

Dear Angel of Dust,

A quick note to say I spoke with Lambert. I didn't recount the dream or go into particulars. I simply asked had he dreamt of "a certain someone," figuring he'd know what I meant if he had. (I didn't want his dreaming the dream, if he hasn't yet but goes on to dream it in the future, to have been influenced by my telling it to him.) He had no idea what I meant. "A certain someone? Meaning who?" he asked. I told him he'd have known if he had. I told him he must not have and that I'd leave it at that, except that if he eventually does dream it he'll know it and to let me know if he does.

So that's it for now, the upshot being it's up in the air, still up in the air. What exactly my dreaming the dream signifies we won't know until we see whether Lambert dreams it too, which could take a while. At what point, if he doesn't do so soon, do we decide he most likely never will? The five or six months it took between the time Penguin last dreamt it and the time I did? More than that? Nine months? A year? We'll see I'd like to say but I'm not sure.

Otherwise, not much is up. We did venture up to Hollywood the other night to a place on the Strip called Club Lingerie, a pop music spot that's been there about ten years, though it's not a place we normally frequent or had even been to before. What took us there was a one-night gig by Ronald Shannon Jackson and the Decoding Society, a band we've heard on records but not live. It was a chance we couldn't pass up, no matter how incongruous the venue seemed to the music or to the way we, at least, hear the music, though on further reflection it made a certain amount of sense, given labels like "free funk" and "avant-funk" that've been applied to it. Anyway, I'm not sure the Club Lingerie crowd was quite ready for what Jackson and his band brought, not sure they knew what hit them. I can't exactly say we were ready or that we ourselves knew what hit us.

For one, even though we'd heard some of their albums—*Eye on You, Street Priest, Mandance, Barbeque Dog*—we weren't prepared for how *physical* they got live and in person, how *physical* the music got. To begin with, the place was packed, teeming with bodies and body heat before a single note was hit, and then when the band began to play it came on *strong, loud, hard*, the guitar amps and the PA system turned up to peak volume it seemed, ear-splitting volume, an impact or effect aided by the piccolo range Jackson likes to compose in (something Ornette pointed him toward, we've heard), the timbral ping the music typically rings with. It made one's head ring, one's bones and body ring, subject to an avant-primal assault bent on recalling the word *avant-garde*'s military roots it seemed, a ringing the club's occasional recourse to strobe lights further assisted. You *felt* the music at least as much as you heard it.

Club Lingerie, our initial senses of it notwithstanding, proved in many ways to be the perfect venue. A young, beautiful, hiply dressed crowd filled it with glamour and gams, miniskirts on the waitresses and on many of the patrons as well, making for a sexy ambience that was lent further sexiness by the very name of the club, its conjuration of chemises, teddies, babydolls, g-strings, corsets, garter belts and stockings, shelf bras and the like. It was Hollywood to the core, Frederick's of Hollywood in another guise, all the more congruent, by virtue of that, with the physicality of Jackson's music, the bodily press it put on, its purveyance of a bodily aromatics the word *funk* attempts to get at. We knew nothing, the band instructed us, the way it got physical, the way it came on, if we ignored the sexiness of sweat, the wet working-out of beauty's mandate.

It would have been impossible not to pick up on all of this. Indeed, Penguin, during the break between sets, remarked that the Decoding Society's brand of funk seemed "exquisitely its own, high-end and, exactly as has been said of it, avant-funk." He went on to liken it, wincing a bit as he spoke, as if the extremity of the figure gave him pause, to "an ever so uric whiff coming off the crotch of a pair of silk panties." It was, though, a figure Aunt Nancy not only agreed with at once but went further with. "Pee and perfume," she said simply, "piss and perfume."

I mention this outing because we appear to've uncovered the origins of the 4/4 shuffle that visited us a year ago at The Studio and once again, in a bit of a teasing, attenuated form, at the Comeback Inn in September. Why we'd never noticed it before will always be a mystery but there it was in Jackson's music, the 4/4 shuffle, in one of the pieces they played that night, "Man Dance" it seemed at the time, though it might've been "Shaman." Drennette was the first to notice, leaning over our table and all but shouting to be heard above the music, "You hear that? It's the 4/4 shuffle." We all picked up on it eventually, buried as it somewhat was beneath an extended shiver the horns maintained.

On our way out of the club, after the second set ended, it all came back to Aunt Nancy, who had introduced the shuffle during the gig at The Studio, that a couple of Cecil Taylor records, *3 Phasis* and *Live in the Black Forest*, made while Jackson was in the band, had probably been her subliminal prompt. I gave both records a listen earlier today and I could definitely hear it, on the second side, as it turns out, of each record—the second half of *3 Phasis* and what's a bit like the same piece under a different title on *Live in the Black Forest*, "Sperichill on Calling." It seems to me, in fact, to epitomize the difference Jackson made in Cecil's band.

It was reassuring to hear the shuffle come up in Cecil's music, to hear it could be avant without the funk. It relieved us of some of our qualms about it, our fear of a certain concession to pop. We enjoy the Decoding Society and we had a good time at Club Lingerie, but we wouldn't want our music to go as far as they go in that direction. The venue and the music did fit, as I've already said—the glamour, the sexual glitz, the not so oblique appeal. Lambert summed it up as we were leaving: "I'm surprised the balloons didn't show up."

Yours,

N.

Dear Angel of Dust,

As Lee would say: Boy, what a night! The owner of the Comeback Inn called Lambert earlier in the day and said it was his wife's birthday, that he wanted to do something special for the occasion and he was wondering if we were available, wondering if we'd be willing to play. He said something about coming back to the Comeback Inn or coming back into the Comeback Inn, Lambert told us, with or without a straight face, he added, he couldn't say, seeing as they were on the phone. Be that as it may, Lambert went on, he answered yes and they settled on the money and what time we'd be there. Talking about the gig after Lambert let us know, we decided it might be a good time, as good as any at least, to try handing out balloons to the audience, the idea I wrote you about a few letters back. There'd likely be balloons decorating the place for the occasion anyway, so why not? This would give us a kind of camouflage Penguin pointed out, doing so without saying why he thought we might need it, a potential nit the rest of us chose not to pick. We agreed it was all the more reason to give it a try.

I'd actually grown to be a little reserved about the idea since I last wrote you about it, more and more coming to see it in relation to the night I sat in with the Crossroads Choir, the "Only One" balloon the audience kept afloat during "Body and Soul." I had already been there it seemed, been there and done that it seemed. I already knew the participant quantum that contained air in the hands of an audience could be, in their hands or just outside them, either way. Would it be a return to that I wondered, knowing in particular I wanted no more of the halfway-around-the-world romance I had recourse to that night, no mere mention even. At some level I knew there was no reason to think the balloons would bear such baggage but at another level they seemed as bound up with it as the "Only One" balloon had been that night. Warmed-over romance I called it, dismissing it with a sneer, haunted, even so, by the possibility that an equally warmed-over social romance, a stale albeit yet to be achieved romance of collectivity, took its place in what we thought the balloons might do or what I thought they might do. Did I want us to revisit the "Only One" balloon, revise it, in some way pluralize it?

Just thinking about it, problematize it though I did, conjured a musical motif whose contour had the feel of having come the way my way out of my qualm would track and retrace, a bent-winged bird of a motif my lips veritably itched to work out on a mouthpiece, reed or brass no matter, a lick-driven theorem concerning the one, the two and the many. (Listen, to hear what I mean by lick-driven, to Wilber Morris's "Miss Mack" on his *Wilber Force* release or to Dewey Redman and Ed Blackwell's "Willisee" on *Red and Black in Willisau*.) Could a lick be said to grow legs or a motif to grow them for it, that's what what I heard sounded like, what the motif I had in mind would do. I heard a symphonette of sorts, a micro-symphonette wound up in a four-bar motif whose unwinding one would never complete, return to the tonic no matter, the one, the two and the many each only more active the more apparently moot.

There would be or might as well have been, that is, an "Only Two" balloon and there would be or might as well have been an "Only Many" balloon, "only" by turns a valorizing claim to singularity (*one* two, *one* many) and a dampening, a disclaimer, putative singularity disavowed (*merely* two, *merely* many). Two would be one only as the many would be one, a social predicate or a political prerequisite I'd advance with an austere pucker (it more and more appeared to be brass I had in mind), an austere pucker free of all recourse to recollected sex—as though, I wanted to say, one "wet" one's lips with dry ice, as though what would again have been touted as closure came off as cosmetic arrest.

"Marginal center," I said instead, as much tonguing the eventual mouthpiece as muttering it to myself. I meant no more than to stencil a self-correcting wobble, sonically rendered or regraded warble, a slaptongue sputter as high as the horn would go. So it was I not so much overcame as incorporated the reservation I'd come to feel. I was ready for whatever lay in store at the Comeback Inn, as were the rest of the band.

We got there a little before 8:00 as Lambert and the owner had agreed, having set up and run thru a sound check late in the afternoon, left and come back. Not as many tables had been cleared away as when we played there in September (they were expecting a larger turnout), so the space in the corner that served as a stage was even tighter than before. It reminded me of the time in the late sixties I went to hear Sun Ra at Slugs', the twenty-piece arkestra packed onto and spilling off of a stage that appeared to be the size of a dining table, two at most, "Space Is the Place" given a whole new meaning by the cramped quarters they issued the music from. I thought it a miraculous negotiation of shrunken premises. I thought back and thought something of the same would be required of us, nowhere near twenty pieces large but backed into a corner somewhat.

When we got there the place was already full, every table taken, every seat as well. There were indeed balloons decorating the room, lining the door we walked in thru as well as the walls inside, balloons of all colors. Of more than one size, some were strung along the walls where they met the ceiling, some from ceiling to floor where one wall met another. The mood was upbeat, festive, people ready to party, most of them friends of the owner and his wife we assumed, some already doing so. This, I have to admit, gave us misgivings. We don't consider festivity to be exactly our thing and we began to wonder had it been a good idea to accept the gig.

Penguin was the first to say it. "I'm not sure about this," he said once we got to the storage room that served as our green room. "I'm not sure about playing for a birthday party," he went on. "I'm especially not sure this is the gig to try passing out balloons, despite what I said earlier about camouflage. Too much chance of them taking it the wrong way." He went on in this way for a bit and the rest of us admitted we had the same apprehensions. Aunt Nancy, however, having allowed she felt exactly such qualms, went on to say that we were there and that there wasn't much else we could do but go on with it, play ("The show must go on," she even said), make the most of it. She got the look of hard thought on her face just before asking, "Remember the time we played the Scarab and someone yelled out 'Uterine hoofbeat!' as we played 'Bottomed Out'?" With the exception of Drennette, who wasn't yet in the band when we played that gig, whom we hadn't, in fact, even met, we all nodded yes. Aunt Nancy went on to say it was up to us to set the tone, to darken festivity or strike a note of dark festivity, that it was exactly the understanding of birth bound up in the "Uterine hoofbeat!" cry we needed to bring to bear, that the run of apocalyptic beat, repercussion and possession thereby implied (the Four Horsemen allied with Haitian vodoun) was ours to introduce, a complicating note we would insist accrues to each natal occasion, the owner's wife's no exception.

We all knew what she meant. It was a dread, gnostic note she was insisting on, birth as an issue of misconception, conception itself as an issue of misconception, dubious arrival into a miscreant world. Dubious cause for celebration, dubious or at best ambiguous cause for celebration, birth, we needed to insist and get them to see, was a bottoming out, a slippery descent down what she said was "the chute of incarnation," bodily being a forfeiture of immaterial essence, bodily being material exile, detour. She suggested we open with "Bottomed Out." We agreed and then decided the other pieces we'd play. She rolled coach, cheerleader and gospel diva into one, exhorting, just as we went out, "Let's wreck this place!"

So it fell to Penguin to set the tone, "Bottomed Out" opening, as it does, with him solo. He more than rose to the occasion—natal, dark, anti-festive in one swipe—or I should rather say he descended to it, more than descended, taking the baritone to his mouth and muscling a low B-flat from it, a call to order calling for close attention, dialing the party atmosphere down. Most of the patrons heeded his call, ceasing to speak and turning their attention to the music, though there continued to be something of a buzz at several tables, conversations carried on with lowered voices and with not so low voices now and then, an outburst of laughter rising out of the buzz.

As always with his entrance into "Bottomed Out," Penguin plied a "Lost Generation" line or allusion, a reference to and a reabsorption of Sonny Simmons's piece, only here he freighted it with something new, something we hadn't quite heard before, the very dread, gnostic strain or insistence Aunt Nancy had prompted us with, primed us with. He parsed a certain seepage in the horn's low register, a low-to-the-ground if not below-the-ground shuttle or shift, stealing away from concept or conception. Reconsideration proposed as concept, conception as misconception, the triplet-laced line he pressed or pursued equated lost generation with generating loss. It was nothing if not the unbottoming of birth, a caveat so severe, so categorical, it uprooted all track not in some way sealed by trepidation. No one yelled "Uterine hoofbeat!" and no one would, but uterine tread, uterine trot, uterine gallop were very much with us, there not all that long after Penguin started playing, low buzz notwithstanding.

Penguin worked his low-to-the-ground or below-the-ground shuttle or shift into a medicinal sweat, the all-out shimmy or shake of a body possessed, a hatching pool of heat. He shook as though powered or possessed by the keys of the horn, shook in such a way as to make the horn rattle. Each key was a peyote button, shriven cactus toughness, a bitter, withered vestige his finger could almost taste.

With the advent of all-out shimmy or shake the crowd turned more attentive. The few tables at which conversation had continued fell into silence, everyone's eyes and ears turned toward Penguin, whose pooling hatch turned out to be more feint than shimmy or shake. He now had them exactly where he wanted them, where we wanted them, and it was at this point that Aunt Nancy, on congas, and Drennette, on batá drum, joined in, the implied, immaterial hooves (vodoun horses, lucumí horses, santería horses) more palpably afoot. Aunt Nancy and Drennette's drumbeats were hits to the head, kicks to the head, horse's hooves intent on awakening any who remained inattentive, alerting all to the uterine bottomlessness they trod.

Penguin let the triplet figure go and let himself be lifted by the uterine carpet the congas and the batá drum rolled out, the uterine precinct or premises we were now on or in made all the more obvious, to any who somehow hadn't noticed, by Drennette sitting slightly gap-legged with the latter on her lap, its pinched midriff looking anything but pregnant notwithstanding. The batá's hourglass shape intimated nothing if not time, birth's inauguration of which and the ravages and wear brought with it "Bottomed Out" would be intent on one bearing in mind. Penguin not only rode this awareness or admission but rode it out, leaving the horn's lowest register for a climb into its highest, a raised eyebrow and a rocket launch rolled into one. He ended his climb with a squealing, roll-with-it peal of acceptance that grew falsetto-like, a peal he held for sixteen measures before coming back down.

It was as if only after making all this clear, clearing the way in a sense, only after the natal, dark, anti-festive note had been struck, could anything approaching festivity be indulged. Penguin's approach was to calibrate his peyote-button plea or appeal as longstanding romance, returning to the bottom of the horn to recall Ronnie Cuber on Eddie Palmieri's "Yo No Sé," an approach whose low annunciativity and quizzicality rolled into one, whose namesake agnostic tone if not timbre, was nothing if not the foot in the door locked-out festivity needed. Someone in the crowd shouted, "Alright!" It was on.

The rest of the piece, indeed the rest of the evening, would prove to be a standoff, sometimes fluid, sometimes tense, between a will or a willingness to party and the music's more austere demands. Penguin dangled his Cuberesque salsa riff, his bolero riff, long enough to let the audience know it was there, no more than a passing taste to let them know romance and festivity were a part of our repertoire, withheld, whenever withheld, neither out of inabiliity nor disinclination but in the interest of a larger design, a certain rigor and recognition. Having served up that taste, he fell back into his triplet-heavy quandary, kicked and had at by the congas and the batá he made it seem, a thrashing bob and weave outmaneuvering would-be assault, as though, knowing every reason to despair, he chose not to. By way of a stoptime pivot opening like velvet stage curtains, he went again to Cuber's matinee-idol suavity and sagesse, not only not despairing but dancing instead. There was no shout of "Alright!" this time. The audience could sense he simply visited the salsa motif. They knew he was not there to stay. Indeed, he was again plying his triplet-laden qualms before long and back to the salsa motif not long after that. It was this back and forth he now lingered with, limning the contours of the mixed-emotional occasion he took birth to be.

Aunt Nancy and Drennette chose to linger as well. Not so much underneath what Penguin played as around it, they built a serrated, bentlegged amble founded on an aspect of godly limp, a gallop true liquidity accrued to, horses at ocean's edge it seemed. The batá rang with echoic reach, a watery, concussive lilt it was all one could do to keep one's feet upon hearing, a sweet-wood sonance, water notwithstanding. One found oneself asking, "Maple? Cedar?" The congas meanwhile plied a bass tack, lengthier legs than those the batá stepped with, a deeper, asymmetrical step taken twice for each the batá took. Anyone familiar with lucumí and santería recognized the interplay of congas and batá as the pattern consecrated to Yemaya, the orisha of the sea and of motherhood. Aunt Nancy and Drennette sought to season if not in some way temper Penguin's mixed emotions it seemed, advancing a more accepting, celebratory take on birth, mixed in its own way though it was, acknowledging the saltiness of birth.

Aunt Nancy was nothing if not the mother and the mistress of mixed possibility. Each conga leg stepped into a hole, a giving way of ground if not the ground being lower than expected, foot missing a rung or a stairstep thought to be there, a giving out of leg or an extension of leg. The tone she'd insisted we set she thereby deepened, an exemplum she invited the audience to ponder, peel back.

The audience did exactly that. The introspective space Aunt Nancy's "drop step" apprised one of they now occupied. The low buzz gone, they sat silently, caught up in the music, attentive to every inflection, caught up in thought. Each of them listened closely, brows furrowed in some cases, visibly given pause by Aunt Nancy's leg-in-a-hole polymetrics.

As always in "Bottomed Out," Penguin pled a certain weakness, a watery-kneed insecurity of limb he called out for support from. Drennette and Aunt Nancy offered that support, the cane or the crutch or the ushering arm around his waist he cried out he needed, but this went only so far. It came to be time for Djamilaa, Lambert and I to join in, which we did, odd as it sounded or seemed, with a waltz-like figure not unlike Billy Harper's "Cry of Hunger," a cradling, chorusing, to-the-rescue riff that was anything but without bottom. Djamilaa was on piano, Lambert played tenor and I played trumpet, offering a unison statement of the line that we repeated again and again, Penguin, recalling Shepp's version of "Frankenstein" on *The Way Ahead*, growing more distraught each time we played it.

It was as though rescue, would-be rescue, only made Penguin more aware of his predicament, more painfully aware of his predicament. He thrashed and bellowed, fought as though caught in quicksand.

I'd been wondering how the owner and his wife were taking to the new tone we set, festivity's hallowing-cum-harrowing, Penguin's predicative distress. I caught a glimpse of them out of the corner of my eye as Lambert, Djamilaa and I bore down on the cradling rescue riff, spotting them over to the right toward the back of the room. I could've sworn I saw the owner's wife blow us a kiss. It might only have been me, I'm not sure, but, not only that, even more than that, it seemed all the souls there'd ever been and all there'd ever be sat in bleachers looking down at the stage we stood on, poor excuse for one though it was. It was as if the Comeback Inn had turned into a stadium and a Renaissance memory theater rolled into one, elastic locality suddenly on the ascendant. It seemed as though the Comeback Inn had become a balloon, an inflated premise that was more than one premise, a gradually pneumatic enlargement equating place with play as well as play with proliferation, locality and prolixity rolled into utmost palimpsest.

This was only a glimpse ahead to what was to come it turned out, a sideways glance lasting only an instant might it be said to have lasted at all. But for an instant (if it was, if that's what it was) the bleachers climbed toward the heavens in a flash exposing us all to the sky, soul seated beside soul, soul seated above and below soul, souls packed in, piled high.

Ahead somehow lay to the side I noted to myself, there though not yet there, eventuality's lateral outpost, festivity's debt or dispatch. No sooner did the thought arise than I put it away, though to say the thought was taken away might be more exact, swept along as everything so abruptly was. Penguin's opening gambit gave way, that is, to a tricky ensemble section—key changes, tempo changes, dotted notes, double-dotted slurs. Whether we'd really been blown a kiss or it only seemed we'd been blown a kiss one could've wondered but that was now moot. The audience was obviously with us, the owner and his wife included. The steeply ascending bleacher seats, briefly glimpsed and gone, had made it clear everyone was all in.

Our tonal reset, our setting a new tone, had not only taken but taken well and we were on our way. Lambert and Djamilaa took terse, meditative solos, rousing in each its own manner, each an understated tour de force, and the one I took wasn't bad either. At the conclusion of "Bottomed Out" there was a hearty round of applause. Two people, in fact, stood up to applaud, so taken with what was only, we'd make sure they'd see, the beginning. We had the house in the proverbial palms of our hands and we were just getting started.

The mood was more mindful now, not averse to festivity but in touch, even so, with all that would give it pause, the wages whereby festivity would have to be won, had had to be won. We were ever, the tone we set insisted, at a point of having reason to despair but also, having looked at it, seen it, stared it in the eye without blinking, at a point of winning reason to rejoice. It was nothing if not a note of hard-won festivity we struck.

We now felt less uncertain about handing out the balloons. We and the audience were now on the same page we felt, closer if not all the way there in any case; the balloons would not be taken the wrong way. It wasn't, though, that we had a particular way in mind we wanted them taken, only that they not be confused with those decorating the room, that musicial purpose and decorative purpose not be confounded. We were pretty sure but we'd see, we'd wait and see, make sure the new tone persisted. That being the case, we'd hand the balloons out before our final number.

Having opened with one of our older pieces, we played one of our new ones next, "Dredj's Dream," following that with another new one, "1489." We then went back to the older part of our book for "Opposable Thumb at the Water's Edge" and then to another newer one, "Sekhet Aaru Struff," to end the first set. Our intensity grew with each piece, as did the audience's attentiveness, a kind of absorption drawing all of us in. It grew more and more clear, more and more certain, that this was the night to hand out balloons. It grew all the more so when, the "green room" such as it was, we stayed out and mingled with the audience between sets.

Everyone we talked with had something hip to say. "When I closed my eyes during 'Dredj's Dream' I saw a shade-late incision of light" was only one of the interesting comments we got. When Djamilaa and I overheard a man in his thirties remark to Lambert, "It was like the music admitted to time only to suspend it, put birth on hold only to know it all the more, take us back to it. We all were the very thought of life again," she whispered in my ear that she was struck by how much it sounded like something I'd write in a letter to you. It did, I had to admit, nodding my head and made to wonder had our corre-spondence crept into the music, seeped into the music, so seeped in it put words in our listeners' mouths. A woman with dreads wearing a UCLA sweatshirt did say to Aunt Nancy that "Sekhet Aaru Struff" was "a beautiful woman's face conjugated into limnings of stride and striation, an implied walk compounded of structure and stroll." Others, on the other hand, were content to let it go with "You guys kicked ass, mucho ass," "You really tore it up" and the like. Still, I wondered.

The mood was good, fun but not frantic, a festive sense being somewhat low-key made more abiding. The party vibe was definitely still there. Drink flowed freely and food abounded of course. Laughter was no stranger of course. The balloons on the wall, of course, did say something about lightness and color, something about pneumatic provision, the tenuous, necessary containment of aerobic endowment. The music had let no one forget the balloons were breath's bounty, an always tenuous bequest.

We played five pieces for the second set, as we had for the first, opening with a newer one, "Fossil Flow." From there we went to something we hadn't played in a while, Shepp's "Like a Blessed Baby Lamb," then to a couple of our older pieces again, "Aggravated Assent" and "Tosaut Strut." We decided we'd put matters in the audience's hands in more ways than one, performing another older one, "Drennethology," as the ostensibly last number, reserving "Some Sunday" for an encore should they demand one. It would be right before this encore, were there one, we'd hand out the balloons. The chance of there not being one, of the audience not demanding one, was a snowball's in hell we felt. We would do what we could to make sure.

The level of intensity we left off on at the end of the first set we started on to begin the second, starting out as on fire as we'd been and building to be more on fire. "Fossil Flow" got its best reading yet, punctuated by a number of what Rahsaan would call bright moments, setting the stage for yet even more. Indeed, there were more such moments in the pieces that followed than I can go into other than sketchily, mentioning one or two to represent them all. Lambert, to mention one, soloed on "Like a Blessed Baby Lamb" in a way that went off-script or perhaps pre-script, working an expectorant, self-excavating vein worthy of Joe Henderson at his five-o'clock-shadow best. It seemed he proposed a radically articulate clearing of the throat, a veritable book of clearing the throat upping the ante on his "Book of Opening the Mouth." It was as though such clearing were no longer preparatory to speech or as though, better,

it were prior to being preparatory to speech, as though such clear-
ing constituted speech—or, if it were indeed preparatory, it remained
adamantly preparatory, promising an arrival preparation preempted,
endlessly prior, endlessly proto-, a seeming endlessness packed into a
four-minute solo, a four-minute string of ahems. Throat-clearing took
the place of talk in a gruff serenade insisting thus would its book be,
talk not arrived at as such, talk already there otherwise. Less exposi-
tory than agonistic (exposing nothing, that is, if not exposition's inse-
cure ground), the solo purveyed a beautifully possessed hemming and
hawing, expectorant scratch attenuated by namesake bleat. It culled a
particular tension and it kept the audience on the edges of their seats,
an expectant stress it offered, in the end, no release from, simply end-
ing mid-hem (or was it mid-haw?) as Lambert backed away from the
mike. The audience, finding themselves more negatively capable than
they'd have otherwise thought, burst into wild applause, as though
declaring themselves to be the release the solo had so impeccably
withheld. Aunt Nancy, who followed, was more than a few bars into
her solo by the time they settled down.

Djamilaa, to quickly mention another, brought an inrush of East-
ern undulation into "Aggravated Assent," quoting from Gurdjieff
and de Hartmann's "Reading of a Sacred Book" behind Penguin's
alto solo. Giving Gurdjieff and de Hartmann's austere Central Asian
modalities a more southerly, Persian bent, she drew from another
recording I know she listens to a lot, Nasser Rastegar-Nejad's *Music
of Iran: Santur Recital, Volume 2*. She teased out the slightly mallet-like
attack one hears in "Reading of a Sacred Book," the ringing hammer
held in check but held, one clearly hears, nonetheless. She held it less
in check, moving over into what it hovers on the edge of, remind-
ing us the piano does deploy mallets while exacting ictic, hammering
runs that brought nothing if not the santur to mind. She did more
than simply accompany the solo, daring Penguin, with a jabbing per-
sistence reminiscent of Monk, to ride the swell her tremulous left
hand kept advancing. It had a way of building and backing off a bit
and then building and backing off a bit again, potentially going on that
way forever. She plied an Ibrahimic reach into the center of the earth
that was also a stairway to the stars. It oddly amalgamated climb and
cascade, a watery stairway made of watery cloth Penguin bounded

upon more than outright rode, an unrolling rug or an unwinding scarf he trod securely on, an escalating splash after his own heart it seemed. It was after everyone else's too it seemed, so effortlessly did the other four of us work behind them (Lambert and me riffing under Penguin's lead), so far forward did the audience, holding its collective breath one sensed, lean and let themselves be hit by the aggregate hammer it all, for the moment and, for a while, moment to moment, turned out to be, all but unbearably beautiful, borne up and out and all the more enduring we irrevocably knew. "Quantum-qualitative" doesn't even come close.

Let these two suffice. What I most want to get into is how things went when we handed out the balloons. The audience did indeed demand an encore when we finished or ostensibly finished with "Drennethology." They applauded loudly, whistling here and there and here and there shouting out an "Oh yeah!" They rose to their feet as we bowed and they remained standing as we made our way back to the "green room." We walked single file, carrying ourselves as we'd agreed beforehand we would, our bodies given over to a stolid rectitude. Their eyes followed us into the "green room" and we closed the door once inside, at which point the applause grew louder. We let it go on for a while, the whistles and the shouts escalating, and then, each of us grabbing a package of balloons from the box we'd brought them in and ripping it open, we opened the door and went back out. They were still standing. Each of us, as we'd agreed beforehand we would, took a different route back to the performing area, handing balloons out to the audience as we did.

Everyone had quieted down and sat back down by the time we made it to the performing area. Lambert stepped to the mike and explained why we'd handed out the balloons, instructing the audience to each use the balloon as he or she saw fit to contribute to the music, a new piece called "Some Sunday" we were about to play that I'd written. He made a point of not suggesting how they might use the balloons, saying nothing about blowing the balloon up and letting the air out, blowing the balloon up and rubbing it, stretching the balloon and twanging it without blowing it up, blowing the balloon up and thumping it, stretching the balloon and snapping it without blowing it up, blowing the balloon up and popping it with a pin, blowing the balloon up, putting it on the floor and stomping it, etc. He simply suggested that they join in as they saw fit when he gave them the sign, which would be him raising his right arm and quickly bringing it back down. He would indicate when they were to stop, he explained, by making the halt sign with his right hand.

We started the piece off with Djamilaa, unaccompanied, repeating the folk song-sounding, children's song-sounding phrase on piano, a vamp-till-ready we let go on for a while. Djamilaa gave it just the right beginner's touch, a sometimes heavy left hand that bordered on losing the time and did in fact lose it now and again, only to quickly regain it. Pointedly unpolished, mock-awkward, "amateur" by its own lights, it made me think of Don Cherry's remark that too many people make a religion of professionalism, a not very satisfying religion he'd found, and there was indeed something reminiscent of his piano work on the *"Mu"* date about Djamilaa's playing. This was all the more apt by way of entrance into a piece we had invited the audience to take part in, as if to say it was okay to be amateurs, okay to be other than polished or professional, okay to be rough and ready, even more rough than ready. Poignancy took the place of polish in Djamilaa's vamp, as if to say, reiterate and insist we're all beginners when it comes to love, especially the Sunday kind Etta James sings about, not to mention the millenarian, great-gettin'-up-Sunday collective love we all so badly want.

It was as if it were the childhood or even the infancy of some new order she was auditioning and it wouldn't be going too far to say that Drennette's conga beats, when she finally came in, making the vamp a duo, were, threaded into everything else they were, the "patter of little feet." They made it echo in our heads, the remote broadcast of some ideal order yet to come, a conceptual impendence one ached and winced and almost wept on hearing. (Had I looked out and glimpsed an audience member or two wipe a tear from his or her eye I wouldn't have been surprised.) The conga-laced piano vamp advanced a nascent ascendancy of all any heart could want. It grew stark in the stitched iterativity it moved by way of, rhapsody met with impediment, pendency's boon and bequest.

Djamilaa and Drennette reasoned against reason it seemed, played as if to placate a ghost. The vamp jumped and ran, a run of lost and rewon time that rayed and rippled, nothing if not a swell and then nothing if not a subsidence, done again and again as though it would never end. Its echo grew more and more inscriptive, an introspective "letter to the world" one wrote without intending to, sound all instinctual plea, appeal or epistle, a recess all proprioception fell into.

Just at the point where it began to appear the vamp would really go on forever the rest of us came in. Lambert's alto jumped out with an elliptical whimsy he might've floated away on were it not for the bottom Aunt Nancy's bass and Penguin's bari put under us all. He went from whimsy to bittersweet anthem in no time at all, a march-worthy solemnity and lilt reminiscent of Jesper Zeuthen's solo on "To Alhaji Bai Konte," one of the cuts on *Brikama*, the new Pierre Dorge album we've been listening to a lot. I put the mute on my trumpet, a quivering blade I wielded or wove underneath and inside the line he laid down, a needling thread abetting the aspirate cloud he plied. March-worthy though it was, we kept to the near side of march, Aunt Nancy's bass unpredictable and volcanic even as it proffered, along with Penguin's bari, what bottom there was. Scott LaFaro's collateral chatter, the eruptive, side colloquy he used to go at in Bill Evans's trio, seemed to be her model, her muse, a kicking up she sprung us away from march meter with, fall into a groove though we otherwise did, grumble and go.

Lambert wasted no time getting the audience involved. At the top of a run one would say put butterscotch in bittersweet's place he took his right hand from the horn, raised his arm and quickly brought it back down, continuing his high flight or flotation with his left hand on the spoons even as he did so, putting bittersweet back in its place as a consequence, intended or not. The audience responded on cue, addressing the balloons in every way we'd imagined they might. Some blew their balloons up and let the air out, some blew their balloons up and rubbed them, some pulled their balloons taut and twanged them without blowing them up, some blew their balloons up and thumped them, some pulled their balloons taut and snapped them without blowing them up, some blew their balloons up and popped them with pins, some blew their balloons up, put them on the floor and stomped on them and so on. It made for a loud, raucous noise, a not unjoyful noise though not always joyful, a devotional sound or song even so.

We found ourselves lifted, oddly buoyed by what amounted to a balloon choir, an additive chorus by whose cacophonous ledger we were called to account. As we looked out at the balloons being rubbed, popped, twanged, emptied of air, snapped, stomped on and so forth, we couldn't help feeling we were being arraigned even as we were being apprised of a corroborative seam or support. That seam, we heard as well as saw, heard even more than saw, paraded haptic amenities before us, audiotactile grip and grain we were called out to chorus and carol with or against in turn. Rise and arraignment rolled into one, the audience's balloon valences broke thru to a vein of strike, stretch, kick, scratch and scour that offered accompaniment and discontent in like measure, deepseated grievance and regret one would've sworn railed against birth itself. What were we doing where we were and what were they doing where they were were only the simplest of the queries they involved us in.

I stole a glance at Djamilaa and saw that she sat at the piano in the most royal way imaginable (regal straightness of back, regal litheness of arms, regal groundedness of rump, regal fingertip élan), a way of abiding balloon arraignment we could all learn from I felt. She continued with her mock beginner's tack, a "tentativity" at times that cried out for support, coronation's darling or doll though she clearly was, royal command and recourse though one knew she had access to. What we were doing where we were was what they were doing where they were she made it clear, no matter she sat enthroned, Queen of Soon-Come Sunday, for we all sat enthroned, whether we sat or stood, we where we were, they where they were, Queen or King of Soon-Come Sunday.

I stood straighter, having stolen that glance, and I noticed that others must have stolen one too, for not only did Penguin, Lambert and Aunt Nancy stand straighter, not only did Drennette sit at her drumset straighter, but everyone in the audience now sat or stood straighter. We all found ourselves draped in regality and rectitude, the odd, unexpected bequest balloon arraignment bestowed on each of us, the surprise endowment the pressure it put on birth blessed us with.

Meanwhile, Lambert kept in mind the "bruised bell" instruction I gave him the first time we played the piece. Neither bittersweet nor butterscotch had anything to do with it now, or, if either did, only in the most angular, at-many-removes way, a warm sound that was as wounded as it was warm, a wounded sound that was as warm as it was wounded, reception and incision, warmth and wound, run as one. Bruised bell met balloon arraignment with a whimsicality or quizzicality à la John Tchicai that, atop Djamilaa's iterative piano, made one beat back tears. Balloon valence, it said, was nothing if not feeling's inflated premises, felt no less for real, felt no less intensely, no matter now known as such. He picked and played off strike, stretch, kick, scratch, scour and so on at will, inflated premises' match at every turn, mixed emotions' match at every turn, a wincing, tangential feint titrating woundedness and warmth over every array.

We had decided beforehand that for this rendition of "Some Sunday" Lambert would not be the only one to solo, that he'd be followed by Penguin, me and finally Drennette with a drum solo before we went back to the head. Before ending his solo Lambert took his right hand from the horn, extended his arm toward the audience and made the halt sign. He went on playing as the balloon choir subsided and the remainder of his solo, albeit continuing the bruised bell vein he'd been working, sounded as if launched by the balloon hubbub it left behind.

Lambert went on for another minute or two, followed by Penguin, me and Drennette. Shortly into each of our solos Lambert gave the audience the sign to join in, later giving them the sign to stop, having himself been given a nod to do so by the soloist. To begin to end what's already a very long letter, I'll let it go at saying that Penguin and I both acquitted ourselves well, negotiating the briar patch balloon arraignment tossed us into with Brer Rabbit-worthy aplomb. Penguin was indeed magisterial, working a bass vein he posed as foil to Lambert's high flight or flotation, a baptismal, often abyssal plunge that even the balloons went under with, but what I want to get to is what happened during Drennette's drum solo. It was during her solo that the comic-strip balloons emerged.

I should note that the audience more and more warmed up to their role the further we moved into the piece, that they more adeptly addressed the balloons and that each of them brought something more like a plan to his or her contribution. With each successive solo, they grew more attentive not only to what the soloist was doing but to the rest of the band and, best of all, to each other as well. Some of those who twanged their uninflated balloons and some of those who snapped theirs could be seen coordinating their respective attacks, not only relative to one another but with an eye and a ear toward Aunt Nancy's bass, an eruptive amen corner that kept stride with her as best they could. Some of those who rubbed their inflated balloons did so with increasing finesse, eking out, in some cases, sounds not unlike those made by a cuica, running the gamut between moan and squeal, whine and whimper, as they advanced a patient, melodic parsing adumbrating the soon-come Sunday we attested to. Some of those who thumped their inflated balloons and some of those who stomped theirs increasingly waited for just the right crescendoed-into moment, a bomb atop a bomb they kept their eyes on Drennette to calibrate. Others, however, especially those who popped their balloons with pins, eschewed coordination, opting for a randomness and surprise tantamount to an irreverent "boo," asymmetric occurrence an end in itself.

It amounted, oddly enough, to the brer patch I wrote you about a year ago, a divinatory field advancing peppered accord, peppered kinship claim. What we were doing where we were and what they were doing where they were made for a tenuous, precarious connection, an on-again, off-again mesh. We were in sync and out of sync by turns, balloon choristers with or without balloons. Balloon-advanced brer patch extended a multiplex field freighted with a feel for polyrhythmicity, vibe-societal strike, stretch, kick, scratch and scour. What we were doing where we were and what they were doing where they were was that.

The audience appeared to be enjoying itself as well, more and more so as we moved further into the piece and they more confidently found their way. Some shouted, "Alright!" Some shouted, "That's it!" Some shouted, "I hear you!" Some, without shouting, beamed in such a way as to loudly announce a certain delight, a certain attunement, their faces lit with the glow they felt fitting into the mix. Engagement registered on the faces of others in different ways, intense concentration or deliberateness in some cases, closed-eyed, trancelike absorption in some cases, lips moving as if counting or mouthing lyrics in some cases, head bowed reverently in some cases. I caught a glimpse of the owner and his wife and saw that they fell into the beaming group, a big, toothy smile on each of their faces as, respectively, they thumped and rubbed the balloons they held in their hands.

Penguin ended his solo shortly after nodding to Lambert to give the audience the halt sign, which Lambert did. The balloon choir fell silent as Penguin continued his low rove, capping off his low rove with a rummaging run in the bari's lowest register. It was a breathy but oddly subaqueous creep whereby he went foraging on the ocean floor, the rival of any octopus the way his tone seemed to spread and to reach and to scurry, covering ground one would never have imagined it could. The solo ended with a climb to the horn's upper register one semiheard and semisaw, the wistful run of notes a string of bubbles rising to the surface, balloons rising to the surface one semithought. We all fell silent as these final notes floated away, all except Drennette, whose turn it now was to solo.

Drennette's opening gambit was unprepossessing enough. She sat with the conga to the right of the parade snare, the conga held at a slight angle in a stand that allowed her to play it while seated at the drumset. Indeed, this allowed her to address either the conga or the drumset or both the conga and the drumset, the latter being what she began her solo by doing. Back straight, head high, Queen of Soon-Come Sunday, she sat with the drum stool turned somewhat to her right, having put away the stick she'd been using in her right hand while continuing to strike the orchestra snare with the stick in her left. She began beating the conga with her right hand, drumming on the orchestra snare still, tip of stick and palm of hand dealing in timbral shadings it appeared to have become her sole purpose in life to inspect and allow us to hear. Everything slowed down. She struck the orchestra snare, letting the sound hang in the air until it faded, then she slapped the conga, doing the same with the sound it made. She went back and forth that way between orchestra snare and conga, insisting we hear not only distinctions between the two but subtler distinctions between different deployments of stick and between different deployments of hand. It was a low-key start for a drum solo, sublime testing or sublime tinkering though Drennette conveyed it to be.

A beginner's tack to the max, Drennette's minimalist outset was, as I've already said, an inauspicious, unprepossessing start. No one would've guessed it would be during her solo that the balloons would emerge. I'm not suggesting flamboyance has at all to do with whether or not the balloons appear. We're not sure what does and I'm not saying that. But, thought of in relation to the eventfulness of the balloons emerging, her opening gambit appears almost pointedly uneventful, certainly, if nothing else, a pointed withholding of the virtuosic display drum solos are famous (or infamous) for. In any case, there appears to have been some occult or in some other way recondite hydraulics whereby legibility of the sort the balloons deliver accrued to deferred buildup.

A deferred buildup was exactly Drennette's tack, beginner's or not, a buildup she invited the audience to join her in. She gradually worked the parade snare and the cymbals into her left hand's repertoire while adding heel, fingertips and even fingernails to her right hand's address of the conga's head, moving on to ever more complex combinations, ever more multifaceted patterns. "Take your time," Penguin encouraged her at one point, which she did, slowly bringing a wider range of timbres, rhythmic motifs and tempi into play. When it got to where she'd set the table to her satisfaction, laid out the repertoire she sought to activate, she gave Lambert the nod and he gave the audience its cue.

The balloon choir came on strong, an aggressive onslaught of pent-up energy let loose, more aggressive than what Drennette had in mind, too loud—so much so she took her right hand from the conga and lowered it, whereupon the audience took the volume down. What she wanted, it gradually became clear, was a quiet, accretional field of haptic intensities, a quiet, slowly quickening submission to an accretional muse, aggressive given time as well as loud given time. Accordingly, not as many balloons were popped, either by pins or by being stomped on, as during the earlier solos, many more now being twanged, snapped and, especially, rubbed. What aleatory knocking is to the opening section of Marion Brown's "Afternoon of a Georgia Faun" aleatory tug, touch and rubbing were to Drennette's balloon-assisted sonic field, an abiding, aleatory patience allowing what would accrete to accrete, what would accrue to accrue.

Rub, as I've said, was the address of choice for the majority of the audience, an address ranging from quiet, caressive strokes to longer, more cuica-sounding moans made by pulling the thumb along the length of the balloon. Rub's predominance accorded with Sunday love's eroticism, suggesting, as it did, epidermal touch, epidermal regard, epidermal warmth. It was clear to everyone that rub, in its multiple senses, applied, epidermal flare well within its range of implication, epidermal friction well within that range as well. Obstruction, difficulty, abrasion, complication and all related meanings along that line were present as well, notwithstanding Sunday love's utopic promise. Everyone, it was clear, brought his or her own experience to bear, from felicitous meow to saturnian groan, not to mention all the gradations between.

Rub indeed ruled. A composite, aggregate apprehension, it truly moved, animated by Drennette's increasingly propulsive recourse to the full complement afforded by the drumset—cymbal shots, paradiddles, bass thumps and such, played with as well as against the conga beats her right hand steadily put forth, she herself on occasion trafficking in rub by pushing the heel or the edge of her hand across the conga's head, scraping, scrubbing, sliding. Again, briar and burr had as much to do with it as purr, a divinatory field haptic amenity two-handedly drove.

Conductor as well as Queen of Soon-Come Sunday, Drennette took her hand from the conga every now and then and lifted it, palm facing upward, cueing the balloon choir to take the volume up. It all grew louder over time, more intense over time, collateral repercussion and pop increasingly part of it, a few more audience members popping balloons with pins, a few more popping them by stomping on them on the floor. When the volume and the intensity neared their peak, Drennette pulled her right hand from the conga and took up the drumstick, turned a bit to her left and addressed the drumset full-tilt, all-out, as formidable a display of power drumming as one could want, quantum drumming.

It was with this step or this quantum step that the comic-strip balloons began to emerge. They did so, when they did, not from Drennette's drumset but from the balloons the balloon choir held, from each and every one of them in fact, whether rubbed, plucked, popped, stomped, twanged, snapped, whatever. The sound had reached a fever pitch, the rich cacophony of a philharmonic orchestra warming up, squealing, keening, groaning, squalling, when the first set of balloons appeared. They arose from each and every balloon choir balloon, all of them bearing the same inscription: *By whatever birth was, back at some beginning, I lay on my back unable to see past my belly, legs up, legs bent, legs open, knee on either side of my belly barely visible. I'd been riding a horse I thought was a bicycle, a bucking horse I was thrown by. I lay on the ground bleeding. I lay bleeding on asphalt, meaning it must have been a bicycle I rode. I lay bleeding in the dirt, meaning it must have been a horse I rode.*

Aunt Nancy, Djamilaa, Lambert, Penguin and I looked on, taken aback. We all looked at one another, perplexed, all of us, that is, except Drennette, who kept on drumming, looking out at the balloon choir, nonplussed—in fact, with a gleam in her eyes and a grin on her lips that seemed to say she knew something we didn't. The audience, the balloon choir, seemed also to be taken aback, albeit, following Drennette's lead, they pressed on, unperturbed, balloon arraignment engaging their energy and their attention all the more. The sound got louder, more complicated, more intense. Balloon valence was now balloon-on-balloon valence.

The first set of balloons disappeared, followed, a few measures later, by another, each bearing these words: *Unprepossessed, my horse told me get off, get a life. It bucked and reared up and threw me to the dirt, threw me to the pavement, a bicycle I did a wheelie on. Thrown off, unsure where I was, was it asphalt or dirt I was on, unsure what it was I'd been on, I lay on my back, a ballooning belly's dispatch, I lay bleeding. My lips bled, blood I took to be a kiss.* Balloon-on-balloon valence made for a thicketed feeling, a thicketed field, a density of atmosphere the Comeback Inn could barely contain, a thickness of air. A hothouse compactedness reigned, implication and legibility at once at odds and in league with each other. This was deferred buildup's bequest, nothing if not hothouse complication.

Things had sped up. When the second set of balloons disappeared another quickly followed, inside each of which were these words: *Sweet rotundity. Fecund recess. Ride had been all there'd been, ride was all I wanted. Thrown off as to where I was, what I'd been on, my long legs straddling my horse, my long legs pedaling, I lay on my back riding myself hard, I lay on my back giving birth to myself. My ballooning belly took the place of the hill I'd begun to climb, the hill at whose base my bicycle's pedal broke, at whose base my foot slipped from the stirrup, causing my horse to buck and rear up.* Aunt Nancy, Djamilaa, Lambert, Penguin and I looked at one another again, taken aback all over again. The balloons appeared to be channeling Drennette's bike ride with Rick, the concussive spill she says taught her percussive spirit. Their apparent equation of spill with birth especially caught our attention we all agreed later, as did their confounding of the bicycle with a Haitian vodoun horse.

Taken aback notwithstanding, we urged her and the balloon choir on, the five of us a rooting section now, offering such exhortations as "Drive it!" and "Take it out!" Drennette did exactly that, putting together a run of rolls that were to a drummer what circular breathing is to a horn player, the rolls a set of uroboric wheels balloon arraignment and balloon-on-balloon valence rode for dear life, the balloon choir doing all it could to keep up, straining to keep up, hothouse compactedness bringing sweat to many a brow.

The moment the third set of balloons disappeared Aunt Nancy yelled out, "Kick it!" Drennette, with a flurry of thumps, was all over the bass drum pedal, almost, one thought, as though it were the broken bicycle pedal come back to life. This took things up a notch, a notch no one, the balloon choir least of all, knew was there, though, well before they knew it, that's exactly where they were. The rubbing was much louder now, riddled with screeches and squeals, and the popping accelerated, aleatory detonation taken to a new high. It had gotten to the point where the poppers, whether stomping or wielding a pin, worked in pairs to speed the process up, one person inflating the balloon and then handing it to the other to pop. The proverbial mine field, brer patch could not have been more explosive.

It took a couple of measures for the fourth set of balloons to emerge. They bore these words: *A flood ran down the far side of the hill, blood gushed at its base. I lay on my back bleeding between my legs, legs bent, legs up, legs open, the lips between them bleeding, blood I knew could only be a kiss, a kiss boats bearing a message were afloat on. They floated leaving the hill behind, each of their sails having the same thing written on them: "Tell my house it's hot in here." So spoke my sailor boy, hot to be with me, my sailor boy who was all but back, due back on Sunday, a Sunday that couldn't come soon enough.*

When the fourth set of balloons disappeared the fifth emerged: *I tore myself to be whole, tore myself to possess myself, no matter how unprepossessing, no matter how unprepossessed. I lay thrown off better to know what on was, my host part horse, part bicycle, house hot church, house heat's ashram, house blood's hot retreat. I lay thrown off better to get back up, sit sweating deep in yogic labor once up. My sailor boy more me than I was, blood lotus, I lay, legs uncrossed, recuperating. I lay percussing, I lay getting ready to sit, repercussing, I lay repossessing myself.*

Balloon arraignment, all said and done, kicked as hard as Drennette did. The inscriptions' ballooning belly took balloon valence to another power, balloon-on-balloon-on-balloon valence, a run of introjection tending outward. The sound hit like aspirated static by now, an unremitting rush the balloons rode like pneumatic surf. They kept emerging, a sixth, a seventh, an eighth, on and on, ringing changes on *birth, blood, lay, sit, house, horse, kiss, hill, bicycle, legs, lips, labor, sweat, heat, boat, belly, possession, percussion, lotus* and the like that would never, it seemed, end but did. The final set of balloons bore these words: *Having been thrown off taught me what on was. I found myself on the far side of my ballooning belly, blood-soaked, smothered with kisses. When I sat up I sat on having been thrown. I made a throne of having been thrown, having been thrown the throne I sat on, lotusheaded, legs crossed, Queen of No-Show Sunday, my sailor boy's home but to be gone.* Drennette, shortly after these balloons emerged, nodded to Lambert to give the audience the halt sign. He did so, whereupon they stopped on the proverbial dime, the balloons disappeared, Drennette soloed a few more measures and then nodded for us to come back in, which we did, restating the head to end the piece.

The audience was on their feet right away with a loud standing ovation. Most of them simply clapped but some shouted, some whistled and some went at it on their balloons again. They all knew, as did we, that something phenomenal, even by balloon standards, had occurred. The ovation was long as well as loud, more heartfelt, I thought, than any we'd ever received before. The experiment, we felt, had succeeded beyond our wildest dreams. Many a thought was provoked and many a question raised, thoughts and questions we were quick to discuss on our way from the gig.

As to what we made of the evening's events, I'd have to say it's too soon to say more than what I began by saying: Boy, what a night! Drennette, for example, insisted, right off the bat, that she didn't, as we thought she might, know anything we didn't know. We'll be talking about it for days I'm sure. I'll let you know what comes of it.

As ever,
N.

Dear Angel of Dust,

It turns out a writer for one of the local alternative papers, *Santa Monica Weekly* (Aunt Nancy calls it *Santa Monica Weakly*), was at the Comeback Inn the other night. He wrote it up and his review (I guess you'd call it) is in the issue that just came out. The balloons, not surprisingly, get most of the attention, beginning with the headline: "The Molimo M'Atet Makes Peace With Its Balloons." He expands on this right away, opening with an assertion that he's always sensed "a certain keeping of the balloons at bay" in our public statements as well as in comments acquaintances of his who happen to know us recount having heard us make in private conversation. Why this is, he goes on, he's never quite been able to figure out, though his guess would be, he ventures to say, that what he would term "a confusion of artistry with austerity" wouldn't let us come to terms with "the bid for attention the balloons can't but be augurs of." He allows that there might well be something noble about this, something valiant about our "holding out against easy acclaim, commercialism, sensationalism and the like."

He devotes a good deal of space to describing the décor at the Comeback Inn Sunday night, detailing the arrangement of the tables, the location and dimensions of the performing space, the lighting and so on, saving the balloons lining the door and strung along the walls for last. Referring to the balloons as "a foretaste of what was to come," he notes the range and variety of their sizes, colors and shapes before announcing that Sunday night marked "an epochal transition point in the band's career to date." By this, he goes on to explain, he means that "on this particular gig, at this particular place, on this particular night," we made peace with the balloons, "came not simply to bear but to embrace them." He resorts to metaphor in his reiteration of this point, referring to our "détente" with the balloons, our "extending an olive branch" to them, our "smoking the peace pipe" with them.

He delays going into exactly what he's referring to by this even while admitting some readers may already, by way of the grapevine, have "gotten word of the goings-on" he'll in a moment get to. He then proceeds to discuss the music we played, the music the two sets were comprised of, addressing it piece by piece, saying a little about each, on the whole positive, albeit not without the obligatory quibble ("Fossil Flow" could've been longer, "Bottomed Out" shorter and so on), but quickly and not with a great deal of detail, saving a more sustained, more lingering approach for the encore, the balloon-assisted version of "Some Sunday," the "goings-on" he delays going into while being anxious to go into. Once he gets to that, that is, he takes his time, carefully narrating our return to the performing area, recounting the passing out of the balloons with great attentiveness to who covered what part of the room, repeating Lambert's instructions verbatim. This, the passing out of the balloons, he announces, "the peace overture, the peace offensive," was our epoch-making move.

He goes on to spare no hyperbole, pull no rhetorical punches, peaking, I think, when he calls it our "come-to-Jesus moment." He waxes patronizing, paternalistic and psychoanalytic rolled into one, praise notwithstanding, writing that it's us coming to terms with our need for attention, "getting beyond a conflicted desire to reach a wider audience." Having dwelt on this a while, he caps it off by saying "their nobility of abstention, their nobility of abeyance, is hereby moved on from in favor of a greater nobility, that of diving in, joining the fray, putting the hay on the ground where the horses can reach it." He then turns to the encore itself, the music itself, the balloon-assisted "Some Sunday."

First off, he writes, he has to "confess to being one of said horses," to "admit to having joined in and fully enjoyed it." He goes from this to a detailed account of "Some Sunday"—Djamilaa's long lead-in, Lambert's, Penguin's, Drennette's and my solos, and especially the balloon choir's participation. He's happy, he writes, to have been "a participant-observer," from which perspective, he admits, he "can't but have experienced it all in a special way," a special way he's not sure, try as he will, he can do justice to. We next read a good deal about him choosing how to address the balloon (he decided to rub it), the challenges of hearing oneself while hearing the band and the other balloon players as well, his and the other balloon players' "gains in confidence and competence" as the piece moved along, his and the other balloon players' "delighted surprise" when the comic-strip balloons appeared.

He has nothing but praise for our "decision to embrace the balloons and the audience both in one bold stroke," calling the passing out of the balloons "not simply the turning of a corner but collectivity's deep dream come true." Not only did we open ourselves to the balloons "more wholeheartedly" than ever before, he writes, we "tapped a live, open vein of musicianship in the audience one wouldn't otherwise have known was there." He himself, he adds, despite having no prior musical experience, "discovered a resident, recondite prowess the band and the balloons apprised one of." He crescendoes to this conclusion: "In making peace with their balloons the Molimo m'Atet made them our balloons. May they long let the balloons take us all higher."

It was Aunt Nancy who phoned and said, "We've got a problem." She was the first to see the review and she quickly gave each of us a call to alert us to it. She said we should pick up a copy of the latest *Santa Monica W-e-a-k-l-y* (she spelled it out) and we'd find a review of the Comeback Inn gig. She gave us the gist of it but again insisted we each pick up a copy and read it. She said she considers the problem the review makes apparent a crisis, a crisis calling for what she termed an emergency summit. She insisted we meet at Gorky's a few hours later to discuss it, which we agreed to do.

Gorky's is a place we go to from time to time, either all together or in smaller groups, an all-night cafeteria downtown on Eighth Street that opened two or three years ago. It's gotten to be a bohemian café, a hangout for artists, catering to and something of a creature of the loft scene downtown, featuring cheap food, coffee and beer, an interesting clientele, live music (usually not much to our liking) every now and then. Anyway, we all went out and got copies of the *Weekly*, read the review and headed there, Lambert the last to straggle in. Our feelings were mixed, as you can imagine, both individually and as a group. It is, after all, a positive, at points ecstatic review, lavishing praise upon us and the music in multiple ways, and we ourselves consider the experiment a success. The pitch of the praise, the assumptions underlying it and the framing of it, though, confirm our reservations about the balloons.

Aunt Nancy could hardly wait to talk about it and she got us going as soon as Lambert arrived, not waiting for him to get food and drink as the rest of us had. Her being the one who came up with the idea of passing out the balloons may have had something to do with her sense of urgency but the review was something we all felt we needed to air our thoughts about. Queen of nothing if not irony, she spoke for all of us by saying, to kick things off, that what bothered her was the reviewer's literal-mindedness, "a kind of tone-deaf earnestness that misses our mock literalness or mocking literalness, our mixed-emotional 'embrace' of the balloons." This was a risk we knew we were running we reminded ourselves, Lambert going on to point out that the prophylaxis the literal balloons were to perform turned anaphylactic in the reviewer's hands. "The balloons embody their own self-critique," he said, "a hedge against what they otherwise embody, advancing legibility as an inflated claim. The reviewer misses that."

We went around on it for a long while. Djamilaa, for example, said she resented "the condescension, the turning of something we did into a command or a mandate to do it, an after-the-fact mandate or an after-the-fact command, as though the reviewer were somehow in charge." Drennette, for another, talked, as Aunt Nancy and Lambert did, about what the reviewer missed, taking up his trope only to qualify it, torque it, saying that "if it was an accord it was a sideways accord we came to with the balloons or they came to with us." After a pause of only a beat she added, "It was, after all, No-Show Sunday's throne they put us on." Penguin, to give yet another, agreed. "Not to mention," he said, "the horsecycle," at which we all laughed.

We kicked it around, as I've already said, for a long while, got more and more into the ambience at Gorky's and went off on tangents. We got off track and went on tangents quite a lot in fact, as more and more food and drink came to the table. We ended up hanging out for a few hours and we had a good time. There was no live music, so it was easy to talk, to hear and be heard. A couple of painters came over to our table at one point, saying they recognized us and that they were big fans of our music. We all shook hands and they stood chatting with us for a while. Frank (their names were Frank and Renée) said he listens to *Orphic Bend* while he paints, that it's become for him what *Kind of Blue* was for painters during the sixties. He said he's in fact working on a painting called "Orphic Bend" and he'd like us to visit his studio and see it when it's finished. We exchanged contact info and they went back to their table.

What we'll do next we didn't decide. Hold a press conference? Issue another press release? Never pass balloons out again? We don't know.

Yours,
N.

Dear Angel of Dust,

Djamilaa and I awoke with a balloon between us. It lay in the space between our pillows. She sat up and stretched, her light cotton nightie exposing her close-to-the-bone shoulders, her dimpled elbows and her elegant, outstretched fingers a true boon above her head. She yawned. I followed suit, yawning as I sat up and stretched. It was as we turned to each other, smiling, and said good morning that we noticed it, the balloon nestled between our pillows, a third head or an extra pillow bearing these words: *I walked around inside a mall where I was to meet a certain someone, music deeper in my ear the longer I walked. The someone I'd come to see wasn't there. A strong wind blew the roof off and the stores were suddenly booths. The music inside my ear visited booth after booth, a late arcade it kept me wandering in all night.*

The smile left Djamilaa's face. "I see you've been at it again," she said.

"Been at what again?" I asked.

"Dreaming about a certain someone," she said.

"Not necessarily," I said, immediately noticing how weak it sounded and how weak it was but having said it before giving it any thought.

Djamilaa got out of bed and stood up, her back to me. I couldn't help looking at her ass, whose bottom half her nightie left exposed. I gave a thought to the workings of the carnal plan, the carnal setup, the carnal eye, her ass's magnetic draw. I stared as though her pendant cheeks and the cleft between them proffered a magic exit from all that was fallen and profane, fallen and profane though they themselves were thought to be. "Denial makes it worse," she said, sitting back down on the bed, looking over her shoulder, her ass no longer exposed.

"I'm not denying," I said, "I'm complicating. Didn't you say it was Penguin's dream, not mine?"

"That only makes it worse. Your thing for a certain someone has to be pretty strong to have to go thru channels."

"A certain someone is no one," I said, more confident now, "No-Show Sunday's bequest."

The balloon disappeared as I spoke, an evaporative remit appearing to confirm the disendowment I noted, a certain someone's inveterate nonchalance, chronic no-show, the someone one could only not know, nearly know.

"I'd like to say, 'Well, now that you put it that way,'" Djamilaa said, "but I won't." She stood up again, her ass's redolent cleft exposed again, carnal provision posed, it seemed, against disendowment, an immaterial musk filling the air clouding my mind if not the air, an imagined musk where there was no musk, all the more intoxicant not being one. I wanted all the more, that is, to whiff the musk that was, press my nose to Djamilaa's ass's redolent cleft as to an actual rent in time (chronic rift, crack in the cosmic egg), the rending of time whose proffered exit took me out.

"What if I were to swoon?" I said, syncope's famous last words it turned out. I spoke them as I succumbed to a rush and fell forward Djamilaa told me a few seconds later when I came to. She was beside me now, in the middle of the bed, cradling my head in the crook of her arm, my head against her breast. My face was close to her cleavage, another cleft, my nostrils wide with the overnight smell on her skin, the morning musk I love so much.

"I was teasing," I said, nose between her breasts, nuzzling her cleavage, her close-to-the-bone beauty all over me, the cracked cosmic egg's repair. The heady smell of her skin kept my nostrils dilated. "A certain someone," I whispered, "is no one but you, you know. The balloon was right between your pillow and my pillow. It was no more my dream than yours."

The smell of Djamilaa's honey-based lotion joined by overnight sweat suffused her nightie, a light, penetrant funk my nose filled with and would've followed to the end of the earth. I wanted its translation more than the musk itself perhaps but words fell teasingly short when it came to capturing it. I imagined a work of audiotactile sculpture that would, her light funk's pheromonal embrace rendered equal parts haptic and sonic. I semiheard, semitouched an atomized, ambient advance one would apprehend as a cystic self-equation cut or carved out of capric dispatch. Djamilaa's goatlike beauty, that is, assailed my inner eye, my inner ear and the fingertips of my inner hand, my overt nose's introvert accomplices, her long-faced forbearance a boon given over to study, aesthetic remit.

Djamilaa-the-Muse was in full effect, Djamilaa-the-Beautiful-One-Has-Come in full effect. The sweat-accented, honey-based lotion smell took me in as much as out, a mustiness of cleft and contained space and a cystic attar opening a faintly beckoning realm. I whiffed and whiffed again and again a remote, redolent beacon broadcasting intimately from afar, a synaesthetic transfer tendering mustiness as light, light funk's multiplied import. There was a deep inwardness, awayness and nearness her smell reposited, inwardness, awayness and nearness rolled into one.

It was a nearness as near as I'd ever know but somehow, nonetheless, not available, an everlasting no-show allure a certain someone or a certain no one was known for, not to be known otherwise, an awayness as near as any I'd ever know. The reticent, so-near-so-far sound of a French horn might be its aural analogue.

"Well, now that you put it that way," Djamilaa said, "I agree. Yes, here we are, two no-shows, erstwhile no-shows I'd say, two certain someones who might also be no ones, each the anyone the oneiric arcade parades all night." Her voice was low-pitched and husky, a kind of catch in it as though lemon and honey might be in order. The faint suggestion of the latter, combined with the sweat-accented smell of her honey-based lotion, took my inner frenzy further, a would-be match for her synaesthetic beacon's far cry.

I sat up, pulling away from Djamilaa's cleavage, catching, as I did, a whiff that came up from farther down, a more pungent waft coming off her loins and what lay between them, a less light, more penetrant musk rising from the hair that lay there and what lay under it. Oboe, English horn or bassoon to her sweat-accented honey-based lotion smell's French horn, it pierced my nostrils and pervaded my thought to a degree that threw me farther atilt. Oboe, English horn or bassoon, I wasn't sure which, as it may have been all three blown as one or blown in unison, a chorusing call or cry of come-home or come-hither, home's far reach and provenance, inner frenzy's far reach and rule. I was nothing if not such reach's vassal, low-lying musk the principality I swore love and loyalty to.

"I'd like to write something," I said as Djamilaa slid to the edge of the bed and stood up again, her ass's redolent cleft synaesthetically broadcasting again, "not simply a musical piece but something that would be that plus what visual artists call an installation."

Djamilaa was standing and she turned around to face me. The carnal plan, the carnal provision, the carnal setup occurred to me again as the tuft of hair between her legs below her nightie's hem caught my eye, so casually, nonchalantly there it furthered my inner frenzy a bit more.

"Audiotactile sculpture I call it," I went on. "I want the listener to be able to step into the piece. I want it to be a step taken off a ledge to be unexpectedly caught by a pocket the air offers, a pulverous nodule cut into empty space. I want it filled with streaming powder, uniformly blown powder perhaps, powder the listener leans into as it catches him or her, coming toward him or her like tactile, particulate wind. I want it to hit like a dry, particulate emission propelled from an enormous aerosol can. I want it to feel caressive and custom-fit, pointillistically tensile and precise, an enveloping provision of support. I'd like to call it 'Copacetic Syncope.'"

So I spoke at the time. If I had it to do over, I'd add that the streaming powder would have a rushlike quality to it, as though it were the inversion or, more exactly, the inverse mold of a swoon or a keeling over, convexity to the swoon's or the keeling over's concavity, concavity to the swoon's or the keeling over's convexity, the music's haptic equivalent custom-fit.

Djamilaa stood listening as I spoke, her pubic hair's visibility incidental and moot if she were aware of it at all. She was attentive to what I was saying but she also seemed a bit distracted, as though on her way somewhere else or to something else. When I finished she said, "Sounds good."

Djamilaa sniffed the air a couple of times, having caught a whiff of something it seemed. She lifted her right arm, turned her head to her armpit and sniffed it. She then lifted the hem of her nightie to her nose and sniffed it, her belly and the full extent of her pubic hair visible as she did so, offhandedly, nothing if not blasé, me further atilt even so, especially so.

After she let her nightie back down she looked at me and said, "I need a shower." She turned around and headed for the bathroom.

Sincerely,
Dredj

Dear Angel of Dust,

Yes, another cowrie shell attack. All the fuss about the balloons must have brought it on. The balloon-on-balloon visitation and valence at the Comeback Inn gave us lots to think about, the unpredictability of the comic-strip balloon appearances, the anaphylactic effect passing out the literal balloons possibly had, the balloons' apparent channeling of Drennette's bicycle ride with Rick, their dystopian tweak of "Some Sunday's" great-gettin'-up morning expectation not the least of it. Then there was the simpleminded review in *Santa Monica Weekly*, which not only gave us more to think about, more worry, but generated some controversy as well. This week's issue carried a few letters to the editor that were written in response to the review, ranging from ringing endorsement to variously critical, the latter complaining that the reviewer "drank the Kool-Aid" at one end of the spectrum and that he got us all wrong, praised us for all the wrong reasons, at the other. Not to mention the queries, comments and opinions of friends and acquaintances. All the buzz, the balloons again upstaging the music, must've gotten to me.

It was as Djamilaa and I sat in bed talking about the balloons the other morning that it hit. I'm not sure it was anything in particular she or I said that set it off so much as the overall strain of having to think and talk about them so much, simply that of having to think and talk about them at all perhaps. In any case, that's what we were doing when I began to feel a tightening in my forehead, the usual sign of the onset of an attack. I had just said, "There can be no adequation," but, as I've said, I'm not sure that's what triggered it. Whatever the trigger, cumulative or momentary, the attack chose to assume what I've come to think of as its classic form—the shattered shells embedded in my brow, the packed or compacted transparency everything seemed encased in, Ornette's "Embraceable You" piped into my head and so on—though not without some of its more recent features.

Djamilaa says it was clear to her right away what was happening, that after announcing, "There can be no adequation," I broke off speaking, went sort of blank and when I spoke again asked for pencil and paper, which she got up and got for me. For my part, I felt I sat at Dredj's desk, Dredj's hand had hold of mine. What I wrote was the letter you received a few days ago. The attack subsided, thanks to Djamilaa's presence and care I think, a few hours later, with no need for a trip to the ER or a hospital stay.

I like Dredj's "Copacetic Syncope" idea. I can't promise to deliver on the audiotactile sculpture part but I'd like to write something with that title, something along the lines suggested in the letter. For one, it put the sound of the French horn in my head so indelibly I haven't been able to get it out. The ring it has or the reminder it gives of a faraway haunt, a faraway hunt, a faraway homing, won't let me be. I'd want French horn to be a large part of the piece. Ideally there'd be three or four of them, a French horn choir chorusing the harmonic equivalent of "What but that solace, that but what other solace," repeatedly plying that qualm, that claim. Going at it ourselves, we'd have to make do with Penguin on bassoon and me on flugelhorn (barring a crash course on French horn) chorusing behind Lambert's tenor. The inflectional weave and the harmonic wrinkle that would encode "What but that solace, that but what other solace" of course remain to be worked out, as does pretty much, I'll admit, everything else. But Dredj got me going and "Copacetic Syncope," I guarantee, even if I do have to take a crash course on French horn, is on its way.

Dredj's evocation of Djamilaa's exposed ass and pubic hair (just happening to be there, just happening to be devastating) keeps at me, a vulgar, vulnerable regard the French horn's muted howl would harken back to, a retractive sound as of a world more near than far but not enough with us. I wonder if what he means by "a pulverous nodule cut into empty space" is a compensatory step one takes wishing it were otherwise, a would-be, wished-for presence or plenum that, would and wish notwithstanding, conduces to dust—an aggressive, propelled, propellant dust fitting one like a glove. I see root people convening at water's edge, low boat-hauling voices deep in their throats and lungs, "There can be no adequation's" rejoinder. Or is it a reconvening, a round or return whose recursive charge obeys Dredj's "enveloping provision of support's" mandate? I see gopher holes eaten into atavistic ground. I hear "What but that solace, that but what other solace" beaded on a thread Penguin's bassoon lets hang, lets dangle, love's don't-get-me-started reluctance and woo.

As ever,
N.

—————————————

Dear Angel of Dust,

Thank you for your thoughts on Dredj's "late arcade." I'm not sure I see it the way you do. In fact, I'm sure I don't. I even think I'd like to see it that way, but I don't. I don't hear a lament for times past. I don't read the roof blown off the mall as a critique of the present, "a redemptive critique hearkening back to sturdier social relations," as you put it. Dredj was getting at something deeper than that old chestnut. We tend, I think, to forget that the annals of the past are not the past. We confuse the felicity of the book, the felicity of the museum, the felicity of reminiscence itself with a lost felicity actually lived in the past. It's too easy to throw rocks at the present, too easy to make fun of the mall. Dredj, I'm sure, was up to something else.

What that something else was I'm not sure how to say. He said the music went deeper into his ear the longer he walked. He said the stores turned into booths after the wind blew the roof off the mall. The wind, he seems to say, converted the mall into a bazaar or a Renaissance faire, which does imply a reversion to the past, I admit, but he goes on to say that the music in his ear kept him up all night, kept him visiting booth after booth, which I'm not convinced is necessarily a happy situation. What's a late-night, insomniac promenade offering temporally remote solace, the sought-after someone lost, but a lament for the present, nostalgia for, if anything, the present, a dismissal of past amenities (if that's what they were) as irrelevant, insufficent, moot? This is the present dressed in past accoutrements only to emphasize they don't apply.

He said, in fact, that it was the music in his ear that visited booth after booth. Did he mean that the music traverses compensatory ground, that the music is a consolation prize or that it seeks to be, that it shops, as in olden days and vainly it would seem, for the thing that would deliver solace, consolation, compensation? Again, that's not, it seems to me, a categorical felicity. A certain someone not present, the present itself not present enough, seems a lament for the present, not the past, a post-expectant lament borne by see-thru auspices, inertial everydayness's return. The balloon bearing "late arcade" was a third eye (a fifth eye really) that lay between Dredj and Djamilaa, shared by Dredj and Djamilaa, a shared, post-expectant arraignment of any such trappings of the past as booth and bazaar. It augured a necessary appeal to the ordinary, the everyday, the unspectacular abidance I'll continue to call post-expectant.

Unspectacular notwithstanding, "late arcade" works deeply allied with "copacetic syncope" I suspect.

Yours,
N.

Dear Angel of Dust,

We couldn't resist any longer. We've thought of issuing another press release following the *Santa Monica Weekly* review but we kept deciding against it. We can't respond every time someone gets the music wrong we've told ourselves ever since putting the first press release out. But Braxton's advice or idea or insistence that one has to provide the terms for understanding one's music, develop a language listeners can learn from and deepen their listening thru, has long spoken to us as well. The hubbub surrounding the balloons' most recent appearance, given the spark the *Santa Monica Weekly* review gave it, finally got to us and we decided another press release, a second post-expectant press release, was in order.

Enclosed you'll find a copy. It was a group effort, everyone contributing input (you'll notice we went with Aunt Nancy's insistence we use her coinage *Santa Monica Weakly*), and I think it pretty much speaks for itself. We were a little surprised, in fact, to find ourselves speaking with such authority and, at points, so didactically about something we're so bewildered by. It's as if the review's easy presumption of knowledge nudged us into knowing by not knowing, a position of knowing that would acknowledge not knowing.

If you have any thoughts I'd love to hear them.

As ever,
N.

POST-EXPECTANT PRESS RELEASE #2

Santa Monica Weakly got it all wrong. It wasn't a matter of making peace with the balloons. No one knows them better than us—no one, that is, knows better than us that they're not to be known—and our experience has been that no peace is to be made with them. Legibility, we know, is an inflated claim, the very claim, were it that simple, the balloons embody. But it's not that simple. The balloons are a hedge against that which they otherwise embody, ostensibly embody. True self-critique or disingenuous dodge, they are not to be bargained with or bartered with, either way. We intended the literal balloons not as a peace pipe, an olive branch or a peace offering but, as one of our members put it, a prophylactic. That they turned out to be anaphylactic proves our point.

What *Santa Monica Weakly* fails to note (or only, at best, implicitly notes) is that the balloons are a bluelit brigade freighted with our wildest wishes, a wildness or a wilderness of wish we sought to bring the audience abreast of at the Comeback Inn. It wasn't so much about the balloons as about them, which is to say about us, our shared arraignment of a hope hoped against hope, the knock, hard albeit soft, of what would not (could not) be. *Santa Monica Weakly* fails to note that a low throb knocked at our door and we let it in, a faint beat that was nothing but anaphylactic willingness, wish and fulfillment, the fullness of which we knew to be fleeting, secret, discreet.

We also notice no mention is made of the gig's occasion, the Comeback Inn's owner's wife's birthday, which seems to us infinitely more relevant than the peace accords the *Weakly* wants the gig to have been. It seems to us that what we had, what can be said to have summoned the balloons, was something of a return to initial premises, premises to which nothing speaks more resonantly than birth. We who make the music remember that the balloons' inaugural appearance two years ago in Seattle burst with intimations of pregnant air, pregnant wind, pregnant swell, a ballooning remit lodged in alternate ground we term wouldly. What but the airiness of natal occasion's commemorative occasion gets at wouldliness, the nothing-if-not-that-and-so-nothing event or eventuality the balloons not only announce and inure us to but are, thinly contained pockets of air that they are? Who remembers birth? What could be more wouldly than birthdays? One commemorates an event one can't remember but at which one was present, the event with which being present began.

The implications of "No-Show Sunday" need not be belabored we thought but the *Weakly*'s unalloyed jubilation makes us think otherwise. We still don't mean to belabor them so much as point the main one out: Sunday never comes or, better, was there but not there. The *Weakly*'s Sunday might've been all there but ours both was and wasn't, a tale of two Sundays, a tale of two sets of balloons. Literal meaning aside, "two" signifies noncontainment, a default on the very containment the *Weakly*'s read would have. We find the review wishful, painfully unaware of itself, not the arraignment or the ironic fulfillment of wish our passing out the balloons was intended for. We again stress that it was a birthday gig, a meditation on birth, wouldly pregnancy, wouldly wind, an endlessly blown wish to wrap walls around wouldly breath. Unimpatient expectancy, we've come to know, is a lesson one has to be long on learning. The *Weakly* would move into the mansion without a single brick being laid. The *Weakly* would have it all too quickly.

This is what we must do, this is what we ever so slowly, ever so gradually, ever so painstakingly, all but asymptotically approach: 1) Commit to a fast of not reaching, commit as though fast and feast were the same. No easily presumed arrival will do, no easy applause. 2) See that it has to do with finitude, that "it all has to do with it," as Trane said of something else, this wanting to have arrived once and for all, a wished-for arrival the band dallies with by way of the balloons but also knows the dangers of. See that dalliance and danger are the balloons' two bodies, an escaped kingship or queenship whose throne would-be arrival seats us on. See too that wouldly breath keeps both at bay. 3) Come ever more deeply to know that shape is tactility at a distance, balloon curvature a boon at whose behest we bend away from capture, our own as well as theirs, which is both good news and bad. Good and bad apportion, as worth or negative worth, respectively, wouldly weave, wouldly welter.

The balloons are dispossessed lungs, inspiration less objectively drawn than objectified, a fix or a fetish made of something we know to be fleet, fluid—"peace," were such to be had, beyond any and all patness, which is nothing if not the balloons' exact proffer. Bicycle and horse rolled into one, the balloons are the gift horse whose mouth we scrutinize, possibly a Trojan horse. We don't trust them, never have, never will. We will continue to keep our distance, B'Loon's ingenuous look notwithstanding.

Dear Angel of Dust,

It seems like forever since I last wrote you though it's been only a few days. I don't mean to be dramatic but I can't help saying everything has changed. Watershed, turning point, call it what you will, the Comeback Inn gig, with its array of repercussions (the *Santa Monica Weekly* review, our "Post-Expectant Press Release," Dredj's visit), appears to have prompted the change. To say we've turned a corner puts it too mildly. Gone over a cliff is maybe more like it, a precipitous plunge into what only a falling leaf might live to tell about, some stark incumbency upon us now to be that leaf, brake short of shooting star, falling star, burnt-out star. But maybe it's just me. Maybe I load it with weight only to be bogged down. Maybe weight, a possible anchor, speaks too persuasively now, not so much weight as counterweight, a would-be, wished-for antidote against floataway onset, the across-the-board leavening balloon epiphany apprised us of—backed up or gone back to, for me, by Dredj's translation of body-and-bone solidity into floataway musk, evanescent nearness, the fleet funk Djamilaa's nightie dilated his nostrils with. I keep wanting to say, "Just let me get next to you," some running plea or some lover's prayer (would-be lover's prayer) running from King Pleasure to Tower of Power, as though nextness or nearness were the always asymptotic falling short it's motored by.

A copacetic plummet I'd call it except I wonder what rubs off and what sticks to have put it so. This chasm I feel to have opened up between then and now, before and after, the cliff we went over and the chasm we fell into, stretches time to where I'm not sure when I last wrote you though I know I wrote you only days ago. Is it that all nextness or nearness got spirited away by some quantum turn we took, not only Ellison's bit about seeing around corners but cornering a certain claim, a charismatic "no-show" claim the balloons admonished us with but would, even so, package and contain and commoditize? I feel my head bent sideways even as I ask. It's not so much a chasm or a canyon I see as a gray morning, misty coastal fog on a downhill street going toward the ocean, a foggy morning prospect in as ordinary a place as Long Beach or San Pedro, if not ennui a diffuse being-at-loose-ends in a small harbor town. Such would be the tone poem I'd write, copacetic plummet downing the ante on Dredj's "Copacetic Syncope." The bumpy logic it would move by evades me at the moment but that's neither here nor there, much less the point of this letter.

More than one person has told me I have an old soul. Maybe that's what this is, the jostling around of what the Rastas call "anciency," but also more. I'd repeat *prospect* only to say *peril*, repeat *peril* only to say *pearl*, repeat *pearl* to imply an irritant ploy whereby time doubles back to audit itself. Some dislodgement intervenes between pebble and ointment, a secreted sheen whose girth and gap we come in time to summon. To have gotten one's head around that, as the saying goes, may well be what time's work is, all it is, all so near nothing nearness can't but be the wall we fall arrested by. A qualitative audit I'd call it, head turned, head gone to or gotten to and so on, arrivance's matte perfume.

Maybe all I mean is that it all feels thicker, portentous, packed with variability so immense it's not at all evident where to begin. I don't remember feeling this way ever except maybe the moment I turned to music as what I'd do with my life. Is this a new beginning, a new life, *la vita nuova*? Thick time, heavy time, the weight shadows carry could shadows carry weight, is what this is, I think, a ponderous vamp-till-ready perhaps. Of the Comeback Inn gig and what it opened up I'd say *cloak* only to repeat it, repeat *cloak* only to say *cloth*, repeat *cloth* only to say *knotted*, meaning by that a dense traffic of shade let loose, all accent, bend and inflection, a quickened and quickening membrane it fell to it to flow thru. Whatever corner we came to would turn to take us in, whatever edge we came toward come to meet us. This was the Comeback Inn gig's bequest, a fund of confidence if nothing else, no matter whatever outer misgiving.

So we hold tight, sit tight in our perch, a risen prospect nothing if not misgiving affords. Call it vigilance. Call it a sensed imminence. We sit bumped up in some way we can't yet specify, an effect of the bumpy logic we'd make music of and will. No, it's not just me. Something real is afoot.

Please forgive this. It may strike you, I know, as more a mood than a letter, a mood piece or a pep talk to myself, the working out of a mood, the working thru it.

Yours,
N.

Dear Angel of Dust,

I woke up with a pounding headache this morning. A repetitive, riverine figure had at my head from inside my head, a sawtooth guitar lick of nine notes, each ever so often let linger with a postulant twang. Such twang sought both entry and release it seemed, a complicated order of induction it cried out for. The river it rode ran dappled by sunlight, a slow promenade so white with sun it forced one to shut one's eyes. I looked on with an inner eye more ear than eye, the procession of pocked whiteness an auditive report blind witness made sing. A benign headache I hasten to call it, benign and low-key. It bordered on but pulled up short of a shattered cowrie shell attack.

"Twang" may be the wrong word. A cross between fishing line and piano wire, a point or a ping somewhere between the two, might be a better way to put it. Whatever it was, it wanted to light out at some damped oblique angle, ringing but all the while reined in, no toll if not exacted of itself, dues and destination rolled into one. In that way it was like everything else, a universality it modestly preferred, a sense of itself as not exempt it advanced with exact restraint. Light's late arcade I was tempted to call it, a deferred arrival portended or carried by the cave or cathedral voice it was the accompaniment for—crystalline, echoic, slightly husky at points, rounded by an encounter with collapse.

It was Milton Nascimento's "Cais" come to haunt me, a friendly ghost, the ghost or the trace of what was already a ghost or a trace, the benign guitar lick in league with a benign organ surge. I put it on last night, not having listened to it for what felt like ages, and found that, having listened to it once, I put it on again and, having listened to it twice, put it on again and, having listened to it a third time, put it on again—on and on like that, listening to it over and over, until I'd listened to it I don't know how many times. Something about it got to me, spoke to me all over again as though for the first time, as though when I heard it ages ago I heard it without really hearing it. It did this again and again.

It wasn't that when I listened to it ages ago I wasn't really listening. It was more a matter of time having been taken out of alignment, a jutting shelf I stood on listening anew, not merely more but entirely such a matter of time staggering or having staggered. Time waits was the last thing I'd have thought I'd ever say but I did. "Time waits," I whispered, all but under my breath. "Bud was right."

Or was it that "Cais" itself waited, lay in wait, held back or held some of itself back, only to have at me all the more later, years later that would seem like ages later? Was the shelf or the shift in alignment the song's eponymous pier, nothing if not Milton's invention ("Invento o cais," he sings—"I invent the pier"), the pier one would let go and go forth from? Was it, to go maybe a little further, anything but a shelving of itself time, in the song's guise, tabled itself on? "Cais" lay in wait or "Cais" crept up on me all these years that have come to feel like ages—crept and continues to creep on conga beats, benign conga beats I hear as padded feet. It launches an invented love ("Invento o amor," he sings—"I invent love"), an invented sea ("Invento o mar," he sings—"I invent the sea"), an invented path ("Tenho o caminho do que sempre quis," he sings—"I hold to the path I've always wanted"), an invented boat ("E um saveiro pronto pra partir," he sings—"And a boat ready to leave"), all of which, separately and as a whole, I'm tempted to call love's late ark, love's late arcade, love's last arcade perhaps.

Come legless to the sea I'm tempted to say. I'm tempted to say love's last arcade might be its first, come to such extremity one's back at some beginning, again the beginner one is when it comes to love. Such, at least, I'm led to say by the pounding, the piano ostinato that breaks in toward the end of "Cais" and on which it fades, Milton singing wordlessly alongside. It takes me back to Djamilaa's beginner's tack on "Some Sunday" at the Comeback Inn, back to my very conception of the piece, its mock-awkward loss of time and its folk song-sounding recovery of time, the verge upon a children's song or a child practicing it treads. "Cais" goes even further, the piano ostinato recalling "Chopsticks."

Where that leaves me I'm figuring out. The pounding, I insist, is benign. Is it a prompt to revisit "Some Sunday" or the advent of a new composition? Is it perhaps a combination of the two, a sequel to "Some Sunday" I might call "Another Sunday" or "Some Other Sunday," in the tradition, titular at least, of James Baldwin's *Another Country*, Gary Bartz's *Another Earth*, Jimmy Lyons's *Other Afternoons*, Grachan Moncur III's *Some Other Stuff* and so on, not to mention Arthur Herzog and Irene Kitchings's "Some Other Spring"?

The "Chopsticks"-like pounding driving my headache took me back to another Nascimento piece, "Pablo," whose piano ostinato is even more like "Chopsticks" than the one on "Cais." I got out the two versions I have, the Portuguese version on *Milagre dos Peixes* and the English version on *Journey to Dawn*, and I've been listening to them, both of them confirming the sense of lost time, lost and recovered time, I took to be at issue in "Cais." "Pablo" takes it even further, making a more explicit reference to childhood in both versions: on *Milagre dos Peixes*, the song is sung by a young boy; on *Journey to Dawn*, Milton sings it with a boyish falsetto and is joined by a children's chorus halfway thru.

I remember one of my college professors critiquing Dostoevsky's use of children in his work (Polya in *Crime and Punishment*, Ilyusha in *The Brothers Karamazov*, Matryosha in *Demons*, etc.), calling it barefaced, blatant, unabashed. He'd probably say the same about Milton but I find myself wanting to be exactly that, wanting to find a place for a child singer or a children's chorus in "Another Sunday" or "Some Other Sunday" (whichever it turns out to be called).

Sometimes you have to go for the jugular. Sometimes you have to show circumspection the heel of your hand. Sometimes, put upon by dilatory compliance, you have to shove more than suggest. Especially under threat of No-Show Sunday, you have to shout.

As ever,

N.

Dear Angel of Dust,

It seemed if I could only 1) angle at the exact amount of incline, 2) lard lead-in with absence in the most parsed and plotted manner possible, lace or load it in such fashion as to make tread trepidatious, the ground trepidatious, trepidation the ground itself, 3) titrate touch in such a way as to build while disbursing twinge, verge on twinkle perhaps, 4) coax or connive, eke sound out, so situate twitch or its adumbration as to extenuate love's least integer, so reside within extenuation as to mitigate timbral collapse, 5) wring the notes as much as play them, *wring* fully in league with an implied play on *toll*, twist each note as though it were cloth and the drop squeezed out of it both, 6) placate momentum's demand while recruiting an abiding pocket, a cyst or an insistence indigenous to suasion or swell, 7) confess to a certain dismay or admit my impatience, pound against time until the beat wore ragged, 8) ply layers of waywardness, an annunciative ken peppered with and paced by hesitancy throughout, an arrhythmic hitch cognate or conjugal with nothing if not rhythm, 9) be at large in a twilit fallback, relaxed albeit beset by combinatory chagrin, fallen shade's fluency and fount, all would be right with the world.

All would be right, at the very least, I thought, with the solo I was at the beginning of. By combinatory chagrin I meant a sense I've gotten in dreams, the sense of returning to a place I've been to before, dreamt of before, dreamt I've been to outside of dreams before, as though to dream was not to make up scenery but to traverse and revisit stable terrain, actual ground and what's built on it, this or that house, this or that room inside. These houses give off the feel of a combination of houses, places I've lived or visited given an odd yet familiar aspect, teasingly familiar but not to be precisely placed. Something about the approach to one of these houses might suggest the promontory to a friend's house in Pasadena while, once inside, the stairway to the second floor would recall, ever so faintly, that of the flat I lived in in Oakland and so on. One of these rooms might seem compounded of the living room of our apartment in Miami when I was a child, the library cubby I studied in when I was in college and more. It's as if all the aspects, facets and features of these places were bits of glass in a kaleidoscope, subject to changing arrangement and permutation while maintaining a sense of real premises, real provenance, more than simply concocted, more than merely dreamt-up.

Chagrin, though, in that, coming upon or coming into these places, I always feel I've forgotten something I meant to remember. These rooms, halls and houses appear to be part of some mnemonic practice, a memory theater of the sort Frances Yates writes about perhaps. I despair each time that I've lost the key that would unlock the familiarity I sense but can't entirely call forth, the legend that would mete out place and punctuality, dispel the tease or taunt of what appears partly "on," partly "off." In some of these dreams I feel like a ghost in the Winchester House, combinatory largesse only so many stairways and doors that lead nowhere. I feel toyed with, the Bible's "In my Father's house are many mansions" brought to mind, a trickster's pitch.

So it was with the notes and sonic tactics at my disposal at my solo's outset. Even so, I wanted to step onto such oneiric ground and into such oneiric housing, have my solo be the means of doing so or even be such ground and housing, my own such instructed tenancy and tread. I wanted to be like the man spoken of in my antithetical opera, "both hands tied, trying to build a house with his voice while sitting on a cot in his jail cell." I wanted my solo, by the time I was done, to say what Rick Holmes used to say on KBCA, "We have built!" I was bent on a masonic outcome for my chagrin.

This was during a gig at The Studio we finished a few hours ago. We were playing "Like a Blessed Baby Lamb." I was on soprano. We'd recently played it at the Comeback Inn and we go back to it now and then at rehearsals. We've played around with different instrumentations, different ways of voicing it, and Lambert wanted to give one of the new ones a try at the gig—him on tenor, me on soprano, Penguin on alto clarinet, Aunt Nancy on violin, Djamilaa on harmonium and Drennette on tablas. How to open up and open out from the gruff stamp Archie put on the piece and how to work the time in a way that keeps to a certain signature drag (as though tar were stuck to the soles of our shoes) but keeps to it otherwise is what we've been asking. How to get gruff stamp and signature drag to coexist with Eastern sinuosity and cut is what we've been asking.

I was the last to solo. The order was Lambert, Aunt Nancy, Penguin, Djamilaa, then me. The violin and the harmonium did exactly what we had in mind. Aunt Nancy and Djamilaa lent signature drag a vectored swell, a diagonal swell, an upward and onward tending, tumescent lilt. ("Lilt" puts it too lightly. It was nothing short of hallowed what they brought to an essentially profane wager, titular lamb notwithstanding. "Lift" says it better, "coronal lift.") They gave it a keening, devotional air, Drennette's tablas adding duly acute prance, due traction. This they did without speeding up the tempo, turning signature drag into Baul-Bengali saunter.

Djamilaa's solo had drawn us into a sacred cave, drawn us in and drawn us in effigy on its walls. It was a crystal cave, a sphere rayed out in all directions like fireworks exploding, shooting radii the spokes of a ball that would swell and contract, the harmonium's bellows lungs and hallows both. Things had gotten religious, as in fact, Djamilaa implied or insisted, they always are. She had taken the title's wager to heart. When she finished and the applause died down, the ground I found myself on, the cave I found myself in, gave me pause. I stepped into my solo with a phobic, philosophic tread, a duly fearful tread.

I tend toward Pharoah's way of playing soprano. I like a little constriction in my sound, long on shading, not the tabula rasa sound we were taught was the goal. I like a nasal burr or a nasal buzz along the edges, a bit of abrasion. The soprano's ability to glide, the auto-pilot sense it can fall into, needs to be guarded against, as does its ability to soar. Room has to be made for creak and squeal, subdued crackle, a ducklike sotto voce, not without an R&B twinge. Pharoah tends to glide and soar more than I felt was called for, so it was Wayne's ictic, foraging way on "Dindi," which, as you know, I've never gotten over and will never get over, that was more the tack I took. It was a more grounded sound I sought or at least a sound that sought to be grounded, a sound that felt its way, even groped its way, seeking ground.

Djamilaa's harmonium had subsided to a carpetlike lowing, ecumenical seep and support. Aunt Nancy's violin was a holding action, airborne glimmer if not watery glare atop distant asphalt on a summer day. Drennette's tablas partly kept time, partly bought it, marking it no matter which, a pinged, ringing press or appeal that tolled an announcement of dues accrued. I stepped cautiously into this coven or cave as though barefoot on a bed of hot coals, tread nothing if not trepidation and vice versa, hesitant from heel to toe, tentative, testing. I temporized for a few bars before what I've come to call the Nine Golden Precepts, the desiderata I listed above, came to me in a flash. I repeat them here for emphasis:

THE NINE GOLDEN PRECEPTS

1. *Angle at the exact amount of incline.*

2. *Lard lead-in with absence in the most parsed and plotted manner possible, lace or load it in such fashion as to make tread trepidatious, the ground trepidatious, trepidation the ground itself.*

3. *Titrate touch in such a way as to build while disbursing twinge, verge on twinkle perhaps.*

4. *Coax or connive, eke sound out, so situate twitch or its adumbration as to extenuate love's least integer, so reside within extenuation as to mitigate timbral collapse.*

5. *Wring the notes as much as play them,* wring *fully in league with an implied play on toll, twist each note as though it were cloth and the drop squeezed out of it both.*

6. *Placate momentum's demand while recruiting an abiding pocket, a cyst or an insistence indigenous to suasion or swell.*

7. *Confess to a certain dismay or admit my impatience, pound against time until the beat wears ragged.*

8. *Ply layers of waywardness, an annunciative ken peppered with and paced by hesitancy throughout, an arrhythmic hitch cognate or conjugal with nothing if not rhythm.*

9. *Be at large in a twilit fallback, relaxed albeit beset by combinatory chagrin, fallen shade's fluency and fount.*

After temporizing for those few bars, I went on, I can say without bragging, to make good on all nine.

I'm not saying this was the best or the most dazzling solo I've ever taken. There's something about the Precepts coming to me the way they did, incumbent upon me all of a sudden as if I took dictation, a suddenly scribal providence or at least provision on the tips of my fingers, on my lips, teeth and tongue, on my diaphragm and in my lungs, that made it get to me and stay with me, still stay with me, to such an extent I haven't been able to get to sleep. Was it the suddenly scribal providence or provision or was it Djamilaa sitting on the floor crosslegged and lotuslike before the harmonium, dress modestly pulled over her knees, covering her open thighs, that did and does it? Was it the unquenchable glimpse I closed my eyes and imagined I got of what lay under her dress, the bulge of hair beneath cotton or silk, such fit I felt exhorted by, rich beard and lift and betweenness, that did and does it? Was it that the harmonium seemed as much incense holder as axe, the ecumenical seep and support it disbursed as much musk as music, the very floataway musk Djamilaa's nightie dilated Dredj's nostrils with? Was it that I could've sworn I sniffed it wafting from under her dress, a newly mixed Vedic neroli, an infusive attar, an infinitely penetrant perfume? Was it this that did and does it?

It was all these things. Djamilaa is my muse and will always be, the someone I need and will need on my bond, as the old song says. She led and leads me thru love's long-tenured bazaar, love's late arcade. Whatever probity, whatever duly theophobic tread, theophanic tread, I acquitted myself with (and my solo did, I know, do nothing if not that), I owe to her inspiration. The Nine Golden Precepts themselves, I'm sure, were the work of her inspiration. Even now, going on five in the morning, I feel I can't but be longer with it.

The Golden Precepts readied my way. Such bearings as they gave me gotten, I left off temporizing with an annunciative, almost airless flutter, a fledgling, asthmatic burst whose asthmaticity rhetoricially asked how to speak of things of which one does not speak. Aunt Nancy, Drennette and Djamilaa knew this to be rhetorical, understood it as a preamble to doing exactly that. We would indeed speak the unspeakable Drennette affirmed with a run of karate chops to the tablas, shunting my almost airless flutter along. Aunt Nancy and

Djamilaa were likewise all horizontality, Aunt Nancy with a series of tonic-tending bowswipes, Djamilaa with a sirening ride of the harmonium's high end.

That played or that said, I told myself, "Take your time." I let my embouchure go loose as I played the first seven notes of the head, cutting it off as if interrupted by a better option than mere completion, had at or put upon by some lateral enchantment. Aunt Nancy's bow was that enchantment, as commanding as Cupid's arrow, picking up and repeating the first five of those notes, identification, if not identity, up to more than identification. Djamilaa meanwhile settled into a low-lying, mist-on-the-moors creep, a droning amble ever close to the floor, the stage floor it made feel earthen, rolling earth. Drennette had increasing recourse to the heels of her hands on the tablas, coaxing a fat sound out of them, all reach and rotundity, itself a rolling aspect as well, fat wheels we rode.

My loose embouchure caught air and the vibrating reed was a drill or a jackhammer against my teeth, bodily abidance's dues, I meant to insist or insinuate, nothing more. Djamilaa, who knew my mouth as no one knew my mouth and whose recondite musk had my nose open, at once caught my insinuation. She answered with a skein of sound, a ribbon of sound, still close to the earthen floor, bodily abidance's reap or condolence. She pulled it from the harmonium's bass register, a grumbling, organlike run Alice Coltrane would've been proud to call her own.

The Nine Precepts ushered me along, Djamilaa's undulance under cloth an abiding bond and trust, rolling bulge, rolling fit, rolling traipse I felt furthered by, a whiff-quickened wraith of myself chasing myself. Robert Johnson's hellhounds were a walk in the park up against the chase I gave myself, a counterintuitive, slow-tempo chase I now tightened my embouchure to ante up on—eked-out advance, eked-out inveterate lag, eked-out inconsequence.

I took my time. My sound opened up, unpinched, not the zero degree at which the horn extends the esophagus without seam or serration, the sound Oliver Nelson, for example, gets on soprano, but less given to the pulverous fray around its edges I started with. Dust off a moth's wing was there to be heard even so, but less of it, my sound as open-throated as it gets. It was cool, collected, not entirely without strain but backing away from it, pointedly announcing a part-ing of ways with it. I thought of when I was a kid and of my mother's friend Mary who'd always say, when things were getting to her, "I can't be strainin'-up here," which was always exactly what she was doing. Everyone called her Strainin'-up Mary. Strainin'-up soprano was the horn I blew.

Things were getting to me. The coven or the cave I'd been inducted into or stepped into played briar patch to my Brer Rabbit, no place I more wanted to be. Announcedly not strainin'-up, I remained calm and collected, my backing away from strain belied by moth-wing dust though it was. Even as things got to me in what was at bottom a good way, my response above bottom was nothing if not mixed. Cool and collected as I was, I played scared, wanted to be scared and grew scared of the very place I wanted to be, feet shod, so to speak, in theophobic, theogonic tread. Djamilaa, Drennette and Aunt Nancy, my three witches, were divinatory and divine in laying down, ladies though they were, the brer patch it was now incumbent on me to traverse.

I couldn't be strainin'-up but I was ever so detectably strainin'-up, moth-wing dust my boon and my betrayal. Strainin'-up Mary was to me as Trane's Cousin Mary had been to him or as Horace Tap-scott's Drunken Mary had been to him, a makeshift Madonna or a makeshift Magdalene or a third, entirely makeshift muse for the oc-casion. Cauldron Mary I wanted to rename her, a fourth, faraway witch in league with the three with whom I played, but Drennette, sensing this it seemed, gave one of the tablas, which might as well have been my head, a resounding slap. I stood by tradition and stayed with "Strainin'-up."

Horace's Mary was more than a passing thought. Strainin'-up Mary was known to have a drink or two or three throughout the day. "Drunken Mary's" head seemed exactly the groove to "Like a Blessed Baby Lamb's" tongue, so I paired it now with the full first ten notes of the latter's head, a joint or a joining I parsed out using Horace's tipsy waltz time approach. This gave it as much jaunt as our slow tempo could accommodate. We did so without at all speeding up.

I bleated lamblike, reminiscent of Wayne's "Dindi," a connect-the-dots tack with which I stated the two heads, conjugated the two heads, all the while observing the Nine Precepts to the letter. Djami-laa's bellowing hallows put me in churchical stead, though Aunt Nan-cy's wicked bowswipes and bowsweeps were yet another matter, as were Drennette's crescendoing tabla slaps, not to mention a certain way in which I scared myself. My tipsy traverse of the brer patch was, by turns and at times concurrently, god-fearing, goddess-fearing, witch-fearing, propriophobic, whichever as the case might be.

Strainin'-up Mary showed me the way. She magnified and illumined the way the Nine Precepts had made ready. I staggered, bounding laterally and at times diagonally between lamblike bleat and capric slur, Djamilaa's goatlike beauty a heady brew aligned with Strainin'-up's unsecured walk. I stole a peek at her seated at the harmonium. She shot me a grin. Undulance under cloth, I couldn't help noticing, had nowhere near subsided. "Waft be thy name," I hummed into the horn, a recourse to heteroglossic traipse Djamilaa met with harmo-lodic tryst, sounding organlike again, Larry Young meets Ornette.

Drennette was all fingertips now, digital dispatch and acrobatic display, a boon to my every capric slur. I walked sonically cool and collected even so, incongruous capric aplomb. Had I been walking nonsonically I'd have turned sideways and dragged a leg, harked back to a dance we did when I was a kid called The Stroll, a dance that danced us as much as we danced it, a dance I've never been able to shake. Thus the slur, the slide away from collectedness, its merger with incongruous aplomb.

Aunt Nancy picked up on Drennette's fingertip attack and went from arco to pizzicato, from swipe and sweep to pinch and pluck. Djamilaa picked up as well, now dispensing staccato runs as if at the wheel of a car, pumping the brakes. The ground we crossed was all the more a brer patch now, bristling with divinatory aspect and pop, divine, prestidigitator snap.

Brer patch was hopping ground, a dense arena rocked by ricochet, detonation, ignition. Vex and revisitation ran side to side, to and fro. I lowered the horn and pointed its bell at the floor, bent over the way I've seen Miles bend over, listening for a certain sound. I was still all lamblike bleat and capric slur, at the brer patch's mercy it seemed I was told later, coaxed, baited and beset by prestidigitator bristle, pinch and pop. I wanted a hollowed-out sound if not a hallowed or haloed sound, moth-wing dust mixed and congealed with ambient humidity, for all its airborne humors a conical or cylindrical wrap of paste.

A conical or cylindrical compress applied to the open wound the air itself now was, the sound I wanted was buoyed by Aunt Nancy, Djamilaa and Drennette's brer patch rotunda, churchical girth I tried in vain, straining, to get my arms around. Churchical girth would not be gotten around, not be embraced but at a distance, an ever so discreet hydraulics of approach it demanded, mandated. The sound I wanted was the sound I went down and got, bent over, horn pointed at the floor, an expectorant howl, no longer cool, collected, an expectorant croon that brought up a shake-the-rafters descent into the horn's low register, a rafters-rattling landing on the horn's lowest note.

The sound I wanted, not quite knowing I wanted it, was the sound of the shaken rafters, the rafters rattling. I now saw what I wanted, that this was the sound I wanted, the highest rafters of a wooden palace rattled by the note I hit and held, wood rubbed to a sheen by oneiric return and revisitation, another strangely familiar house I dreamt I was in. I didn't open my eyes and I didn't need to. I knew we were in that house, that palace. I kept holding the note (holding on, as Bobby Womack would say), doing so with circular breathing. Aunt Nancy, Djamilaa and Drennette kept their plucked and popping rotunda alive and played louder now. I knew we were in that house, that place, that palace.

The audience had begun loudly applauding as I held the note and the rotunda popped and bristled, Pharoah's "Let Us Go into the House of the Lord" having nothing on our stringent, less unctuous approach. I didn't open my eyes and I didn't let go of the note as Lambert and Penguin came back in, restating the head over my sustained note and the brer patch rotunda, only for us all to stop on a dime at head's end. We had built.

As ever,
N.

Dear Angel of Dust,

Drennette called Penguin on the phone last night about an hour after rehearsal. Balloons had followed her home again, she told him, just like back in November, stowed away in her drumset. After getting home she went to unpack and set up the drumset to practice some more, she said, and, just like before, balloons emerged when she lifted the lid to the parade snare's container. They floated out of the container before she could reach in to take the drum out, rising up from under the lifted lid just like before, as if out of the container's mouth. She sounded upset, Penguin said, telling Lambert and me the story this afternoon.

Drennette had called Aunt Nancy and then Djamilaa but neither answered. She then called Penguin, she explained, shaken by the balloons having shown up again and needing to talk with someone. What made their appearance this time especially creepy, she went on, was that they didn't disappear into the air after a while the way the balloons usually do but hung there, above the parade snare's container, instead. They had emerged one by one, the first bearing these words: *I tread lightly, ever so lightly, in my approach, feet an awkwardness I'd be done with if I were able, so badly I want myself unsoiled and off the ground, free of the ground and of contact with the ground. All for you, I'd be entirely of the air, all for you, treading lightly, light itself. Footless were it mine to decide, I come to your window, a ripple in the breeze, tread of wind at your balcony, you my belovéd.*

The first balloon hung there, Drennette told Penguin, moving to the side to make room for the second when it floated up but still not going away. The second bore these words: *Not to mention heat. Doesn't it go without saying that heat brings me and I bring it, light not lacking heat and heat not lacking light, a harmattan rippling the entirety of air I'd aptly be? I come to your balcony bearing heat, a nuzzling breeze at your neck. I carry your perfume into the surrounding air, belovèd broadcast, happy to have in the least lifted it, the subtlest waft I'd be.* The second balloon took its place next to the first, hanging there above the parade snare's container, hanging there still, Drennette explained to Penguin, even as she spoke with him on the phone, as did the third.

The second balloon had moved over to make room for the third when it floated up out of the container. The third bore these words: *All aspect and approach I'd be, beauteous tread not quite arriving. An away-ness infinitesimal but palpably felt I'd be, could airy entirety be said to know touch. So it is I come to speak of touch, prime among the unmentionables, gone without saying or scared away by saying, so it is I come not to speak of touch. I pledge fealty to that which remains unshown or, shown, unspoken-of, un-mentionability's own, liege and lief. No matter what I mention, more remains unmentioned.* It took its place and hung there, Drennette told Penguin, the last to emerge she concluded after waiting a while and seeing no fourth balloon float up.

Penguin had a kind of laid-back ease and assurance that's not quite like him as he spoke to me and Lambert. "I could tell from her voice she was upset," he said. "She asked, 'Don't you think that's weird?' to which I replied, 'Yes, very weird.' Saying yes appeared to bond us in some way, as though I'd uttered a secret password for admission to a guild or a lodge. She spoke more softly now, almost secretively, her voice a little lower and a little huskier than usual, her mouth closer to the receiver's mouthpiece it seemed. 'No telling what could happen,' she said, almost whispering.' I answered, 'Yes, no telling what could happen.'"

Drennette again made the point, Penguin said, that none of the balloons had gone away, that the three still hung in the air above the parade snare's container, hung there as though staring at her she went so far as to say. "'It's eerie,' she said," he said. "'I've tried closing my eyes and opening them again, thinking maybe they'd be gone when I opened them, hoping they'd be gone when I opened them, but they were still there. I've tried leaving the room, going to another room for a while and then coming back, hoping they'd be gone when I came back, but they were still there when I came back.'"

Penguin went from laid-back to bursting when he got to this point, bursting to tell us what she said next and what happened, much more his uncontainable self. Her voice was still low and intimate, he said, he and she still members of whatever guild or lodge or secret society he'd been admitted into. We were at Lambert's place, drinking beer. Lambert interrupted to ask if Penguin and I would like another, to which we both said yes, and when he came back from the kitchen with three fresh beers Penguin continued.

"'They stare at me like stalkers, these three,' she whispered into the phone, her voice husky but vulnerable too," Penguin told us. "Like I said before, I could tell she was upset, though it's not like her to show that kind of thing and she tried to make herself sound nonplussed and merely observational even when saying things like 'No telling what could happen' and 'It's eerie.'" He fell silent, took a sip of his beer and gazed out Lambert's living room window, taking in the scene outside, the tops of palm trees and the sky mainly, as though the key to what happened next lay somewhere in the clouds. Lambert and I held our tongues.

"Then suddenly, after she said that, the thing about the balloons looking at her like stalkers, she paused a moment before saying, in a tone and with an inflection I've never heard her use before, her mouth even closer to the phone's mouthpiece it seemed, 'That's why I called you.' After saying that, she paused again, ever so slightly, then asked, her voice not as low now, girlish, 'Can you come over?'"

Penguin fell silent again and gazed out the living room window again, again as though looking for an answer in the clouds, taking one sip from his beer and then another and then another. Lambert and I held our tongues again but Penguin's silence lasted longer this time. Finally, when it looked like he'd never speak again, I asked, "Then what happened?"

"I went over, of course," Penguin answered, immediately falling silent again.

The silence hung there for a while and then Lambert asked, "And then what happened?"

"I'm not the kiss-and-tell type," was all Penguin would say, gazing out the living room window at the tops of palm trees and the sky.

We drank more beer as the afternoon wore on, a lot more beer, and all three of us got pretty loose. No matter how loose he got and no matter how much Lambert and I pressed him, Penguin would only say about what went on after he went over to Drennette's, "I'm not the kiss-and-tell type."

Yours,
N.

Dear Angel of Dust,

Penguin and Drennette haven't shown any sign that anything happened. Since him telling me and Lambert about her calling him up and asking him over we've been looking to see if there's anything new in their way with each other. I can't say that anything has changed. They still go about their business as before. Last night at rehearsal Lambert even called up "Drennethology," thinking maybe there'd be some blush or some other such telling sign or perhaps a more passionate approach to the piece by him or by her or by both, a new emotion brought to it. No such difference. They were nothing if not businesslike, cool technicians to the point I thought their coolness might be a sign that something had happened. "Maybe what happened is that nothing happened," Lambert said later as he and I talked after rehearsal. "Or maybe they're trying to hide the fact that something did," I said right away.

Time will tell. In the meantime, I'm still wondering how to make good on Dredj's "Copacetic Syncope," struggling with how to make good on it. The squint I was beset by during a cowrie shell attack way back comes back of late, conducing to a Rasta koan or equation, faraway French horn filiating Far-Eye trombone. Processionality's call summons a fetch and a furthering, a fromness (Rico, *Man from Wareika*) and a forwarding (Rico, *That Man Is Forward*) so-near-so-far reticence gets or doesn't get but won't gainsay, all the sway of gathered cloth folding it in. I know what Dredj means by so-near-so-far, which leaves all the more to be said for so-far-so-far. Squint wants to sing something we see best at a distance. I squint and I can barely see, blown particulates' blind beneficiary, *musk*'s near rhyme with *dust* the refrain I'd ply, caroling dark but chorusing light.

It's not that I've decided to add a trombone, much less that I've decided on reggae telemetrics, much less the hurry-up sound of ska. I'd like that sense of going somewhere but I'm not sure I trust it. I like the diffuse, frustrated reflectivity brass imposes on Far-Eye reach, more audible in the strainin'-up sound of French horn than on trombone but a shared come-so-far-to-say-it sonic inheritance none-theless. Brass familiarity, brass familiality, is maybe all I'm getting at, a strained familiarity or a strained familiality announcing exodus or exile in the case of either horn. It was, after all, "I can't be strainin'-up *here*" Strainin'-up Mary used to say.

As ever,
N.

Dear Angel of Dust,

"It's not," Penguin was saying, "that I don't like a woman whose eyes take you in and take you deep, so deep you think you'll drown, you'll never get out. I'm not saying sparkle that far down in her eyes doesn't dazzle, dark though the mascara might make it, a highlight heteronymically come to the fore." The three of us—him, Lambert and I—were in Lambert's car, heading to Dem Bones, a barbecue place in Westwood we like. Lambert and I were in front. Penguin sat in the back seat. We'd been going along quietly when out of the blue he began talking. Lambert kept his eyes on the road and I kept looking straight ahead as well. "It's not," Penguin continued, "that I don't like a woman the shape of whose nose is nothing if not divinatory signage, the harbinger of heavenly form, that I don't like a woman whose lips are full and whose mouth pouty, that I don't like her mouth brimming with teeth and gums, protruding toward a kiss it forever invites or anticipates."

"Who said it was?" was on the tip of my tongue but I let it stay there, sensing Penguin was in a certain space we shouldn't intrude on. Lambert appeared to think likewise. We both kept quiet and kept our eyes on the road.

"I'm not saying there were no balloons there," he continued, "that she lured me there under false pretenses. It's not that it wasn't exactly the way she said on the phone, not that the three balloons weren't still there, hovering above the parade snare's container, inscribed with exactly the words she had told me, read to me, over the phone. I'm not saying I didn't blink my eyes and then close my eyes for a while, as she had, to see if they'd go away, not saying they went away and were not still there when I opened my eyes again, just the way she had said it had been with her. No, I'm not saying that. That's not what I'm saying. No way was it that the wine she offered wasn't good, great in fact, exactly my favorite white, sauvignon blanc, chilled just right to go with the oysters on the half shell she also offered." He paused, savoring the memory of the oysters and wine it seemed to me. Lambert and I remained silent. I looked out the window at a particularly nice row of palm trees, lost in that somewhat until noticing Penguin was speaking again.

"What I'm saying isn't that I don't like the kind of incense she likes," he was saying, "those green neroli sticks the Vedanta Society sells, the ones that have a kind of funkiness to them, a kind of bootiliness or bootiness to them. I don't mean that the smell of that smoke, mixed with that of the scented candles she had burning, the smell of perfume on her neck and a very slight waft of sweat, didn't almost take me out. No, I'm not saying that." He paused before continuing, "It's not that I don't like standing pelvis to pelvis with arms around each other, that thrusting and grinding pelvis to pelvis isn't for me. I don't mean to say I don't like the feel and taste of her tongue, her tongue feeling and tasting my tongue. No, I'm not saying there was anything not to like about her tongue groping and my tongue groping back, anything wrong with the kiss getting deep and slow and a little bit sloppy. I'm not saying that." He paused again, caught up in his own thoughts it felt like, gazing blankly out the window I would've sworn. Lambert and I continued to hold our tongues, continued to keep our eyes straight ahead.

"I'm not saying," Penguin said when he resumed speaking, "that I don't welcome the rotundity of pendant hips in the palms of my hands, that I'm averse to holding her with one of my legs between hers and one of hers between mine. It's not that a pinched waist and a generous, low-hanging ass don't speak to me. No, that's not what I'm saying. No, I'm not saying that. It's not that I'm immune to her nipples hardening against my chest, that her nipple pressed hard against my tongue, stiff between my teeth and lips, doesn't get to me. That I don't like her teeth and tongue on my earlobe and her low, husky voice issuing coarse demands and crude encouragement, whispering sweet endearments as well, is most definitely not what I'm saying. I'm also not saying I don't like the thick hair between her legs or the feel of it against my thigh, that I don't like the wetness of what's underneath it wetting my thigh." He paused.

Lambert and I continued to think it was best not to speak or to turn our heads and look at him. Lambert kept his eyes on the road and I mostly did so too, though I did turn my head and look out the window from time to time. We were coming upon a Carpeteria store on our right as Penguin left off speaking, the company's trademark Aladdin's lamp–style genie looming twenty feet tall atop the store. Grinning, turbanned, holding a large roll of carpet above its head, it never fails to catch my eye and it did so again this time. I turned my head and stared up at it as we passed.

It felt like Penguin was gathering his thoughts, deeper in thought. When he resumed speaking he began by saying, "It's not that I don't like a woman who likes to be gone down on." When Lambert and I heard this we both had the same thought. Lambert kept his eyes on the road but I turned my head to look at Penguin as the two of us said at the same time, "Careful, man. You're telling us way more than we need to know." I left it at that but Lambert went on, "Don't tell us something you're gonna regret telling us."

Penguin's eyes were on the road ahead and did not meet mine. As far as I could tell, he hadn't so much as given the genie a glance. He had an intent look on his face, as though he spoke not on a need-to-know but a need-to-tell basis. "It's not," he went back to what he'd been saying before we broke in, "that I don't like a woman who likes to be gone down on from behind, her ass cleft recruiting one's nose as one's tongue slips between the lips between her legs. I'm not saying I mind her turning over after a while and lying on her back, pulling me up between her legs and on top of her, reaching down and sliding me in. No, I'm not saying that." This was a far cry from "I'm not the kiss-and-tell type," so far from it he might as well have been blowing a horn, blowing the oboe, the high boy, the high would, piping for all heaven, earth and hell to hear, no matter he spoke softly, calmly, self-possessed, giving an all too graphic account of what had gone on between him and Drennette. Had balloons begun to emerge from his mouth I wouldn't have been surprised.

I turned my head and looked forward again, went back to looking straight ahead. There was no stopping him I could see. I looked out the window. We were on Santa Monica now, the street Dem Bones is on. "It's not that I mind being told it feels good and to keep doing it," he continued, "that I've got a big one, a really hard one, a really stiff one and I know how to use it, that she likes the way it fills her, that between her legs is where I belong. No, it's not that. I'm not denying the word 'big,' the word 'hard' and the word 'stiff' never sounded so good, that they never wielded more magic." No, there was no stopping him. Words, it was clear, were his high horn, theirs the horn's piercing, penetrant cry. "It's not that I don't care for her gripping my hips while I'm between her legs," he was now saying, "spreading my cheeks to finger my ass before bringing her finger up to my nose for me to sniff. No, it's absolutely not that. I'm not saying I've got anything against her asking, while doing that, 'Why are we so smelly?' in her you've-been-a-bad-boy voice. I'm not saying that at all."

Let me be clear that there was nothing the least bit lascivious or salacious about the way Penguin spoke. He spoke with absolute sobriety and equanimity, not exactly dispassionately but collectedly, even as the events of which he spoke built, crescendoed and peaked. "It's not," he said, "that I don't like it when her body tightens and it all begins to build to the release we've been moving toward, that I don't like the way her body spasms, bucks and quakes while she tightens her embrace of me and I tighten mine of her, that I've got anything against the feeling of something from deep down and inside being drawn out of me, some inmost extenuation, my very self maybe, not that I'd rather she not moan and, shortening my name to 'Pen,' quietly call it while this goes on."

Penguin didn't stop there. He paused but he didn't stop. He became all the more sober, somber even, certainly serious, meditative, solemn I could feel. I took my eyes from the road and turned and looked at him there in the back seat. As he began to speak again he tilted his head like a bird, looking askance at some new conundrum it seemed, aggrieved and quizzical at the world's illogic. "What it is," he said, "is that the Drennette all this happened with wasn't Drennette, that it happening, necessary no doubt, was insufficient. The Drennette I did all this with and who did all this with me wasn't her. The kissing and the caressing, the whispers and the getting wet, the wafting and the thrusting and the squeezing, the muscle contractions and the getting wetter yet were not the utmost her I wanted, the utmost her I still want, the inmost her it perhaps is I long for and that I still long for."

He fell silent. His eyes hadn't met mine when I turned to look at him and they still didn't meet mine. Had he been talking to us or to himself I wondered and so said nothing. Lambert, however, eyes ahead and on the road still, cleared his throat and spoke up, speaking from hard experience it appeared, delivering a hard-won truth. "Beauty does that," he said, "especially outer and inner beauty combined, exactly the sort it is Drennette has. It makes us see things. It makes us see what can't be touched. It hawks the intangible. No matter how material, no matter how palpable it seems, no matter the low-buttocked angel a rung or two above us leading the way it appears to be, it can't be touched. Tread lightly. Don't go thinking you can grab it, have it, hold it. You can look but ultimately you can't touch." It was a sobering thought.

Penguin, less rather than more sober on the heels of Lambert's remarks, spoke with barely damped passion. "But she was right there," he said in a sotto voce cry, "me pressed up against her, her pressed up against me, there but not there, me in her arms and she in mine but not there, not the"—he paused, chasing a thought, reaching for a word—"Drennethological Drennette I so wanted and still want. I was surrounded by water but thirsty, thirsty in the middle of the sea. Beauty was indeed water spiked with salt, water I could look at, not drink. Proximity, tangibility, was the bait on beauty's hook."

Penguin fell silent again, lost in thought it seemed, at a loss as to where what he'd said left him. He came out of it quickly and at last his eyes met mine. He turned his head and looked toward Lambert, whose attention was on pulling into an empty parking space that, luckily, was almost directly in front of Dem Bones, just a few spaces farther up from it. It was clear to me that, no matter whether Penguin had been talking to himself or to us earlier, it was to us he'd been talking this last little while and that from us he wanted a response. Having looked toward Lambert, he looked back at me, but I myself was at a loss, unsure how to take up with what I was still afraid he'd later regret having told us.

Met by my silence, Penguin looked back toward Lambert, who by this time had pulled into the parking space, backed up a little, gone forward again straightening out the car, backed up again a bit, turned off the engine and begun to open his door. He looked back over his shoulder at both of us and said, "We're here. I'm hungry. Let's go eat."

Yours,
N.

Dear Angel of Dust,

I don't doubt that what Penguin intimated happened in fact happened. It's not that he made it with an imaginary Drennette, as you say, but exactly the opposite. Wasn't that his complaint, that the Drennette of his dreams, his "Drennethological Drennette," remained unavailable, not to be known corporeally, impervious to bodily embrace? Wasn't his complaint that he didn't—couldn't—make it with the utmost or the inmost her, the very her of her, the her that, ostensible contact notwithstanding, could only be conceptual, only apprehended by the mind or the imagination? Wasn't his complaint that the gulf between carnal capture and conceptual embrace persisted, unbridgeable, driving a thirst that would not and could not be quenched? Didn't he say he's beset by an ethereal buzz or an immaterial vibe with only bodily address to try reaching it with, an address not only necessary but compelled, yet insufficient?

Anyway, to answer your question, no, the conversation didn't go much further in that vein after we got out of the car at Dem Bones. Penguin tried to pursue it but Lambert and I discouraged that by moving on to other things. "You'll work it out," I told him, which was the last we said of it. Penguin, I'm sure, knew to begin with it wasn't something we could help him solve. He was just getting it out, letting it out. He didn't bring it up again.

The other shoe sort of dropped at rehearsal earlier tonight. Drennette, who doesn't often compose, brought in a piece called "Lapsarian Surfeit," a piece she'd written, she told us, just in the last few days. Lambert and I looked at each other, wondering was the title, "fallen excess" put otherwise, a reference to what Penguin told us had gone on. Drennette, to a certain reading at least, was backing away from what had happened, parallel to but different from Penguin backing away, if that's what it was. I wasn't sure, however, that's what it was, in either case. I wasn't sure falling short of a metaphysical wish is a backing away, that a built-in default can be called backing away. The case with Drennette, I thought at first, seems more a matter of moralistic recoil but it soon occurred to me that "lapsarian" might refer to such a falling short, not necessarily to a fall or to the Fall. Where that left matters I wasn't sure except to say that the title was anything but self-evident and that even "surfeit" might be defying its face value to say something less about excess per se than about incongruity or incommensurability, a lack of adequation or a lack of congruency that is, to put it colloquially, "too much."

So I say sort of dropped as I might also say sort of another shoe. It wasn't clear what to make of the title, jump to an easy conclusion though Lambert and I were guilty of doing. Neither coming in with a composition nor the title of the composition seemed particularly loaded for Drennette. She was her usual self, as was Penguin. Only when she told us the instrumentation did anything happen that might've had implications. This was that when she said the piece called for Penguin to play baritone Penguin thought a while and then asked could he play oboe instead. Lambert and I looked at each other again, thinking the same thought I'm sure. Were we reading too much into it to wonder whether Penguin felt a judgment implied by his assignment to the low-pitched horn, that he too felt the piece might have to do with what had lately transpired between them, that he sought to reverse that judgment as well as reverse the fall or the falling short they'd undergone by way of recourse to the higher-pitched horn? Perhaps so, but when Drennette stood firm and reiterated that the piece called for him to play bari he put up no further resistance. He let the matter drop and said okay, he'd play bari.

Things went uneventfully otherwise. We got the hang of "Lapsarian Surfeit" pretty quickly and we ran thru it several times. Penguin delivered a full-throated sound that betrayed not the slightest hint of reticence or misgiving. He brought Charles Davis's playing on "Half and Half" on Elvin Jones and Jimmy Garrison's album *Illumination* to mind, both titles possibly relevant and obliquely allusive to his and Drennette's recent tryst I couldn't help thinking, not to mention the circular, running-in-place, treadmill motif "Lapsarian Surfeit" shares with "Half and Half." I may have been reading too much into this I'll admit, but you can see, I'm sure, why Lambert and I wondered might more be going on than met the eye.

"Uneventfully" overstates it perhaps. There were moments during Penguin's solos when he dug into that deep, guttural, expectorant sound Fred Jackson gets on Big John Patton's "The Way I Feel." He thrashed and cursed and spat, a study in frustration, a beast caught in a tarpit, a Sisyphean or Tantalean ordeal one couldn't help feeling had implications beyond the business at hand. That Drennette, during these moments, upped the ante, veritably bashing and more loudly attacking the drums and the cymbals, driving, goading, testing and taunting Penguin, did nothing to negate that feeling. They were moments worthy of Elvin and Trane.

Whatever the source or the array of sources, "Lapsarian Surfeit" adds a gruff, gravelly page to our book.

As ever,
N.

Dear Angel of Dust,

I saw what seemed an immense crystal encasing the extent of the known world. "See how far it stretches," a demure voice in back of me advised. "See how much there is of it, the it you'll have traversed always." I wondered why "always" and how that would work and was it true, wondered had "Some Other Sunday" found me, wondered was I its muse or it mine. I wondered about the sound of the future perfect. It seemed it offered a child's-eye view of it all, magisterial in the sweep and the eventuality it afforded, the world it made one feel one could afford. "Some Other Sunday's" day had come at long last, the song's day and the song's awaited day at last begun. "Some Other Sunday" I knew the title would be, "Another Sunday" not even close.

Prospect and *promontory* were two words that crowded my thoughts, an alliterative consort I heard caroling long and wide. What was it that issued from the ground, I wondered and wished, whatever its contour, what if not a chorusing reward all hope abounded with, hope though it might be, all the sayers concurred, against itself? I was no sayer or I sought not to be at least, say given to what "Some Other Sunday" held in abeyance, on its way toward me if not yet there. A tree trunk's uplift embroiled us I saw. Sound's reconnoiter was what faces were front for.

All sense of limit fell away as the initial notes came in. A children's chorus's trill was what vertebrae were, a twinge whose gamut strung light across the tree's timbral recess, tweak attendant on tweak attendant on tweak attendant on tweak, all done automatically, all within skeletal reach.

My back loosed its bone and it sang, a quiver notes were tipped in, of but athwart the tone world I translated, "Some Other Sunday's" ruse its reason, tunefulness's rise and regret.

I sat up straight as my back burned and smoke lay at the top of my neck. This is why we do this I thought, my last thought before "Some Other Sunday" was finally there.

As ever,
N.

Dear Angel of Dust,

Djamilaa told me Drennette told her and Aunt Nancy all about it. This was after Drennette, who's not one to write much, showed up last night for the second rehearsal in a row with a new piece she'd written. The title, "Rick's Retreat," raised Lambert's and my eyebrows, albeit Penguin, when she announced it, remained neutral, nonplussed, allowing not the slightest facial expression or any change in body language. Lambert and I couldn't help wondering was this finally the other shoe, truly the shoe "Lapsarian Surfeit" only sort of was. Djamilaa and Aunt Nancy weren't struck so much by the title, knowing nothing at that point of Penguin and Drennette's get-together. They took note, Djamilaa says, of the fact that Drennette had brought in a second new composition so close on the heels of the first. Something had to be up, she says, and they wondered what. It was to find out that they suggested the three of them go for a drink after rehearsal, a drink and a little "girl talk."

They took note as well, no doubt, of the tenor and tone of the piece. Lambert and I certainly did. Title notwithstanding (or, more precisely, title the flipside of what it announces, title inverted, title reversed), it brims with advance. Moreover, it brims with a distinctly military advance, march meter, a decidedly martial thrust in which Drennette's drumming plays a conspicuous part. After opening with a 7/4 march figure introduced by the drums alone, it settles into a peculiar structure allotted in thirteen-bar segments in which it returns to the march figure throughout, alternating five bars of 7/4 with eight bars of 4/4. The piece brings the rhythm section to the forefront,

Djamilaa serving up tall, resolute chords, Aunt Nancy gone well beyond walking to indeed be marching on bass. It reminded me a little of Horace Tapscott's "Lino's Pad," which came out on one of the *Live at Lobero* albums two or three years ago, except the drums are much more out in front than they are there. It has Penguin, Lambert and me on soprano, clarinet and cornet, respectively, the head something of a round or a catch. It has us not so much playing as piping, blowing with a certain fierceness, blowing like Furies, blowing as if to clear the air, blow something away.

"Rick's retreat," it almost goes without saying, seems another way of saying "Drennette's advance," a way of militantly saying it. The bearing on this of what recently went on between her and Penguin could hardly not occur to Lambert and me—or, for that matter, to Penguin as well. Lambert and I wondered was this her way of saying the memory of Rick had been exorcised, that her tryst with Penguin had blown the memory of Rick away, swept it away. It certainly seemed so, an appearance borne out by what Djamilaa told me later.

Djamilaa says they were a little hungry and decided to go to Café Figaro and that, once there, they talked about this, that and the other before getting to Aunt Nancy asking Drennette what had brought on the burst of writing she's been doing. "I don't know," Drennette said at first, "it's been like ice melting, a glacier retreating." She hesitated a moment but then she wasted no time, as Djamilaa puts it, getting to the heart of the matter. "I think it all goes back," she said, "to a certain someone we call Penguin. I've lately gotten to know him in a way I never knew him before. I'll go so far as to say I never knew a certain someone we call Penguin at all until now and that a certain someone we call Penguin never knew me." It was odd, Djamilaa says, the way she referred to him, but she continued to do so throughout the conversation. She never simply called him Penguin but referred to him as "a certain someone we call Penguin," perhaps even (there was no way of knowing, Djamilaa says, though the way she said it and insisted on repeating it made it seem possible) "A Certain Someone We Call Penguin."

I was struck by how differently she and Penguin have reacted. While Penguin despairs of there being a Drennette he can't come close to, an auratic or a supplemental Drennette that's more than meets the eye and that sensory perception can't reach, a "Drennetho-logical Drennette" not even carnal knowledge knows, she exults over them now knowing each other, at last knowing each other, insisting that before such knowledge they didn't know each other and perhaps couldn't have known each other. Did this make her a true romantic or an epistemic sensualist I wondered as Djamilaa told me all of this. Djamilaa says it didn't take much coaxing to get all the details of her and Penguin's "breakthru night" (Drennette's words) out of her. They sat huddled at their table, she says, leaning over their food and drinks like grand conspirators, no detail and no particular too inti-mate for Drennette not only to relate but to relate with great relish, blush somewhat though she did.

I won't say I never knew "girl talk" could get as graphic as Djamilaa tells me theirs got, only that it surprises me Drennette engaged in it at all, let alone enjoyed it and, it appears, encouraged it, so stalwart, no-nonsense and all she comes across as. When I mentioned this to Lambert he said, "I'm not so surprised." He then went on to add something I think I understand though I'm not entirely sure. "It's the reticent ones you have to watch out for," he said, "the needle-in-a-haystack types." Anyway, Djamilaa says Drennette did repeat that the recent writing has to do with a kind of thaw, the retreat of a glacier she admits to be Rick or her feelings for Rick, a complicated figure that also had "glacial retreat" referring to her feelings toward men after her breakup with Rick, so that the thaw was in part her "glacial retreat's retreat." She made no bones, Djamilaa says, about attributing this to Penguin and their get-together the other night. "A certain someone we call Penguin," she said, changing metaphors, "completely flushed Rick out of my system."

Drennette's kiss-and-tell account, according to Djamilaa, was in-deed long on metaphor as well as intimate detail, anatomical detail, graphic action, graphic mise en scène, a "rich mix of registers," as she puts it, that had them going from smile to giggle to loud laughter more than once, shushing Drennette and telling her to stop. "We left no door closed. There was no door we didn't enter, no door we didn't go in thru. We left no depth unplumbed," Djamilaa says she said at one point, pausing to look them in the eye, the beginnings of a grin on her lips, "no orifice unexplored," whereupon they broke out laughing and ordered another round of drinks.

So we would seem to have confirmation now, were such needed. This thing is definitely afoot, afloat, going or stopping where, as the Temptations would say, "nobody knows."

Yours,
N.

Dear Angel of Dust,

Lambert wore a long, heavy overcoat steeped in sound. Sadness was the coat he wore. It was a cloak of sound like Stanley's "Walk On By," the weight of a tear and a warlock's come-on athwart complaint. It was time walking by, time walking on, with which, for the first time, he was reconciled, with which, for the first time, he was okay. Time's bouquet was the bitter beer we all drank it seemed he said, the first and forever church of hardheadedness reconvened. He was there, if not for that, he said, for nothing. It was heavy but light as a tear at the same time.

Now and again he got to a point where his intonation got away from him (or so, at least, it seemed, so, at least, it sounded like), a ragged, frayed edge of sound or a collapsing core of cloth, a hoarse extenuation he could only let have its way. He told us later that out of the blue his affection for Marvin Gaye's "Stubborn Kind of Fellow" when he was a teenager came back to him, a recollection of walking to school and hearing it on his transistor radio. It was the part where Marvin's voice breaks and goes hoarse that came back to him he told us, the lines "Oh, I have kissed a few, / I tell you, a few have kissed me too," the pleading way his voice gives out and recovers, gives out and comes back to itself on the word "too." It wasn't so much his intonation getting away from him as it was it sounding like that, him having it sound like that, him imitating or trying to imitate Marvin's momentary loss of voice, his fleet, pleading hoarseness, the rough tenuity it for a moment falls into. It was nothing if not the stubborn, mind-made-up ministry his hardheaded church was or would eventually be known for.

I took up my tenor and joined him. We were a two-horned bellowing beast, avowed monophysite twins whose affray was love's last recourse. Death was in the house one could hear, neither of us not with its chill on our breath. We spoke with a quake in our voice. I almost immediately contracted Lambert's hoarseness, a rough tenuity I found my intonation, like his, intermittently fell into. A contagious rash it might've been, so raw, so abraded, so sensitive to touch we winced as we played. While I wasn't aware at the time of Lambert's Marvin Gaye reminiscence, I was struck by one of my own, not of Marvin Gaye but of Dionne Warwick, whom Lambert's Turrentine cloak had brought to mind. It wasn't "Walk On By" but "I Say a Little Prayer" that came back to me, a certain weakness for which I found I couldn't help confessing, a weakness for the perky Burt Bacharach brass that punctuates it. Something very bright and upbeat and optimistic about Bacharach's use of brass, even on a sad song like "Walk On By," where a burnished underglow speaks resolve, has always gotten to me. It seems to arise from or reach out to a utopic horizon, all the more so in a song like "I Say a Little Prayer," bordering on naïve in the bounding felicity it announces having arrived at, reporting prayer where there's exactly no need for it.

This was the recollection that hit me as Lambert and I bellowed and brayed. It wasn't at all that I tried to get that sound on tenor but that the very impossibility of doing so and the analogous impossibility of the simple felicity and resolve, the simply happy life it celebrated, ever being arrived at goaded and got to me. Cognate with Lambert's hardheaded, mind-made-up abrasion, it occurs to me in retrospect, was my own stubborn lament for what I knew and will always know to have been impossible from the start, damned or doomed from the start, impossibility perhaps the crux of its appeal. I bellowed and brayed and cursed the simple accord Bacharach's perky brass wanted one to believe was available, the damned auratic resolve and felicity it teased one with. I bellowed and brayed and cursed myself for having taken the bait, blew as if to blow away my weakness for what I knew and will always know is only a cartoon kind of happiness, an ad man's happiness, the unlikely accord I simultaneously confessed my sweet tooth for.

Bacharach's perky, burnished brass was a dangling carrot I chased and I blew to disavow my chase, a guilty pleasure I damned and disowned my indulgence in. It was an odd way to go about playing, an odd motive, as though reed envied brass almost, an insinuation Lambert would have fumed had he known he blew complicit with, stubborn kind of preachment and/or mind-made-up appeal in league with perk, albeit a disavowed attraction to perk. The very thought of it induced a lightness, a lightheadedness, that threatened to spirit me away, a floataway loss of weight I was all but lifted by, an infectious balloon blurb or blip I needed, I knew, to find anchorage against.

I found recourse in Aretha's cover of "I Say a Little Prayer," which opportunely popped into my head. I told myself to keep my ear on the prize, the prize being Aretha's deep churchical bite and benediction, the gravitas her low gospel chords, rolling gospel chords, bestow on her version from the very outset—no brass, no bounce, no perk, just piano. Her voice's cutting dip into tenor, bottoming low from the outset, likewise proved an answer to perk, nothing if not the anchor that would steady my way.

Aretha's remembered hums and moans kept bubbly lift at bay, champagne brass's floataway auspices held in check. Lambert and I had gotten low and we stayed low, rummaging the horns' low register, grazing black, piquant soil it seemed, the lips of our tenors' bells nuzzling loam. Lambert's tortuous "too" enlisted my low-lying "prayer" exactly where memory and sentiment met, albeit unbeknown to us at the time. We purveyed a run of rapid-fire, quick-trigger ignition allied with hiccuping rhythmic relay that brought Trane and Pharoah on a piece like "Leo" to mind we were told later. That we got there via deeply rooted pop reminiscence unbeknown to each other made it all the more post-expectant, all the more the quantum-qualitative increment it was.

This was during Lambert's solo on "Sekhet Aaru Strut" at Onaje's last night, a solo that at one point hit me in such a way I just jumped in, unexpected, unplanned, we two "soloing" at once. Everyone says it was the high point of the night.

I felt a corner of some sort had been turned, some sort of lesson learned, another in a long line of lessons come upon. I felt we learned something very important, very new and very subtle, something so subtle I can't exactly say what.

Enclosed is a tape. Let me know what you think.

As ever,
N.

Dear Angel of Dust,

There's a review of *Orphic Bend* in the latest *Cadence*. We didn't expect it to get any such attention, so this comes as a surprise. It's the first review it's gotten. The reviewer we neither know nor have heard of, but he seems to know the music and he has positive things to say. It's not that there's not the inevitable quibble here and there, but he does hand out a great deal of praise. One would definitely have to call it a good review. Indeed, friends are congratulating us, calling it a *rave* review. We don't go that far, happy though we were to see it, and even if it were a rave we'd want to draw back, not get too excited.

As it turned out, we were surprised not only by the review but by our consumption of it, the elation we initially felt upon seeing it, caught out or caught offguard by how happy we were to see it, how greedily, at first at least, we ate it up. It was as though it was this that we put the album out for, as though we recorded it to be reviewed, written about. There was not only the question of why we were so invested in being reviewed and in what the review said but a certain disappointment, both with such investment and with our elation's failure to live up to expectation, simply on its own terms and on the face of it, an expectation that, post-expectant as we'd have been or thought or wished ourselves to be, we didn't know (or simply hadn't admitted) we harbored. But we did, or had, and it was by that expectation that even our elation, on its own terms and on the face of it, was found wanting. Thus it was that elation mixed with or morphed into letdown. Happy wasn't happy enough. And even if it were, we weren't sure putting out a record to have nice things said about it, written about it, was what being a band amounted to.

The review, then, gave us pause, became the reason or occasion to ask, late to be doing so though it was, why we play. "It's not about reviews," Aunt Nancy emphatically said as we were discussing this at rehearsal. "It's not even about aboutness. It's not about being-about." It was a thought we needed no time to reflect on, no time to digest. We all understood what she meant, all of us in our heart of hearts having long wanted exactly that, only that, to play not for the sake of what could be said but athwart it, play without claim or caption, advancing (if advancing anything) being-in-and-of-itself, self-evidence, hub and horizon rolled into one. We countered claim and caption, coupling or conflating claim and caption, because of the elephant in the room in the review, the reviewer's reference to balloons emerging from his copy of *Orphic Bend*.

It was odd the way we tiptoed around the balloons at first. The review bringing them up made for mixed feelings, if it didn't indeed bug each of us outright. It was our fear of them upstaging the music again. The reviewer's recourse to them as a self-crediting tack, boasting or bragging it seemed, made matters worse. Critical authority seemed to be at stake, visionary credentials even. Such were the insistence and relish he reported having seen the balloons with. Even so, we were slow to get around to it. Perhaps it was all too obvious, going, as they say, without saying. Perhaps we were loath to admit mention of the balloons bothered us, loath to admit anything in a review, least of all that, wasn't just water on a duck's back.

Though we were slow to get around to the balloons we did get around to them. Not long after Aunt Nancy said it wasn't about aboutness, Lambert ventured an equation of claim with inflation, aboutness with inflation, aboutness with would-be containment, cover. "Reviews are balloons," he summed it up by saying. We laughed, relieved it was out in the open. But once the subject had finally been broached we found we felt no need to belabor it. It was enough to know we all knew it was on the table. We briefly kicked it around and went back to rehearsal.

I'm enclosing a new installment of my antithetical opera, a new after-the-fact lecture/libretto called "B'Loon's Blue Skylight." I won't say it was inspired by the review but had the review not appeared it wouldn't have been written.

As ever,
N.

B'LOON'S BLUE SKYLIGHT

or, The Creaking of the Word: After-the-Fact Lecture/Libretto
(Djband Version)

Djband bumped into B'Loon at a newspaper vending box. One of the local weeklies featured a review of Djband's album *Orphic Bend*, a review whose author took pains to announce that balloons had emerged from his copy of the three-record release, doing so not only during the bass solo on a cut called "Dream Thief"—about which, he pointed out, there'd been a good deal of chatter on the underground grapevine—but at a number of other points as well. The reviewer took no small amount of pride alongside the pains he took to make this announcement, as though the balloons' appearance, multiple as it was and occurring at points on the recording not reported by others, bestowed a mark of distinction, made him elect among the elect, confirmed his acuity and taste.

The newspaper vending box stood on the corner of Melrose and Fairfax, across the street from Fairfax High. Djband, spotting the title *Orphic Bend* in the subhead of the front-page review, had opened the door to the box, taken out a copy and read the review, looking up dismissively when finished and humphing, "He thinks it's about him."

"But it *is* about him," an inner voice or an inner B'Loon reminded Djband, "as much about him as about anyone. Why not? Isn't the music for and about each and every listener, there to have made of it what any set of ears can make of it, there for nothing if not laissez-faire audit? Anything goes." The inner voice paused and on deeper reflection allowed, "Well, no, not anything. But where to draw the line is always an issue."

The review was filled with such wording as "insofar," "as it were" and "as if," the language of qualification disqualifying language itself. So it was, the review suggested, the balloons fled language while carrying language, bearing it to more auspicious precincts, Djband's music and any other music, all music. "Music," it said at one point, "is language in exile, exile exponentially borne—that is, owned up to, lived up to." The review went on and on about the balloons, not so much about the reviewer, when it came down to it, as about B'Loon (though the reviewer had no way of knowing the balloons' avatar's name). It waxed alliterative and assonantal regarding "the balloons' détente between containment and contagion, forfeiture and fortitude," as though, in so accenting sound, it sought or asserted its own balloon status, inflating its recourse to sonorous air, "aeriality," sonority's infection or effects. "Sound," it went so far as to say, "is the deep, not so deep tautology of *is*, its flipped ipseity," obliquely alluding to Oliver Lake's *Life Dance of Is*.

Djband wasn't sure what to make of such pronouncements. Using language to question language seemed only a roundabout self-regard. "He thinks it's about language," Djband grumped, "that old chestnut, no more than the balloons by another name. He might as well have called it l'anguish. He thinks it's about the balloons." The review got on Djband's nerves, further mixing mixed feelings about the balloons. Could the intersection of two metropolitan avenues be called a house, B'Loon, a mixed blessing, was in the house.

Djband had been out of sorts to begin with, one of its members having awoken from a troubling dream. Aunt Nancy had dreamt an onslaught of Santa Ana winds dried out her skin, leaving her face, neck, legs and arms ashy. When she went to put lotion on, she dreamt, squeezing the tube nuzzling the palm of her hand, rather than a drop of lotion, albeit looking like one, what came out was a maggot. She immediately awoke, shocked by so brusque a reminder of death. She'd gotten up on the wrong side of the bed and been in a funk all day, Djband's other members, having been told the dream, in it with her.

The lotiondrop maggot continued to spook Djband, a Creaking of the Worm compounding ricketiness with unguent, omen with unctuousness. Djband couldn't help imagining an abruptly desiccated, husklike maggot, a stiff chrysalis rustling in the wind, no longer lotionlike. Knowing it meant skin would lose its luster, flesh be feasted on by worms eventually, Djband wondered what it meant regardless, wondered against knowing, not wanting to know. Knowing but not wanting to know what it came down to, body a balloon of skin with guts inside, "An offal thought," Djband inwardly quipped, at odds with and wanting to make light of the unsettling truth.

Aunt Nancy broke away and spoke. "It's not so much it all redounded to me. I'm not saying that. It's not even it was me it had to do with," she said. "It was anyone's palm, everyone's palm, the lotion came out on. It was anyone's arm, everyone's arm, the worm would eventually eat. It's not that I'm the only one whose head a sword hangs over. No, I'm not saying that. Not even close." She then took two, maybe three steps back, blended back in. "No, not even close," Djband agreed.

Djband staggered along what seemed an exhaust wall, automobile and bus fumes attacking eyes, nose, mouth and throat. A white sedan darted in front of a bus in time to make a right turn from Fairfax onto Melrose, black smoke pouring out of its tailpipe as it sped up, black smoke pouring out of the bus's tailpipe as well. "We'll all die together, choke together," Djband announced.

It was too much, as though, playing Monk, Djband forgot Monk's chuckling grunt, his wry wink. There was none of Monk's extreme right-hand hammering, his making the piano his toy, "Sweet Georgia Brown" turned "Bright Mississippi." It was in fact the contrary, as though "Epistrophe" had been renamed "Entropy," so doleful the note, so to speak, Djband repeatedly struck.

It didn't help that the review described "In Walked Pen" as "Monk salad," a phrase that, meant as a compliment from all indications though it was, got on Djband's nerves. It deliberately mixed its message Djband couldn't help suspecting, hearing overtones of "tossed," "thrown together," "hodgepodge." At best it was merely clumsy. It came off, in any case, in Djband's reading, as flip, too offhand, too casual, assuming unearned familiarity with Monk and Djband both. "Why not talk about a worm on a lettuce leaf as well?" Djband muttered all but inaudibly. "Why not say, 'A worm nibbled away at the romaine,' make an adage of it?" This was what Djband would have none of, a balloon of attitude meant to say, "I'm in the know," a balloon inflating itself at "In Walked Pen's" expense, Monk's expense, trivializing "In Walked Pen," trivializing Monk. "'Monk salad' my ass," Djband added.

Thus it was there was much to be annoyed about. The need for an answering salve or an answering salvo couldn't have been stronger. Neither much appealed to Djband however. A letter to the editor taking issue with the review was anything but the water-off-a-duck's-back aplomb Djband liked to think it was an exemplar of. Salve, at the same time, couldn't help but recall lotion, couldn't help but conjure, in so doing, the lotiondrop maggot, the last thing Djband wanted a reminder of.

Djband turned its head to the right, looked over its right shoulder toward where the sound it suddenly heard seemed to come from. It was a rattling sound, as of bamboo slats knocking against each other. It was the sound of actuality falling short of expectation, the sound of a gap between ideal or imagined reception and actual reception, a discrepant rattle (discrepant rub) the review's nondelivery of ideal audition helped arise and resound.

It wasn't, Djband insisted, that there's a hearing one's mind's ear hears, a hearing that can only be virtual, a hearing no manifest hearing lives up to. This could be argued and it had often been argued but it wasn't what was going on here or it wasn't, were it at all going on, all that was going on. Indeed, Djband quickly admitted, it was in part what was going on, which was that three sets of hearing obtained: a) the hearing one in the act of composition or performance imagines, b) the hearing that in fact takes place, and c) the distance or disjunction between the two, audibly manifest now in the form of a rattling as of bamboo slats, a veritable Creaking of the Heard.

Was it that all reception, all audition, was flawed, inevitably a fall from the imaginal hearing one thought to hear and one hoped would be heard as one penned a piece or executed a run? Or was the Creaking of the Heard a veritable Creaking of the Herd, reception no inevitable fall but instead the outcome of herded audition, corralled by such would-be pundits as the review's author? These were the thoughts that ran thru Djband's head.

Yes, the latter was the case, Djband went on. It wasn't that reception was simply herded however. No, worse than that, it was *hearded*.

Hear's past tense's past tense, *hear* exponentially past, hearded hearing was multiply removed from the present, someone else's having heard presumed to be one's own. It's bad enough to presume to have heard with one's own ears, Djband reflected, worse to allow someone else to have done so for you.

The rattling sound made it clear *Orphic Bend* had been hearded, the review's corral evidently made of bamboo. Clunky wind chimes it occurred to Djband it sounded like, not at all graceful, not subtly insinuative, clumsily intrusive instead. "Clunk salad," Djband muttered under its breath, putting water-off-a-duck's-back aplomb aside for a moment, answering the review in kind.

"I want a big, bodacious onslaught of sound," Aunt Nancy had stepped forward again and was saying, "sound enough to beat back dream thievery, lotiondrop-maggot sleight of hand, an advent sound." She stepped back, blended in again, having had her say. "Yes, exactly," Djband agreed, "a big, bodacious advent sound." The contrast with rattling bamboo couldn't have been more stark.

Defensive, water-off-a-duck's-back aplomb notwithstanding, Djband was an ectoplasmic wall, a stone wall even, petrified by the specter of death. Either way, it was a wall from which its members might occasionally emerge. Up to this point Aunt Nancy was the one who had done so, soloist or soloistic, as though performing a piece rather than standing before a newspaper vending box.

For the moment time was an ancillary matter, not to be disregarded nonetheless. Tacit statements of tempo implied or insisted that point or presence might be other than outright, recalling something Mingus wrote about a leaky faucet in the liner notes to one of his albums. Djband knew itself to be there more as an aggregate shake or as an aggregate shiver than as corpuscular stump, a street corner symphony of mean provenance and prospect, time's "will tell" a window impendence blew thru. It could hear itself no matter the time and the place, time nothing if not a suspended platform by turns made less than it was and made more than it was, a bevy of don't-care notes and a preterite soapbox.

So Djband stood bunched at the "will tell" window, the arthroscopic, worm's-eye glimpse into hearded audition the vending box had become. It heard itself beside the hearded rendition of itself the review purveyed, beside the rattling bamboo that was the gap between the two as well, the latter's lapse or its falling away from the former, along the rickety would-be joint between the two. Hearded audition's noncoincidence with Djband-as-it-heard-itself was only to be expected, Djband reminded itself or consoled itself, even scolded itself, angry at itself to have caught itself out expecting better.

A car's horn caught Djband's attention, a Toyota Corolla cut off by a Jaguar XJ-S changing lanes. The driver pounded the hub of the steering wheel and shook her fist as the Jaguar darted in. Oddly, it blended in perfectly, a staccato garnish to the music Djband would have been playing had it been playing, a defenestrated ragtag pomp.

All advent flew thru the "will tell" window. All admonition stood streetside awaiting it, a cautionary wall Djband did its best to embody or at least evoke, an admonitory shingle if nothing more. Warning both stood and ran, a cathartic *récit* audition sought to be door to, time's indiscreet relay. Djband had seen it all. Warning stood and would always do so, it said and saw, knowing "always" to be the dangerous word it was but daring it, ran and would always run.

Djband pasted a poster on the bare wall it was, the bare shingle, the wall or the shingle it took itself to be. The poster bore After-the-Fact Caveat #1:

> Time, perfect or syncopated time, is when a faucet dribbles from a leaky washer. I'm more than sure an adolescent memory can remember how long the intervals were between each collision of our short-lived drip and its crash into an untidy sink's overfilled coffee cup with murky grime of old cream still clinging to the edges or a tidy rust stained enamel sink that the owner of such has given up on the idea that that maintenance man is ever going to change the rhythm beat of his dripping faucet by just doing his job and changing that rotten old rubber washer before time runs out of time.
>
> Musicians partly come into the circle of various blame which encompasses much more than leaky faucets, rotten washers, or critics. Wow! Critics! How did they get here?
>
> I know. It's Freudian. Faucets and old rotten washers. The innocent audiences that are sent in the direction of prema-

ture musicians—critics who want to play and some who play and study at music and can only encompass soul-wise and technically about someone else what they themselves can comprehend.

It was none other than the passage from Mingus's liner notes to *The Black Saint and the Sinner Lady* that had crossed Djband's mind earlier, could "earlier," down this corridor in which time, faucet leak notwithstanding, was ancillary, be said to matter—no less dangerous, if so, than "always."

Shingle more than wall though neither shingle nor wall, it was a sandwich board the poster was pasted on, not a shingle or a wall Djband was but a sandwich board Djband in fact wore, Mingus's admonitory note gracing both boards, back and front, counseling passersby both coming and going. It was a long, detailed message for a sandwich board. Printed in large letters, it barely fit.

Djband had clearly let its water-off-a-duck's-back aplomb fall by the wayside, answering the review with the sandwich board, fighting back, answering "Monk salad" with Mingus. It was clearly involved, clearly invested, to the point of uncool even, the ensemblist equivalent of a sandwich man, anything but blasé, nothing if not caring, standing on the street advertising its message. Djband laughed at itself, realizing that insofar as to bear a message was to be a balloon it had become a balloon, balloon and sandwich man both, both rolled into one. Djband had not only bumped into B'Loon but become B'Loon, pressed and possessed by the spirit of caption and contention, the former manifestly, the latter more implicitly, bearing on which and whose caption fit. The review itself, one saw clearly now, was nothing if not a caption, nothing if not a balloon, nothing if not a message-bearing bauble, the bane of Djband's proprioceptive audition. It happened quickly, in a flash, balloon and sandwich board bound up as one.

"Myself When I Am Real," Djband reminded itself right after it laughed at itself, Mingus's title more to the point than ever before. A pointed mix of aim and arraignment, "Myself When I Am Real" said it all, could any five words be said to've said it all.

Djband turned toward where the sound of another car horn came from and saw the driver of a Mazda GLC headed west on Melrose give a thumbs up, in approval of the Mingus quote it was clear. How the driver so quickly read so long a text Djband couldn't say but happily nodded to acknowledge the approbation. The sandwich board was making a difference already.

Djband turned sideways between the boards, lifting its arms, elevating the boards as though they were wings. It was now Lambert who stepped forward and spoke. "I want a straw to fall and fill up with air and float," he said. "I want float to be what unlikeliness does. Due to itself or in spite of itself, I want that to be what goes on, float's new leaf turned over, float's new reign and regret." Djband agreed, echoing, "Float's new reign and regret."

"Whatever comes up," Lambert continued, "it will beg the question it costs itself—float lure, float intended, float intransigence. Reed a wet stick in my mouth, I want more, flutter-tongue abandon's new almanac, float's lush life begun." Djband agreed and took up the tailend of what Lambert said, repeating, "Float's lush life begun."

"Float nothing if not a barge I'd be borne along on," Lambert continued, "I want each lick to incubate what float would be." Djband agreed again and repeated, "What float would be." Lambert stepped back and blended in again.

The sandwich board had brought an element of reduction in, Djband brought down to the reviewer's level, fighting fire with fire, balloon with balloon. Lambert's invocation of flight or flotation thus arrived right on time, albeit flotation, Djband was well aware, carried a balloon suggestion one could hardly miss. Still, lift and levitation won out over balloon rut, balloon mire, the bone "float's new leaf" picked with "Monk salad" notwithstanding, that bone the very filled-up, floating straw itself perhaps.

More no doubt than perhaps, Djband decided, embarrassed, underneath it all, by the sandwich board, needing to make a move. Disambiguating float from what balloons do was that move, float's association with balloons its new regret. Float's new reign was nothing if not a resolve to overcome inflation, nothing if not a bone proffering puncture. It remained a willingness to abide by high jive, high jubilation, a resolve to reside on high even so.

To say that at exactly that instant Djband smelled roses would be going too far. Roses did come to mind and they did so in a flash, their characteristic perfume no doubt bound up in the thought but not to the point of Djband actually smelling them. L.A. was way more than a stone's throw from Pasadena but Melrose might as well have been Colorado Boulevard on New Year's morning, so large did Lambert's barge now loom, float parting company with balloon.

It was a visual not an olfactory image, an address of the mind's eye, not the mind's more distant nose. Djband saw Lambert's roses-bedecked barge for an instant, easing down Melrose, Lambert atop it waving to the crowd. Yes, it was New Year's morning, float's new day begun, float's new leaf turned over, float's new reign and regret.

For only a moment were such premises afoot, parade premises. The moment they arose they subsided. Melrose was back to being itself as on any other day, Djband a sandwich man pacing the sidewalk, a modest parade if it could even be said to be that—no barge, no float, no roses. No sandwich board either, Djband quickly decided, lifting the sandwich board over its head and lowering it to the sidewalk, propping it against the newspaper vending box.

Rained-on parade was the theme but Penguin, stepping forward, would have to do with it only ostensibly, obliquely, bending away from it as what he had to say built. "I want a front-row seat at the Apocalypse," he said. "No," he said, quickly correcting himself. "I meant to say at the Apollo, James Brown on his way up, in his prime." "In his prime," Djband chimed in and Penguin went on, "I want to have lost someone or to sing and scream and shout as though I had. I want shout to mean to run around in a circle, led by immanent splendor's allure."

"Immanent splendor's allure," Djband agreed and echoed and Penguin continued, "I want the rump of the cosmos in front of me, barely up against my nose or a bit farther away perhaps, all but in touching distance, infinitesimally out of reach. I want to call out to it, calling it Regenerate Rose Reborn." Djband echoed and agreed again, "Yes, Regenerate Rose Reborn." Nose wide with cosmic whiff, cosmic what-if, Penguin stepped back and again blended in.

Before Djband could do what it would do next, Drennette stepped forward, cosmic vamp and commanding virgin rolled into one. "Yes, do remember," she agreed and exhorted, "how the smell of the cosmos's behind pervades all extension, how the smell of cosmic loins penetrates all space." "Penetrates all space," Djband thought to echo and agree but quickly thought better of it, remaining silent as Drennette, noticing the withheld echo and agreement but not needing it, continued, "Do remember how these two smells enter your nose and take hold of your scrotum." It was a footnote, a blurb, an outburst, a balloon. Djband withheld echo and agreement again. Drennette stepped back and blended in.

Djband reeled and staggered, all but overcome by wafted cosmicity, up-from-under pitch and posteriority, belt and bouquet. It was a ploy, a feinting play on exhaustion, even so. Drennette, Penguin, Aunt Nancy, Lambert, Djamilaa and N. were each only a face on the wall Djband was, the wall Djband affected it was, the exhaust wall it earlier staggered along but now steadied and took inside itself. Immured against hearded audition, a wall against rained-on parade, Djband took a stand and stood tall against critical caption, the review's upstart balloon, cartoon acuity.

What Djband would have done next had briefly been put on hold by Drennette's impromptu boast (which is what, underneath it all but not so underneath after all, it all was). Reeling and staggering standing tall, it did now what it would have done next. It issued a collective, composite swipe of sound aimed at wiping the slate clean, a return to pre-caption premises, an airy gesturality or gist it wanted to say was what life itself is, an airy gesturality or gist gotten or gotten at by nothing quite like music, albeit to say so, to go from wanting to say, was to tie up with tar-baby balloon, tar-baby boast, as though Drennette had simply jumped the gun.

Drennette had in fact jumped the gun. That there was a gun to jump tempered Djband's recoil from cosmic waft. Reeling and staggering standing tall as though she'd held a finger out to be sniffed, a finger it knew underneath it all was coming, Djband issued a funky-butt, low-register burst, Mingusesque, a second swipe of sound, going the other way. This was also, it seemed it wanted to say, what life itself is.

Such expounding upon life, oblique though it was, attracted a crowd. Passersby stopped and looked on. They stood a short distance away, staring at Djband, able to read its thoughts evidently. They heard the music Djband inwardly rehearsed evidently, nodding their heads, popping their fingers, patting their feet. Yes, this was life, they seemed to agree, the what-is of it.

Djband knew there was no wiping the slate clean but made as if to do so anyway. Accretion was all, it knew, whatever would-be cleansing wipe a further murk or mucking up, palimpsestic supplement, palimpsestic struff. In this case, funky-butt struff spoke directly to the claim of a "détente between containment and contagion" the review advanced, agreeing with it only to complicate or contaminate it, wipe running one with swipe in more ways than one. Palimpsestic add-on plied boast on boast, waft on waft, whiff, what-is and what-if rolled into one.

Palimpsestic struff was nothing if not infectious. Several of the on-lookers who'd gathered began to dance, squatting low to the ground at points, letting their asses graze the sidewalk. Reveling in rump cosmicity, they delighted, they let it be known, in having asses, delighted that there were asses to be had. Close to declaring ass what-is's what-if, they drew short of that, lifting skyward from the squat's low point with a pelvic thrust, saying something like what they begged off saying. Lee Morgan's "The Rumproller" had nothing on what they did or on the music they heard or thought they heard Djband rehearse.

"I want not to have seen it all," Djamilaa stepped forward and said. "I want not to have seen this movie before." "Not to have seen this movie before," Djband agreed and repeated, part antiphonal add-on, part set-aside. Djamilaa paused.

"I want," Djamilaa went on after pausing, "the clean slate I know we can't have. I want the meat of our being here truly met, true meet's tally, no mere funky-butt largesse." Djband agreed and repeated, "No mere funky-butt largesse." Djamilaa's advancing meat, meet and romance (cosmic tail, cosmic tale, cosmic tally) went on with her saying, "I want the rose's perfume where pendent cheeks meet, funk sublimated upward, astral crevice, crease." Djband not only echoed and agreed, "Astral crevice, crease," but added, "Ass as in astral, amen." Djamilaa stepped back, again blending in.

The more booty-invested of the dancers, hearing Djamilaa's admonition, dialed it down. A couple of them stopped dancing altogether, stepping back into the crowd, content to nod their heads, pop their fingers, pat their feet.

The now more precisely calibrated serenade made it crystal clear that Djband was no Parliament, no Funkadelic, no Zapp and Roger—crystal clear even as it grew to be pearl opaque, for the review, irritant pebble to Djband's oyster, was coming to be accreted over, contained, gotten over, a tribute to palimpsestic add-on, palimpsestic struff, stick-to-itiveness. The music grew to be pearly smooth as well as pearl opaque, much less bumpy than funk.

It was now a precisely telepathic serenade, the heard rather than hearded audition every band so deeply wants. Sensing this, Djband saw no further need for the sandwich board and picked it up from where it lay propped against the newspaper vending box. N. stepped forward to flip it inside out so that Mingus's words no longer showed and then stepped back and blended in again. Djband again propped it against the newspaper vending box. The blank sides of the two boards glared in the sun.

The crowd of onlookers had grown larger, all of them nodding their heads, popping their fingers, patting their feet. Looking out at Melrose, Djband saw that traffic in both directions had slowed, drivers and passengers looking over at the goings-on around the newspaper vending box, Djband telepathically holding forth, the onlookers looking on. They too, the drivers and passengers, looked on, nodding their heads, popping their fingers and (Djband imagined rather than saw but couldn't have been more certain) patting their feet.

Parade was back. The cars, vans, buses and trucks proceeded at parade pace, not so much cars, vans, buses and trucks as floats, ti-trating, ever so exactingly, the ideal roost and repose Lambert had adumbrated earlier.

Parade was indeed back, as much on the sidewalk, it turned out, as on the street. Emerging from the opening between the two boards of the sandwich board was none other than B'Loon, out in the open for everyone to see—the eyelashes hovering above the head and brow, the poorly defined limbs and extremities, the wistful, noncommittal mouth and all.

B'Loon, small at first but steadily inflating, grew to be as big as the giant balloons at a Macy's Thanksgiving Day parade, rivaling Superman, Kermit the Frog, Snoopy and the rest, floating high above the sidewalk, lifting.

Everyone stared into the sky at B'Loon drifting higher. The crowd of onlookers on the sidewalk stared skyward, as did those in the cars, vans, buses and trucks, leaning out their windows and bringing traffic to a stop. Djband as well stared skyward. Was B'Loon's lift mere exhibition or possibly more, possibly exorcism? It was hard not to wonder.

B'Loon floated higher and higher. Heads tilted farther back and hands became visors as B'Loon drifted higher, everyone more and more straining to see as the image got smaller. Less visible the farther away it floated, B'Loon soon couldn't be seen at all. Thus B'Loon exited the house the intersecting avenues could be said to be.

For a long time after B'Loon floated out of sight everyone kept looking into the sky. The crowd of onlookers on the sidewalk stood staring skyward. Traffic remained at a standstill, those in the cars, vans, buses and trucks continuing to lean out their windows looking up into the sky. Djband continued looking up as well.

Everyone went on staring into the sky, lost in thought. It had all been only a bubble, a moment in the sun, a quick boon, barely embraceable, blown up to be let go.